OF
SOULS

BY

STEPHANIE HUDSON

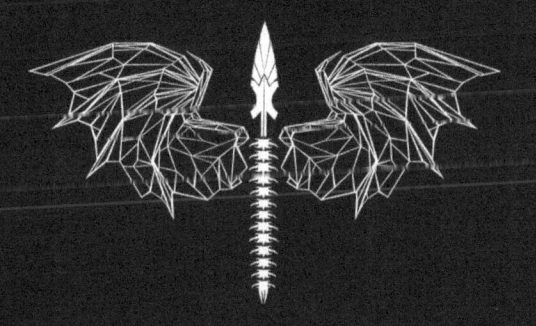

Tree of Souls
The Transfusion Saga #6
Copyright © 2020 Stephanie Hudson
Published by Hudson Indie Ink
www.hudsonindieink.com

This book is licensed for your personal enjoyment only.
This book may not be re-sold or given away to other people. If you would like to share this book with another person, please purchase an additional copy for each recipient. If you're reading this book and did not purchase it, or it wasn't purchased for your use only, then please return to your favourite book retailer and purchase your own copy. Thank you for respecting the hard work of this author.
All rights reserved.
This is a work of fiction. Names, characters, places, brands, media, and incidents are either the product of the authors imagination or are used fictitiously. The author acknowledges the trademark status and trademark owners of various products referred to in this work of fiction, which have been used without permission. The publication/use of these trademarks is not authorised, associated with, or sponsored by the trademark owners.
Tree of Souls/Stephanie Hudson – 2nd ed.
ISBN-13 - 978-1-913769-41-3

I would like to dedicate this book to my dear friend Carrie Anne Gosselin Wyman, who is fighting every day like a warrior queen against the battle of cancer. A true inspiration and a soul of true strength and spirit.
A strength that knows no bounds and a great friend that will always be family in my heart, even when Heaven has claimed an Angel with your soul.

This poem is for you and your family.

Strength.

The strength of hearts beats in times,
Of failing health our body chimes
It tells us it's tired of pain that's too much,
But our strength remains, with the cheeks we touch,

The strength of family that is by our side,
The hearts of others that we pride,
The sounds of laughter replace the sorrow,
For those are the sounds of tomorrow,

Those are the sounds of forevermore,
That is held in the heart of Heaven's open door,

Not the tears to hold beyond
But the sights of smiles, are found and fond

Those memories held so dear
And close to hearts forever near
Will be the sight taken with me
The children I love having on my knee

The giggles and candy wrappers,
The jumpers and the sound of clappers,
The fun of life that fills my soul
With my grandchildren that fill me whole.

With my husband who is so dear,
With his love he's shown every day of the year
My children of which I am so proud,
To hear their voices happy and loud

So I hold your hands and say a prayer
As I face the new life with every last one of you there
The strength of me, will never die,
For I am the strength passed on in each of your lives.

WARNING

This book contains explicit sexual content, some graphic language and a highly additive dominate Vampire King.

This book has been written by an UK Author with a mad sense of humour. Which means the following story contains a mixture of Northern English slang, dialect, regional colloquialisms and other quirky spellings that have been intentionally included to make the story and dialogue more realistic for modern day characters.

Thanks for reading x

PROLOGUE

I RUN TO YOU

The second the song came over the radio I cursed that my hands were full and therefore I was unable to turn off the beautiful notes of Lady Antebellum's 'I run to you' quickly enough. It had been nearly two months of banned love songs and as the lyrics seemed to tell my life's story it was of little wonder why...

'I run from hate, I run from prejudice, I run from pessimists, but I run too late...I run my life, or is it running me?'

And wasn't that just the question right now I thought as I struggled to the table with yet another armful of research papers my friend Yosef had given me. Damn my Spotify account recommending songs!

I quickly got to the table only dropping a few scrolls and one book, doing so just as the lyrics continued with...

'Run from my past, I run too fast, or too slow it seems... when lies become the truth...'

"Yeah, you can say that again!" I said picking up my fallen articles with annoyance and slapping them back on the counter just before grabbing my tablet and turning it off just as the beat kicked up with,

'That's when I run to you... this world keeps spinning faster, into a new disaster so I run to you...I run to you baby'

"Nope, not now and not ever," I commented as I killed the music and the second I did, that was when I felt it. Like a presence so powerful it sucked all the energy from the room and left me near gasping for breath. And that difficulty in breathing wasn't just from the moment you realised that you were no longer alone, but it was more when you realised *who* it was that stole that solitude from you. Because when you were on the run there was only one being out there you hoped not to find in the room with you...

The hunter.

And I knew my time was up when the first words spoken in that smooth hypnotic voice of his told me,

"Now that is a shame."

I sucked in a deep breath, one that felt as though it had the power to suck much more than just the air into my lungs. Which was why I started questioning my sanity the moment I heard it. The voice that I had heard so many times in my dreams. The one that had me crying out his name nearly every night. The one that had me in tears and wishing I could go back. Go back to the beginning, just to relive those perfect moments together. The dreams I had that didn't include the reasons I ran but only the reasons why I never wanted to. The moments where I was his one and only.

But then I would awaken to my reality. One that told me that I could never go back.

Not after what I knew.

It could never be undone.

So, he became a cruel dream I couldn't control. He became the dream I longed sleep for as much as I tried to keep myself awake from having it. But now it wasn't a dream and that cruel temptation was standing in my reality once more. I didn't know why or how he had found me. I had been so careful. I had left no traces. No breadcrumbs to follow.

Not a single scrap of evidence.

But yet found me, *he had.*

I knew this the moment I felt that presence behind me stepping closer. A presence so strong that you could do little but feel it. The way it seemed to consume me. Draining me dry of every emotion before emitting back a force powered from the core of what I knew was a stone-cold heart of a Vampire King who had been hunting me.

Well, the hunt was over.

I had been found.

I had been caught.

And the moment I felt those hands take hold of me I knew with his whispered words, words I had forbidden him to ever speak again, that I had also been,

Captured...

"Found at last, my Khuba."

CHAPTER ONE

LUCIUS

FISTS AND FORGIVENESS

The moment I saw Amelia stepping out from her chosen hiding place it took me just a single look at the devastation on her face to know that the conversation she had heard, hadn't been the same one spoken. I had even started to quickly replay certain parts of it in my mind, ready to begin to rectify the situation as soon as I first overcame what I knew was her urge to run from me.

But then I noticed the blood, after scanning the length of her body, starting with her blood-soaked shoes and trouser hem that continued on as splashes of crimson up her jeans. There were also smear marks on her cream sweater that I knew was from the only blood that belonged to her and was no doubt from the injury I could see on her hand. But there was also something there on the side of her head where her hair was soaked with blood too.

Gods, but what had happened to her this time?! I was fucking furious at the idea and almost grabbed her to me, caring little for what her reaction would be. But then it was the tears in her eyes that stopped the impulse. As I knew that I could heal her body in moments, but I was only free to do so after first attempting at healing what looked to be her damaged heart. Something that, by the looks of things, wasn't going to be easy.

"Oh Gods, Fae! I…we…didn't mean for you to find out this way…we didn't know you…" Keira started to say having no clue where her daughter's mind was really crashing towards. For it was of little doubt in my mind that Keira was thinking the worst of her daughter's heartache was solely based on the fact that her mother's knowledge of our relationship had been kept from her. But the second Amelia snapped back with utter distaste,

"Oh, I know you didn't!" That was when I knew that both Keira and I had far a worse problem on our hands. One that for me personally, seemed as if it was going to become a battle of the past all over again. Which was why I told her,

"It is not what you think it is, my Khu…"

"NO!" she roared at me with such anger I swear I could hear it echoing around me as if the walls were about to crack from the force of her pain.

"You don't EVER, ever get to call me that again!" she screamed at me and I couldn't help but physically react, flinching as she openly scorned my love for her. It was starting to become clearer still, with the level of rage and hurt that she felt had been inflicted by a shadow of the truth. Which was why I raised my hands slowly, knowing any moment I would have no choice but to strike out by reaching for her quickly, to contain her and grab her to me before she fled.

"Lucius, what is happening?" I heard Keira asking in a pained and worried tone that told me the true horror of what her

daughter believed she'd just witnessed was only now just starting to penetrate.

"Alright now, Pet, let's just take a breath and calm things…"

"Calm things down…are you fucking serious right now!?" she snapped, interrupting me after I had ignored her mother's question and focused solely on her. Then she stepped up to me, getting close, and I was seconds from making my move when suddenly she thrust the box into my chest with a hard shove into my body, one I barely remained immobile against, flinching only against the roar of anger she threw at my face when she screamed,

"YOU'RE FUCKING MY MOTHER!" I closed my eyes for a few seconds at the grief throwing those words at me inflicted, knowing the true meaning of pain as they ripped through me. To believe that was what she truly thought of me. To know that after everything I had done, all I had said, all the fucking love I had shown her, every second of it set alight and crumbling to ash at my feet in a single heartbeat…to know she believed it all to be lies just after one moment of mistaken affection shown for someone dear to me.

Gods, the pain of it rendered me unable to move.

Even as I watched as she had already started walking away, I could do nothing but roar in both anger and pain as it tore through my soul. Gods, but I wanted to hate her just as much as I fucking loved her! I was so Gods be damned angry that she could believe her words, I was struck unable to move!

That she could think of me as such was utterly unfathomable!

I vaguely watched as even Keira tried to reach out to her only to get Amelia's venom lashed her way,

"Don't fucking touch me! I never want to see you again! Either of you…you are both…*lost to me!*" She sobbed these last three words in such a way that I knew she had really meant them as something else, words that she couldn't ever take back if spoken. Instead, she ran from the room with tears flooding those beautiful eyes of hers. Turning them into something beyond the realms of beauty...

...but into something breathtakingly haunting.

This was when I snapped.

"FUCK!" I flipped the nearest table closest to me, making the sound of it crashing against the far side of the room become an echoing shadow of my rage. The song of destruction doing little to ease my temper and neither did Keira when she ran to me and begged me to stop. To see reason and calm down before scaring her daughter with my anger. To let her be the one to go to her and explain everything, to show Amelia her thoughts, the images of the conversation before. She blamed herself and with tears streaming down her face she begged me to let her be the one. But I cared nothing for Keira's tears.

I only cared for Amelia's.

Which was why, without even answering her, I walked towards the door and ripped it from its hinges without taking a moment to think about the damage behind me, simply hoping that Keira had enough sense to get out of the way of it. I was both utterly numb and furious at the same time, that I could barely even think. To the point that the second I felt Keira following me out and grabbing me from behind, still begging me to stay, was when I turned to snarl down at her to let me go. But neither of us saw what was coming next...

Or should I say who.

Suddenly, before I could even fully register the reasons behind it, I found myself travelling backwards until I found my body being slammed back, smashing into the fireplace in the library. I groaned through the pain as some of my ribs snapped. Then I gritted my teeth through the process as my body instantly started to mend, fusing the cracks and breaks, along with healing the puncture to my lung. I sucked in air as I started to breathe past the pain and after turning my head slightly, that's when I noticed that the secret doorway into the Janus Gate was ajar. Something I knew wasn't from my impact as I had landed against one of the cast iron sentinels.

Had this been where Amelia had come from? Was this where Dom kept his safe? For she had gotten hold of the box somehow, so it would make sense and might explain her injuries. But it didn't explain the other evidence of blood, which now had me questioning, if this was the witch's doing?

I located the box that in my rage I had thrown to one side, both damning its existence and questioning the reason for her trying to take it. But then these thoughts were ripped away from me the moment I saw the cause for my being back in the library with broken bones, which right now were nothing more than an inconvenience.

I didn't have time for this shit.

I needed to find her!

But then, with one look at the Demonic King who had not an ounce of Angel in sight, then I knew I first had to deal with a son of Hell's wrath.

"YOU KISSED MY WIFE!" his demon roared, and I found myself doing a double take the second he said the last words I believed his reason for attacking me to be.

"What the..." I never got the chance to finish as the asshole was charging at me, his dark wings taking him high first so he could gain leverage on his attack. Then he tried to barrel into me, making me move with only half a second to spare before he would have killed me from it, being as his twin swords extended from his wrists on his downward attack, making his wife scream out,

"DRAVEN, NO!"

Thankfully, my senses returned quickly enough to save myself along with his wife, for had he succeeded, then it would have not only been my end, but hers too. But it was clear he was out of his mind with rage and had given total control over to his demon, who wasn't acting rationally enough to function beyond the need for death and revenge.

"Fuck, Dom, you have it all...fuck!" I ended this the second he lashed out against me with his swords raised, ones that flamed purple and licked out at everything they touched, scoring it black instead of setting it alight.

"DRAVEN, STOP THIS!" Dom paused long enough to snarl at his wife, telling her,

"I will deal with your deceit later, woman!" She jerked back as if he had struck her and I could see for myself her own anger close to erupting and when it did, then I knew it would have been nothing compared to Dom's.

Twin pools of crimson fire were igniting in her eyes but seeing this gave me barely enough time to dodge the blades he continued to swing at me. Meaning that I had no choice but to summon my own blade to my hand, thanking my foresight in having Nesteemia place a summoning spell on the sword of Kings, Caliburnus. A spell which enabled me to feel it start to materialise into a solid weight in my hand. And it was just in time too, for I held it up above my head with barely enough of it appearing in time to save my head as his blades collided with its growing length.

"FUCK DOM, LISTEN!" I roared as I pushed back on the blade making him take a step back allowing my anger to fight his own rage.

"Good, I wanted a fair fight before I see your head fucking roll from your vessel!" he shouted venomously and I snarled back, before swinging the sword around in my hand and showing him that I was ready. Because this time it was a fight I was not going to use my will against him to win. For he would soon discover that I wasn't the same man he had once fought before.

I was something much more and had the Venom of God running through my veins to prove it!

"Then, in doing so, you see your Chosen One fall also!" I reminded him before I lashed out, hitting against his twin blades so quickly he slipped slightly, which was enough that I caught his shoulder with my blade. Because my words had started to penetrate through the demon's rage, and he was weakening to the fact. He even looked towards Keira as if seeing her standing there for the very first time and there was only one emotion now clouding his judgement in the fight...*doubt.*

"Please...don't do this," Keira whispered at him, holding herself rigid as if she were now witnessing her whole world as it came crumbling down around her. As if she had failed in some secret quest. But whatever the cause it finally made an impact on Dom as his demon simmered down.

"I will not kill you, Luc, but that doesn't mean I won't bring you to your fucking knees!" he shouted back the moment he made his mind up about my death.

"I make no such promise in return, old friend!" I snapped back fighting him now with a far more equal footing, allowing my hits to mirror my deadly mood. I was unrelenting with my sword, swinging it so fast he could barely keep up and on a punishing downward slash, he only just managed to block against it. It was clear to me now that the wrath of his demon had relented even further to the emotional reasons behind the fight. Something I used to my advantage when his guard lowered our collided blades enough for me to punch out at his face, feeling the crack of bone crunch in both his nose and my knuckle.

Then I grabbed the front of his shirt and threw him against the wall with my sword held high ready to strike.

"LUCIUS, NO!" I ignored Keira's furious and desperate cries in place of something else. As just when I was about to deliver what I knew would be a damaging blow, I heard Amelia's deep and tortured cry in agony...

A pain I had inflicted.

That was when I lost the fight in me and lowered my weapon. Then I raced to the door, ready to leave the battle behind me in search of one far greater.

The battle for her heart.

"AMELIA!" I shouted her name and nearly made it through the broken doorway when I felt myself being yanked back before a fist connected with my face, jarring my senses.

"No weapons is fine by me!" Dom snarled at me before another fist connected with my jaw this time making me grunt from the impact as my jaw broke.

"Dom, stop it for fuck sake! You have got this all wrong!" Keira shouted at her husband and I blocked the continued hits long enough for my jaw to fix itself and enable me to tell him,

"You should listen to your wife before she puts you on your ass!" Then I brought up my fist and delivered an upper cut punch to his chin, knocking his head back from the force.

"LUCIUS!" Keira roared at me as I took another moment to hit back, giving it my all and caused blood to trickle from his nose the moment I got my second punch in. Of course, I felt my own blood running down my chin from the split in my lip that was at this moment trying to fuse back together from his powerful fist. Dom wiped away his blood with the back of his hand and stared at it, before grinning back, telling me,

"It's been a long time since I have seen my own blood spilled by another...*I look forward to this, Vampire.*" Then he rolled his shoulders and I braced myself for the fighting machine that was my former King. I took a deep breath and told him,

"Fucking bring it, you Demon bastard!" I roared my words and let them fuel my rage just as we both collided. But this was also when Keira had found her limit. And what a fucking limit it was! As the moment our fists connected, a blinding light was all we both saw as our bodies separated from a force. One so great, my bones weren't the only ones that suffered as we were both flung to opposite sides of the room. And there, at the centre of it all, was Keira. Now a glowing figure of white-hot fire that consumed her body, licking out angrily at the air as it crackled around her. She had both her hands out towards us, holding us in place so she could prevent us from fighting further.

She was utterly magnificent, just as she had been the day she had ended a war. A beautifully terrifying picture of Hell's wrath as she panted through her rage. And I wasn't the only one who suffered from it and needed time to heal from the force of her power, as Dom also had fallen victim to his wife's fury. I don't know how long it was that she kept us prisoner for, but long enough for bones to heal and organs to repair. A sight that seemed to flip the switch between thought and deadly action. As it was only then that she managed to get a hold on the power directed through her, one straight from both Heaven and Hell, when the flames finally started to simmer to nothing but a warm glow. She then lowered her arms and we both dropped to the ground, gaining our feet at the same time. After this she turned to her husband and told him in a calm tone that sounded as if it took great effort to do so,

"We did not kiss, Amelia has it all wrong." I then watched as Dom closed his eyes as her words sank in and finally stayed long enough for his demon to evaporate back into the image of a man she knew well. Although, what I knew of Dom's usual temper, then I assumed she knew his demon's image well enough also.

"Then why was she so upset, my Electus?" he asked her with his tone still hard and obviously suspicious. Keira took a deep breath and released it on a sigh, before looking to me and the look of regret on her face said it all. This had been the deception she had been dreading telling her husband and it was one she had no choice but to admit to. So, I nodded for her to do so.

"Keira?" Her name came out as a rumbled warning for her to speak and do so quickly before he lost his patience completely. But then, as she first looked to me and then back to her husband, she must have decided to take action to prevent what she believed would happen next. I knew this when her hand raised and suddenly Dom's body was pushed back against the wall and held there, clearly against his will. He snarled angrily and pushed against her force, making her hand start to glow brighter at the effort she needed to keep him there.

Only after she was assured that he was kept in place did she choose to speak,

"Okay, so there is something I have been keeping from you, but it's not as bad as it sounds, so please...please Draven, just try and hear me out...yes?"

"I must say that I would be more inclined to try if I was not held against my will and therefore released from your grasp... one that I can feel weakening by the second," Dom replied with the threat of movement showing through for he had been fighting her the entire time he had been kept to the other side of the room. A fact that was starting to show with the strain on her face at keeping him from reaching me. Because, as powerful as Keira was, Dominic Draven was equally so, for there weren't many who could defeat such a being, his wife included. No, Dom just needed a little more time to break down his Chosen

One's defences and by the looks of things, he was close to doing so.

"Gods, but how the Hell do I...?" Keira started to say but I'd had enough of this shit! I just wanted to get the fuck out of there so I could find Amelia and explain everything to the only one in my life the truth mattered to.

So, I quickly snapped,

"Oh, for fuck sake!" Then I walked over to him,

"Luc, don't please... just let me..." I then ignored Keira's plea, and said the words I'd wanted to say since the very beginning,

"I am the one dating your daughter, Dom."

CHAPTER TWO

THROUGH THE DEVIL'S FINGERS

The second I said this it took Keira the time to mutter, *"Oh shit,"* before Dom exploded into rage, bursting free from her hold with little effort as her energy was spent and his demon was too strong. Which meant that once again I found myself up against a bookshelf with a fist in my face and for once, it was a series of blows I allowed to happen.

The reason for this was because this time, I knew he needed it and, as much as I hated to admit it, right at that very moment I welcomed the pain. Because it was one I felt as though I deserved. My gut had told me for far too long that I had dealt with this all wrong. That no matter how or when I had told her father, the outcome would have most likely remained the same…but that didn't change facts now.

"DOM, NO!" Keira screamed behind him as I allowed him to rain blow after blow on my face, even as she tried to pry his arm back, he merely roared down at me,

"FIGHT BACK!" But again, I simply took it, knowing that

if we were ever to move past this, then he needed to get it out. So, I calmly said,

"No."

"Fight, damn you! Fucking fight back!"

"Dom please, stop it! Just stop it!" Keira tried when he shrugged off her hold, snarling back at her,

"You betrayed me!" She took a step back, holding her chest as if he had delivered the next blow to her instead of me.

"No...I...I..." she started to stammer weakly.

"You fucking knew!" he threw back at her and just as she whispered his name in a plea to get him to understand, he turned his back to her,

"Enough, I will deal with you later!" At this she found her anger and was about to speak when something finally penetrated my whole entire being.

I could no longer feel Amelia.

Meaning she was no longer inside the building!

This was when the second Dom's fist came at me again, I caught it in my hold and allowed my true nature to take back control, telling him,

"That's the last one you are going to get, now get the fuck out of my way!" Then I forced him back, using my grasp on his fist to do so, letting my true nature ripple through me. The blood dripping down my face started to be absorbed back into my skin as the Venom of God darkened my veins. The cuts, bruises and breaks he had caused, healing instantly this time as my demon rumbled dangerously beneath my vessel wanting to break free and chase down what was rightfully ours.

"Why, so I can just let you run after my daughter, I don't fucking think so!" he shouted back and this time when he tried to swing for me, I moved with deadly calm, ducking out of the way of his throw, causing his fist to embed into the shelves behind me.

TREE OF SOULS

"You are never to see my daughter ever again, do you understand me, Luc, I will fucking kill you, so help me, by the Gods I will end you!" Dom roared at me the second I started to walk away.

"I don't need your fucking approval!" I snarled over my shoulder and just as I was making it out of the library, he made it clear he wasn't finished with me. I was grabbed from behind and pushed face first up against the wall next to the door. My face quickly became part of the plaster as it now had the side of my face imprinted there.

"She's my daughter!" he roared next to my head and I had finally hit my limit, doing something I had once vowed never to do again, not since the last time. And I started by elbowing him back in the face, spinning the moment he loosened his hold so I could face him. Then, just as he was bringing forth his blades one more time, I knew now was the time to end this. So, using the power of my will against him, one that not even he was strong enough to fight against, I forced him to drop to his knees. Then I willed his arms to cross, embedding his blades into the floor to keep them there.

"ARRGH, DAMN YOU!" he thundered in anger, or should I say his demon did, for his vessel was under my control, whether he liked it or not and he was about to find out why. As there was something I had come to understand. It was a fundamental rule that he himself had taught me once. One I had to learn the hard way and one that was a lesson I would now be giving back to him.

For you never got in between a King and his Chosen One.

"Lucius, release him!" Keira shouted making me look back up at her and say,

"Not this time. Not when he stands in my way." Then I took the few steps needed towards him and looked down at him.

"She may be your daughter, Dom…" I told him, pausing

before I could then lean down slightly, getting closer so I could tell him the truth of it all.

"...but she is my Chosen One."

Dom's gasp of shock was one I ignored as I walked towards the door, doing so with purpose, stopping briefly when Keira asked me,

"What are you going to do?"

"I am going to right a wrong...*once and for all,*" I told her with a certainty I felt in my bones.

"It can't be...it can't be true! You can't...Luc, I forbid it, she is my...!" Dom tried to say one last time, but with a slash of my hand I cut him off by force. Then, when I looked down over my shoulder, no longer granting him my expression for only my words of promise were needed,

"She is yours no longer, for she belongs to me now...and you should know, Dom...nothing gets in the way of me claiming what is mine!" Then after this, I allowed his roar of anger to become the background echo to my journey while running to her room. It was the last place I felt her presence, so I was hoping... no, more like fucking praying that she was still in there! That the ache in my heart had been wrong. That pit in my gut that she left was nothing more than misplaced dread. That it was a mistake and she had not left me. For her heart might be damaged but at the very least it was still in the building ready for me to fix!

But the more I ran and the closer I got the less and less that hope held power, for I knew what I would find the second I opened that door.

"Amelia!" I shouted as I burst inside only to find the start of my nightmare playing out.

She was gone.

The moment I saw this I allowed my hands to curl into fists morphing the pain into a controlled anger that I dared not let loose inside this room for fear of destroying her things. Besides, I knew that if I did give into my demon's urge to break free that I would then be no use to anyone, the very least of all to myself.

For starters, I argued the fact that she couldn't have got far, as she didn't even have a car here...*or did she?* Would she have taken one...could she? These were things I needed to know, so without another thought I ran back to the library, knowing that I would find Dom released of his mental bonds and unsurprisingly I found him arguing with his wife, shouting about her deception.

"Amelia is gone!" I snapped the moment I made it back through the door and just at the sight of me, Dom was about to act when I held up a hand and warned,

"Don't make me put you on the floor again, Dom, my Chosen One is fucking missing and could be in danger, now you either help me find her or I will fucking put you on your knees and force your help! Now where the fuck would she go?!" I all but roared this at him making him take pause and think twice now that my words had taken the time to sink in. As, thankfully, the most important part was what he chose in that moment to focus on,

"She is missing?!"

"Oh, God," Keira said covering her mouth, the tears running down her cheeks starting afresh once more. I snarled at them both,

"I don't have fucking time for this! Now, where would she go!?"

"Draven, did she say anything when she saw you?" Keira asked, making me grateful that finally someone was asking the right fucking questions! Dom frowned down at the floor as if recalling the moment before he had flown inside here with the sole intent on killing me for supposedly kissing his wife. Something I assumed Amelia had told him as a way of a diversion, as it had certainly kept me busy enough for her to make her escape.

"No, but it would be easy for her to take one of the cars and…" I didn't listen to the rest as I was already out the door and travelling with unnatural speed down to the lower levels of Afterlife and where I knew Dom kept his car collection. Hell, when I got there under any other circumstances, I would have scoffed at the sight of his Ferraris all lined up. But instead it took me no time at all to see an empty space closest to what I knew was an automatic door that would have been on a sensor.

The second I knew Dom had turned up next to me, I snapped out my question,

"What car is missing?!"

"Ferrari SF90 Stradale," he answered quickly.

"Tracking?" I finally looked to Dom and he dragged a hand through his hair and snapped,

"What do you fucking think, Luc, no one is insane enough to steal from me?!"

"No one other than your daughter!" I snapped back making Keira come running inside with a phone in hand, holding it out to Dom, telling him,

"It's our pilot, he wants to know if he has authorization for the new flight plan to London Gatwick or not…it must be Faith!" Dom grabbed the phone and started telling him,

"No, you fucking…"

"Wait!" I told him, quickly cutting him off.

"Hold on, Curt," Dom said lowering the phone.

"Tell him yes, but to stall the flight."

"But why would he…" Keira was cut off when Dom held up his hand as he understood where my thoughts could potentially lead us to.

"Yes, Curt the flight is approved, but I need you to stall, tell my daughter that due to the last minute flight plan you are just waiting for the ground crew checks to be approved before you're allowed to fly." Dom waited for his pilot to agree, before I snapped,

"Don't let him leave before I fucking get there!" Dom nodded and relayed the order as I went back to scan the extensive garage, having no fucking time to waste.

"I need a car," I told him, making Dom walk towards a panel on the wall that housed all the keys before he grabbed a set. But then, instead of throwing them to me like I was about to demand he do, he walked to the closest car, a Ferrari Roma. A car that, even if I wasn't a fan of the brand, I had to admit was a good-looking car. Of course, it was an opinion I wouldn't be voicing anytime soon.

Dom walked to the driver's side and I frowned asking,

"What are you doing?"

"What the fuck does it look like I am doing, I'm driving, dickhead. Now, get in the fucking car before I change my mind!" he said before nodding for Keira to go to him. The second she did, he gripped her chin, and forced her gaze up to his before he growled down at her,

"First I get our daughter back, then you and I are going to have a very long talk, one that I have a feeling will start some years ago." She nodded letting the tears slip down her cheeks and I tore my eyes from the sight, hearing him whisper to her,

"Don't worry, I will bring her back to us."

"She is going to hate me." I heard her heartbroken admission and I could stand it no longer and got in the car, wishing in that moment I could have just wrestled the keys from his hold and sped off. I ignored his reply to this but instead snapped impatiently,

"We don't have time for this!" I heard Dom's growl in response, but my words rang true as he folded himself in the car and started the engine, watching his wife's small frame, arms wrapped around herself, in the rearview mirror until she went out of sight.

"Please tell me married life hasn't made you fucking soft on the accelerator?" I asked, as if the past fifteen minutes of trying to kill each other hadn't just happened, he looked to me and grinned before telling me,

"What the fuck do you think?" Then, as if to prove his point, he floored the pedal and forced the car to use all its six hundred plus horsepower. After this I was then forced to sit, unable to do more than just wait until we arrived, so I could claim my girl, her father be damned!

"How long, Luc?" His question suddenly cut through the silence. One I had hoped would have lasted until we arrived. *No such luck.*

"Seriously, you want to do this now?" I asked rubbing a hand at the back of my neck in frustration.

"I am driving you to the fucking airport to get my daughter back, Luc, so what do you think?!" he snapped making his point.

"For all I know you're planning to drive me off a fucking cliff and pray locking the doors will help you succeed." He scoffed a laugh.

"As tempting as that would be right now, I think we both know that I can't kill you without risking the life of my Chosen One…besides, I like this car." At this I couldn't refrain from commenting,

"Singing a different tune now I see."

"If I had wanted you dead, then you would be dead, Luc!" he snapped making me laugh.

"Yes, well, being as you are my Chosen One's father and I am pretty sure killing you first would present me with a lifetime of headaches, then right back at you, Dom." At this he held a hand up and said,

"Do me a favour, Luc, let's just stop talking about who you say my daughter is to you…or that cliff might find itself becoming a destination after all." I rolled my eyes and told him,

"Whatever suits and aids me in getting to this fucking plane of yours quicker." After this I continued to watch the world travelling past at a far slower speed than I would have liked, even though Dom was pushing the car as fast as we were physically able to go. Hell, he wasn't just breaking every speed limit, he was no doubt setting new records for speeds driven on these roads.

Of course, his silence also didn't last as he hit out at the steering wheel and growled,

"Fuck me! But I should have seen it sooner!" Naturally this didn't take a high IQ like Amelia possessed to know what he was referring to.

"I thought you didn't want to do this now?" I reminded him, something he ignored when he said,

"Gods, just how fucking blind have I been?!"

"I guess we are doing this now then," I muttered dryly under my breath as he continued to rant.

"I should have known it in my office, I should have fucking known it was you!"

"Yeah, well, what can I say, Dom, it wasn't exactly the time, or at least that is what the woman in your life kept telling me," I told him with the sarcasm more than evident in my tone.

"Oh, so you wanted to tell me but didn't and why, because a woman told you not to…? Yeah, because that sounds like you!" he commented derisively before adding,

"When is it that you let anyone dictate to you what you can or cannot do, let alone a woman?"

"I don't know, Dom, when was it that you found yourself afflicted with the same burden?" I asked knowing that I had made my point when he growled. I then released an exasperated sigh and told him,

"Amelia didn't know how to tell you and feared your reaction, and all things considered, I think she had a right to that, despite how I argued her decision... along with that of your wife's, I may add," I confessed making him bark,

"You should have fucking told me!"

"Yes, well I didn't! No, instead I went against my own wishes and was forced to watch as my Chosen One acted as if I meant little to her and allowed everyone to believe I had no rights to my claim," I bit back angrily, letting him know the toll which this had taken on me.

"A claim I still dispute, I will add!" he said making me growl,

"Dispute it all you want, Dom, but as you know the Fates cannot be denied, nor can they lie, which is why Keira knows and has for some time."

"How long?" he asked quickly.

"That is not my place and you fucking know it!" I told him in return, as the very last place I wanted to be right then was between a married couple who unfortunately happened to be the ones who birthed my Electus! Talk about fucked up!

"The least you can do is give me that!" he argued.

"I don't owe you shit, Dom! For the way I see it, if you had been the type of father and husband that had made it easier for the two women in your life to speak freely of the truth, doing so without them knowing for certain what your reaction would be, then none of this would have fucking happened!" I said giving him a bit of fucking reality.

"You're blaming me for this!?" I shook my head and sighed before telling him,

"Look, I was never fucking expecting a pat on the back and a welcome to the family, Dom, but seeing as you tried to rearrange my face, then yeah, I am blaming you for being their reason to keep this a fucking secret in the first place!" Dom thought on this before nearly destroying the wheel, being forced to ease his grip before he did.

"How long, Luc?"

"Does it fucking matter?" I asked making him shoot me a twisted look of betrayal before he snarled,

"How long has my wife known?"

"And I told you to ask…"

"It is the fucking least you could give me!" he interrupted and in that moment I decided instead of telling him to go fuck himself like I wanted to, I gave him what he asked, seeing as it was the lesser of two evils.

"My understanding is that she has known longer than even I have."

"Lucius," he said my name in warning before gritting out again,

"I asked how long?"

"Since the day she was born," I told him making him curse, *"Fuck!"*

"And she kept it from me…all this fucking time!"

"Yes, and ask yourself why that is, old friend," I said rolling my eyes and looking out the window taking note that we were at least getting there a lot quicker than we had done when first arriving.

"Oh, I know why, because I would have done everything in my fucking power to keep you from her, that's why!" he admitted with ease.

"Exactly and in doing so you would have also been committing the biggest sin as a King that you could, which is fucking with the Fates' plan…or are you forgetting the last time you tried to fight destiny in regard to your own wife? Something that, if I recall, had you been successful at then

Amelia wouldn't have even been born!" I said reminding him of his past and making him frown in frustration.

"And since when did you become so willing to accept the Fates' plans, huh? Only if memory serves, Luc, you have spent a great deal longer singing a very different fucking tune these past few thousand years." I gritted my teeth against the reminder of my own past and threw my own point back at him, being the next one to lash out in this verbal battle of ours.

"Yeah, well, you wanna know what happened?"

"Divine intervention?" he asked sarcastically.

"Your daughter happened, Dom, that's what!" I said making him growl my way, which I ignored and continued,

"But hey, lucky for you when you met your Chosen One you didn't have anyone but your own self getting in the way or holding you back."

"Oh no, I think I recall having someone in my way, Luc, or are you forgetting the Triple Goddess where my wife nearly lost her life too." I shook my head at his version of the past and told him,

"Yeah, well, go right ahead and call this even then, if that is what it takes, Dom, but the fact of the matter remains that I am not going anywhere! I am in your daughter's life and all that is left to discover is if you want to be in it also!"

"Exactly what are you threatening me with here, Luc?" he asked in a dangerous tone I ignored because it meant shit to me.

"Exactly what it sounds like, Dom. You want to try and get between me and my Chosen One, then fucking think again. She is mine and…"

"Oh no she fucking isn't!" he roared back making the car jerk suddenly into the other lane. An action he corrected before he had a head on collision and crashed before we could get there.

"Oh right, I forgot that you have a long list of people lined up ready to extend her life the way her Chosen One can by making her immortal, something you and I both know is only accepted by the Gods if it is fated to be," I reminded him contemptuously, making him tense as he knew I was right.

"Which explains the conversation in my office that night," he muttered to himself.

"I was merely trying to open your eyes to facts, Dom, just as I do now. She is mortal but doesn't need to stay that way and she won't, not by my side as my Queen," I said thinking this was the best way of reminding him that, despite his initial anger, once thought was applied, then really, how bad did he see our union to be. Especially when it meant granting him something he had wanted since discovering his daughter was mortal?

"I swear Luc, that if you start the next sentence by telling me you have already claimed my daughter, I will drive this fucking car into a tree and hope it impales you!"

"Believe what you want, Dom, it won't change a fucking thing!" I snapped back at his narrow mindedness and inability to admit that I was right.

"No, maybe not, but your actions today most certainly might have."

"Make your fucking point, Dom!"

"I think you are missing that the biggest obstacle in your way is no longer me. For have you considered that after what she believes happened between you and Keira today, that she won't want you anymore?" he argued and I swear I wished in that moment I could have knocked him out, left his vessel on the side of the road and driven the car there myself.

"I will make her see the truth," I told him in a firm unyielding tone that nearly cracked my teeth.

"Umm, yes because that is so easily achieved," he muttered mockingly.

"What?" I found myself asking in annoyance.

"I think I have a little more experience in this than you, Luc, you know, seeing as I have been dealing with both my own Chosen One and my daughter's personalities a lot longer than you to know that with all the will of the Gods, you can try and make them see what you want them to...but achieving it is another matter entirely." Unfortunately, that was a point made that I couldn't ignore.

"Yes, well for your sake and hers, I hope that you are wrong," I told him making him foolishly ask,

"Why is that?"

"Because now is not the time for her to disappear through that stubbornness, as she needs as much protection right now that she can get...*from both of us!*" I added this last part on an exasperated growl, seeing as I hated the fact about as much as I knew Dom did.

We both may hate it, but we also had no choice but to work together.

Again.

THE MOMENT we turned up at the private hanger, I knew instantly that something was wrong, even if the plane was still there and seemingly waiting to leave.

"Stop the fucking car!" I snapped and the second he did I jumped out. A moment later, his question heard behind me,

"What's wrong?"

"The Ferrari isn't here," I told him on a growl pushing past that fucking weight in the pit of my stomach that told me the worst of my fears weren't yet at an end but instead...

Only just beginning.

I ignored Dom's hiss of anger behind me and stormed

towards the plane, finding myself up its steps in less than a second of time. Then I saw her, and it was if my heart stopped dead at just the sight. She sat with her back to me wearing what she'd had on earlier, the scent of her blood filling my nostrils and easing my panic.

"Amelia." I whispered her name like a fucking prayer on the wind. I released a deep and regretful sigh the second she purposely didn't turn to face me, and it was only when I made it within reach of her that the truth of those scents started to infiltrate through the lies. Her hair, her skin, and even the blood that coursed around her body…

It was all wrong.

The blood on her sweater was old and the only piece about the figure sat before me now that belonged to her. I reached out and just before I could touch her, the imposter turned around to face me.

"She gave me money." I let my hand drop, forming a fist at my side on a snarl of anger.

"Get out!"

"Excuse…"

"I SAID GET THE FUCK OUT!" I roared making her cry out in fear before getting up and running out of the plane, pushing past Dom as he entered, the sight speaking for itself.

"Gods, no…tell me she didn't…"

"Deceive us all…Yes, Dom, yes she fucking did!" I snapped walking past him myself and back towards the car, doing so with purpose. Because it looked like my girl had given me the slip and run from me, slipping right through my fingers.

Meaning that once again it was time for this King to go…

Hunting.

CHAPTER THREE

A HELLISH FORCE OF HAND

By the time I returned to Afterlife I had issued so many orders, I wasn't sure how many of my people I had out there searching for her, Dante included. So, granted the journey hadn't been a waste of my time, despite cursing her name for half of it and cursing my own for the other.

Of course, I hadn't been the only one to spend the journey barking orders as Dom had also been making his own calls. Although, I couldn't help but point out that most of his would be pointless.

"You won't find her that way," I told him after he'd ordered whoever the fuck it was to monitor her bank accounts and have her passport flagged with all airports.

"Well, she won't get fucking far with no money or use of her passport!" he snapped, making me shake my head as I got out the car once it was back in front of his building.

"I think you will find yourself eating those words when you discover the level of just how cunning your little girl can be," was my irritated reply, hence half the journey spent cursing that very same cunning personality trait.

"Then what would you have me do, just fucking wait?!" he snapped back over the car's roof after first slamming the door shut.

"Not at all, I am just advising you on what your men will find, as will most of my own," I told him raking a frustrated hand at the back of my neck and making it crack.

"And that is?!" he demanded in a less than patient tone. So, as I entered the main doors to his club, I told him,

"Nothing, you will find…" I paused letting him overtake me once inside as suddenly a thought hit me, causing me to whisper the last word to that sentence,

"…*nothing.*" Dom looked back at me as my steps faltered. I then looked off to one side as my mind now focused on all the questions I had started to ask myself when she first stepped out of her hiding place. Questions that were only now starting to become relevant once more. Because, after I had found out she was missing, then nothing else had mattered but getting her back. And that same desperation in achieving this still stood strong but with little to go on, then it was time to find the answers I needed.

"What is it?" Dom asked obviously seeing it on my face as the last moments of her in the library started to play back in my mind. Then, the second I fixated on what I had seen after being flung back inside the library, I took off running. Doing so now with Dom following me and keeping up with my speed.

"You want to tell me what the fuck is going on now?!" he snapped the second I made it through the club, inside his home and back to the library, ignoring the obvious destruction we had caused.

"I am about to find out," I told him as I walked straight up to the hidden door into the Janus Temple that I had noticed was ajar.

"I take it your vault is through here," I commented as I opened the door and looked back at him. He raised a brow at me and nodded before following me inside.

"Amelia had the box in her hand when she found us," I told him making Dom reach out and grab me the second we stepped into one of the Temple's halls, holding me back long enough to tell me,

"She doesn't know where my vault is, Luc." I rumbled out a growl as I looked back towards the bloody footprints that now followed a path to only one door.

"No, but it looks like someone did," I commented with a grim expression.

"You think she was led here by…?" I quickly interrupted his thought process with a growl.

"The witch, *yes I fucking do,*" was my snarled reply before we both continued to follow the path, telling me now why it was that her shoes were soaked, and the hem of her jeans covered in blood.

"What the Hell could have happened?"

"I don't know but this isn't her blood." Dom growled at my answer and snapped,

"Please don't talk about her blood like you are well acquainted with it, as we already destroyed my library."

"And?" I asked with a raised brow.

"And I would prefer not to do the same to half this temple." I scoffed but refrained from telling him it was a little too late for that, for I was more than acquainted with it, I was fucking addicted to it! Of course, the moment I came to the vault door that obviously belonged to Dom due to the family crest that was carved at the centre, I was growling for a different reason.

"Now that is her blood."

"Yes, and I will ignore the reason it is now scented with that of yours," Dom replied in his own scathing tone.

"And how the fuck is it you think I am keeping her eternally young and healthy Dom, a heavy dose of Vitamin C in her morning juice?" I snapped making him snarl,

"Just stop speaking, Luc, for the love of the Gods, just don't say another word!" I smirked at that and focused back on the door, knowing now just looking at the center hole how the injuries to her hand had occurred. My only hope was that there was enough of my essence inside her that she would have healed by now. Along with the injury to the side of her head.

I moved out of the way so Dom could get the fuck on with it and open the door, one that wouldn't have needed half as much blood from him that it most likely had from Amelia. The thought didn't exactly sit well with me and from the hard look on Dom's face, then I would say our thoughts weren't that far apart.

"What the…?" he muttered the moment he opened the door and four inches of blood flowed out around our feet. We both looked inside to find the cause being from a large well situated through a wall of columns. One that could be seen overflowing with thick blood instead of the water that it should have been. Meaning that I knew just by looking at it, that it was no doubt fed by an underground spring that bordered the realms of Hell. Now, the biggest question was how it had turned to blood and had managed to flood the long passageway that led to what I assumed was Dom's vault.

"I take it that this isn't a security feature," I said dryly.

"No, it fucking isn't," was his stern reply as he continued on down the wide entrance hall, seeing for himself what I was, that the blood dripping down from high up on the walls told us that there had been a lot more of it earlier.

"Do you think she ran from this?" Dom asked and I took in

all the evidence I could, seeing that it was likely the doing of a certain witch we wanted to see burn. But there was only one way to know for sure. Which was why, after first swiping a finger down the wall and scenting the blood for myself, I turned to him and said firmly,

"Call your seeker."

AN HOUR later I found myself inside the library going back over everything we had learned so far. Something that, thanks to Takeshi, had started with a vision of myself waking her from a chair she had fallen asleep in. At least it answered how she had been led into the Temple to begin with and it pained me to see her trusting a figure of myself taking her into the dangers that awaited her. I had to give it to this bitch, the witch was turning into a mastermind at manipulating people.

I had, of course, ignored the questioning look I had received from Dom the moment Amelia threw herself into what she believed was my arms, telling me she was sorry. This, of course unbeknown to Dom, was referring to our argument on the rooftop.

But witnessing this all play out meant only one thing, which was that I found myself getting closer and closer to losing my shit with every second I was forced to watch the ghost of the past play out through Takeshi's re-enactment of events.

However, this had been nothing compared to having no choice but to assume force was needed when using Amelia to open the vault. This was something that we couldn't see due to Takeshi's limitations to where we were. But once inside, this hadn't been the case and we were forced to witness the struggle that occurred after the deception was discovered. And from the roar of anger next to me, then I would say I wasn't the only one finding this shit difficult. Especially when Dom's fist found itself embedded in his own image in the statue nearest to him. It reminded me once again of forcing myself to watch the fight between her and the mercs back at Transfusion. Although granted, it helped somewhat that I had seen her since this moment obviously happened, unlike before when she had been taken from me.

And just like that moment, I also found myself in utter awe at her strength and found that the only shred of a silver lining in all of this was that her father was finally getting a chance to witness it too. Because she made herself get to her feet despite the blow she received to the side of the head and run after the witch, fully intent on getting the box back.

Gods, but I didn't know whether to be angry at her for what could have happened or worship at the girl's feet for what she had accomplished when running after her. And it was easy to see that I wasn't the only one who was astounded as Dom's reaction was a mixture of disbelief and blessing the Gods for the gift of such a daughter. Something we were, unsurprisingly, in agreement of.

However, by the time Takeshi had finished showing us images of the past, then the biggest question of all had been how? Neither of us could understand what force had summoned the river of blood in that moment, for it was clear in the worried face of panic that it hadn't been the witch's doing, for she had looked both shocked and surprisingly... scared. It was a question that still plagued us both after Takeshi had admitted that no other trace of power could be detected, so it remained an unknown, something neither I nor Dom, accepted easily. But then Takeshi did also point out that his power was limited within the Temple's walls as the past belonged solely to that of Janus. Once through the doorways, this was another matter. Hence the void in Takeshi's visions.

It quickly had me questioning if consuming my blood wasn't taking some effect that could cause such a connection with the source of Hell's power the river of blood had come from? For that was the most that Dom's Seeker could detect, none of which eased our concern. But this all seemed secondary and cast in the shadows for the time being, seeing as she was still missing!

Dom had even called the authorities reporting the theft hoping to add pressure to finding her. This was after my insistence of course, for I would stop at nothing in my mission of finding her and if getting her put in a jail cell was a way to achieve it, then so be it!

I walked over towards where she had been hiding when watching the wrong end of the conversation between me and her mother, one I would fucking curse until the end of my days. Even now, as I slipped behind the staircase and saw a book on the floor, I continued to replay every word back, trying instead to hear it the way she would have.

Gods, how she could really believe my love for her had been a lie all this time, it made me fucking furious that she could ever believe that! After everything we had been through these last few weeks, did she seriously believe that it meant nothing to me?!

I was as angry at myself, as I was at her. Knowing exactly all the places in the past I had gone wrong and asking myself if there was ever going to be a point with Amelia when I actually started doing things right!?

I lifted the book from the floor on the page it had fallen open seeing for myself the significance of events in those two pages. The double picture depicted was one that looked to have imitated life. A blood-soaked kiss represented her fairy tale unravelling and turning into what now looked to be a poisonous kiss she believed happened between myself and her mother. For

I turned around and tried to see it through her eyes. To see what she had seen and quickly realising now that during that tender moment between Keira and I as old friends, it may have indeed looked like a stolen kiss between lovers.

The thought sickened me! I found my hands fisting the pages and tearing away the image of two lovers kissing, a scene now stained in the blood of heartbreak. Their perfect dream now shredded by demonic claws that forced their way over my fingernails. In fact, the more time passed the harder it became to hold back my demon from taking over completely. The only reason it hadn't been allowed to happen yet was the belief that news would come to me soon and when it did, I needed to be in my right mind to act and act quickly.

Needless to say, that it was a torturous wait.

I left the library, knowing that it held nothing more for me in its discovery. Numb steps soon had me stood outside her bedroom door, cursing the fact that I hadn't gotten there sooner. Along with it, the knowledge that I had been wasting that time in fighting with Dom before being able to get to her in time to stop her from leaving!

I pushed open her door and tried to take in anything that may have been missing, seeing that not one thing had been packed.

She had left with nothing.

Dom assured me that she wouldn't get far with no money and no passport, with nothing to her name but a stolen Ferrari. And I hoped…no, *more like fucking prayed,* that he was right. But something in my gut told me that Amelia wasn't going to be as easily caught as her father liked to think and no amount of hoping for that outcome would change facts. For her intelligence was nothing but a curse set against me.

Even her copy of the map she had taken today had been left on her desk, making me crush it in my hand before I turned back to her geeky little heaven. Which meant that without the box, one that was back in Dom's possession for now, and without the map, then she was making a statement by leaving them both behind…she was done with her mission of discovery.

Just as she assumed that she was done with me.

A fact on which she would soon find herself proven wrong…*very, very wrong.*

I tore my eyes from the bed, tired of seeing her there in my arms like some cruel memory on repeat. For had it not been her room, then I would have found my fist embedded somewhere in space and the centre of the painted wall.

"You!" The second I heard the hiss of anger coming from the door I knew exactly who I would find standing there like some twin image of both mother and father combined.

"I don't have time for you, boy," I commented letting my dark tone speak for itself.

"I don't give a fuck if you do! You did this! You pushed her away just like the first time!" Theo roared at me, storming his heavy frame inside her room and making me snarl at him for doing so. Right now, this room was off limits.

"You know nothing of which you speak and therefore this will be the only warning you get…back the fuck off, Theo!" I growled in a dangerous way, one the brazen youth didn't take seriously.

"Man, you got some fucking nerve, you treat my sister like that and expect me to just what, let you get away with it. I don't give a shit if what she saw wasn't…"

"You spoke to her?!" I snapped, suddenly realising it and hearing it in his voice for myself.

"I didn't say that, but the way I look at it, seeing as she left you then it's no longer your business even if she did!" The second he said this was when I officially lost my shit, releasing the firm hold I'd had on my demonic side and relishing the moment of furious freedom!

"Big. Fucking. Mistake!" I snarled low and menacing before I made my move. Theo braced just in time for me to fly into him, forcing him back through the door so we wouldn't destroy anything Amelia treasured.

We ended up crashing into one of the many stone walls in Afterlife, before I grabbed him and threw him down the hallway, one that was getting closer to my intended target. But then the asshole simply shook it off and barreled right back into me, causing us both to go crashing into some antique sideboard that almost crumbled on impact.

I felt a fist in my gut, just as my own connected with his jaw for the second time that day. However, the longer this continued, the more and more my demon seeped through and before long I couldn't stop it as the leather on my glove ignited into Hellish flames. Meaning that if I didn't put a stop to this, then I would end up doing something that couldn't be undone the moment I touched him.

For a single touch by the hand of the Venom of God was all it would take to,

Kill a Draven.

"ENOUGH!" I roared and forced him to his knees using my will against him, just as I had done with his father. Only this time, he didn't know it, but it was done so more for his sake than mine. So, despite making it less than a fair fight, the alternative would have undoubtably been far worse. Besides, I needed to get to the bottom of that call and fast.

"Now you will tell me where she is?!"

"Fuck…AHHH!" He ended this insult in pain as I twisted my fist, mimicking his spine.

"Lucius, stop!" Keira shouted coming out of Dom's office, clearly still upset shown by the tears streaming down her face.

"I will, just as soon as he tells me what I demand to know!" I informed her calmly despite my demonic appearance. Then I felt her hand on mine, the only being in the world able to touch my hand and survive. This was due to the same Venom of God in her blood, being why she was unaffected by it.

Her touch startled me enough that I dropped my hold on the boy's mind and staggered back, feeling my wings hitting the wall first before my back followed.

"He doesn't know where she is, she wouldn't tell him, just as she wouldn't tell me," Keira admitted in a devastated tone.

"You spoke to her!? When, what did she say?!" I demanded in a rush of words.

"Luc, please just calm down and…"

"NO! For fuck sake, Keira, don't you see, all this deception, all these fucking lies are the reason I am now stood here without my Chosen One! She ran because I agreed to do as you asked of me!" I said verbally lashing out at her.

"I know…I know, but please if you will just listen to me and let me explain then I…"

"NO! No… FUCK NO! I am done listening! I have never once gone against you or said no to you, Keira, but I am fucking done! No more, No fucking more! Because all the lies, the secrets, where has it got me…WHERE IS MY GIRL!?" I roared losing it and I only knew this when Theo rose slowly and positioned his mother behind him, protecting her now and staring at my exposed hand.

"Easy now, Luc…let's just take a breath," Theo said in a calming tone that was meant to bring me back from whatever had claimed my vessel, aiming for my mind next. So, I followed their fearful gaze and looked down at my own hand, feeling it pulsating with Hell's power like the Devil's own limb was attached to me. And that wasn't far from what I found, for it was only a glimpse of the charred black scarred skin that I had been used to seeing whenever I finally removed the glove.

However, now in the height of my wrath, it was more like volcanic rock with glowing magma showing through the cracks, as it had arisen from Hell's own rivers of fire with the sole purpose of causing death and destruction as it was currently creating an opening in the floor. A growing circle of energy where I was unknowingly summoning up that same liquid fire I seemed able to command, and it was now flowing up through the opening I had made and being absorbed into the tips of my molten crusted fingers, each digit cursed for an eternity. It was as if it was reaching for its demonic puppet master, the edges of the flames licking out and scorching the stone floor, turning it black like my own burnt skin. Its infection spreading like soul weed, snapping outwards with every inch grown from the glowing hot serpents that continued to reach for me, as it was obvious that I was the one dragging them up from the portal I had made from Hell.

"Lucius, *let go.*" I heard Dom's voice coming closer, after first taking hold of Keira's shoulders and pulling her further back, nodding to his son to protect her as he took their place.

"I am not sure I can," I confessed, my voice barely being that of my own, as it only just made it through the hold this undiluted rage had on my demon.

"Yes, you can my friend, you just need to fight it." I looked up at him and saw the sincerity of those words in his purple gaze, his own dark wings now hiding his family from my view.

"She ran from me," I told him, giving him the root of my rage.

"She ran from us all."

"But she is mine." My demon growled for us both as I felt the first tentacles of flames curling around my arm, feeding the venom in my flesh with a power I could barely contain. Dom

looked to my hand and closed his eyes a second longer than what was needed, for it was the first time he had seen it since I'd lost it completely all those years ago.

"Then the Fates will grant her back to you," he told me in a strained tone that said so much more.

"You can't know that," I said gritting my teeth at the very thought of the words I spoke.

"Oh, but I can, for they granted me back my own," he said looking behind him and lowering a side of his wing to see his wife, who had tears in her eyes. But I found the sight too painful to look at anymore…for he had his Chosen One. He had fought for her and won! I snarled down at my hand, the hand now cursed by the first sinful act of an Angel of God and one that turned to poison. The one I had no choice but to sacrifice at the gates of Tartarus before it grew back into little more than a cursed hand of the Gods!

"Luc, don't go back there…don't listen to what that hand is telling you to do," Dom said for he knew what it wanted me to do. It wanted me to burn the entire place down beyond its foundations and even past the realms of Earth, sinking it into a portal in Hell I knew I had the power to open. I wanted his happiness consumed and twisted back into the hatred of mankind!

I wanted a war.
I wanted death.
And I wanted destruction!

I wanted to scorch the Earth, ridding it of all life until there was nothing in it but her! I wanted nothing in this world but her by my side for all of eternity!

"I want her back!" I snarled fisting my Devil's hand. Dom released a sigh and told me,

"I know."

"I WANT HER BACK, DOM!" I roared again, now looking

back at him and he closed his eyes once more before telling me in earnest this time,

"I know, my friend." I forced the hard lump of pain down my throat before I felt as if I would choke on it and heard Dom take in another breath before telling me,

"I will help you...I will help you get her back, Luc." I took another breath, one that didn't come easily, for I knew how hard those words had been for him to say and therefore the true meaning behind them.

"Then you accept my claim?" I asked near fucking ready to follow through with the destructive nature of my hand should he say anything but what I wanted him to say.

But this time when he closed his eyes, he didn't open them again until after he answered me, making even his wife hold her breath.

"Yes, I accept your claim on my daughter," he finally admitted, and it was a sentence that seemed as if it had been torn from him, forcing others to lay witness to his acceptance. I, too, found myself closing my eyes as the true meaning of this moment branded itself to my soul.

It was a decree he could never take back.

"Good, because I promise you this, the moment I find her again, then make no mistake, Dom..." I said taking pause and extinguishing the flames of Hell with nothing but a click of my fingers. Doing so with ease now that my mind was back to being centered and focused on only two things, one was finding her and the second was the promise I then made to her father,

A promise not even the Gods could prevent...

"Make no mistake...*I am making her my wife!*"

CHAPTER FOUR

AMELIA

BRIBES AND PHONE CALLS

Once I left the airport, I found myself driving until I could stand it no longer. I didn't know how long it had been, but it was now dark, and I knew that if I didn't fill up the car soon, then this journey would come to an end a lot quicker than I first anticipated. Now, that was the problem with stealing a twin turbocharged V8 engine that kicked out 986 horsepower…it was damn expensive to fill up the tank!

Now, if only my father had parked one of his electric sports cars nearer to the entrance then this little getaway of mine would have been a lot cheaper, as the electric part of this engine gave you all of about fifteen miles and that was it, although it did help air in making it go faster, so that was something at least. Damn it though, why couldn't I have stolen a Tesla, his two-seater roadster could do about 600 miles on one charge.

Which meant that it was time to form the next stage of my plan. To be quite honest, I had been surprised I had even made it this far, knowing that by now my father had no doubt called the cops and reported the theft. Which meant that I needed to ditch the car as soon as I could, and to do that, I needed first to use it as collateral. Which was why the second stage of my plan was admittedly an insane one. But then again…

What did I have left to lose?

My heart was shattered.

My life was in pieces.

My future gone.

All I had left was my mind and before I would allow it to fully submerge in the self-loathing, self-pitying, bitter hatred, pathetic part of the night, I first had to use it to get the Hell out of Dodge. Which was why I had been ignoring all the tears that escaped, trying instead to focus on the road and not the sight of my own heartbreak in the mirror.

I barely knew how my mind had even managed to get this far, but it had. It had all started when I had run back into my room and just found myself standing in the centre of what had once been my entire world. But all I found myself saying over and over again whilst looking up at the ceiling was,

'Lies, lies, lies…nothing but lies.'

I had then looked around the room and in the end knew I had no time to take any of it. I had no time to pack. I even grabbed my bag but then realised that I wouldn't have been able to use anything inside it. Not my phone, not my bank cards, not even my passport…everything could be traced.

So, in the end, I grabbed the only thing that I knew was worth enough for me to make it as far as I did. Then, I pulled the map from my bag and placed it on my desk in plain sight, knowing that it would be found. Doing so in hopes of fooling whoever found it into believing that the last thing on my mind was anything to do with the problems we faced. After this I had run out of there and doing so to the sound of destruction as my father and Lucius obviously fought it out.

In fact, it brought me so much pain that I found myself falling into the wall and crying out in agony, knowing that I had caused the fight. Gods, but what if my father really hurt him... surely he wouldn't go too far...surely he wouldn't risk my own mother's life? Because although I hated them both that didn't mean I wanted either of them hurt by my own doing.

They could suffer with the knowledge of what they had done to me. From the knowledge that they had broken our family apart and hurt those they had deceived. But that was the extent of the pain I wanted them to suffer. Which was why I looked to the library and took a few steps towards it before stopping myself. I did this twice more before crying out in anger, hitting the side of my fist to the wall before running in the opposite direction, ignoring the pain to my hand or to the side of my head. I knew the cuts I had suffered, thanks to the deception of the witch, had already started to heal and it sickened me to know why.

Lucius' essence was still a part of me.

After this decision was made, I continued running until I got to my father's garage and stole the keys to the car nearest to the door. After that I had broken every speed limit and thanked whatever luck I had left in my life that I wasn't pulled over by the cops on the way to the airport. But this wasn't all I did. As after I had angrily swiped away my tears it then took me all of about two minutes of driving to form the first part of my plan.

Because I needed to disappear. I needed to leave once and for all. I could no longer be a part of that world...my father's world...the world Lucius belonged to. It pained me to think of my parents splitting up or my father being in the same amount of pain as I was feeling. But then no matter how much I loved Lucius, I knew deep down that for my father it would be worse.

So much worse.

Which was why, after the first part of my plan was out of the way, I knew that I needed to call him. Just the once. I needed to know he was alright before leaving for good. But before that call, first came the one to my father's pilot. A number that was thankfully still in the history of calls in the car's fancy system. So, a few taps later and I was making plans with him to take me to London, knowing that his next call would be to my father asking his permission. After that I was relying on only one factor left and that was greed.

Which then meant that I had no time at all before I was pulling the car close to the plane and running on board ready to make a deal with the flight attendant, really hoping that she had a thing for diamonds.

I hated myself for doing it, seeing as it had been a gift from my parents on my twenty first birthday. The necklace was called a Pluie de Cartier and was a collar of twenty-one vertical and horizontal lines of diamonds equating to 27.7 carats. Each line was framed by even more diamonds that were all set in 18K white gold. Naturally, I had only worn it once, being utterly terrified of losing it or damaging it in some way. Or even worse, having it stolen, which was why it had remained at Afterlife with all the other jewellery my family had bought me over the years.

But I told myself that one day I would get it back, no matter how much it would cost me. Even though, knowing my father's taste, then I would no doubt have to sell my flat to do so! However, it was my only ticket out of here, so I used it to gain my part time identity. So, I took one look at her and sent up a quick thank you to the Gods that she was at the very least a brunette, because if she had been blonde then this might have a been a little harder at the whole convincing thing.

After this I took out the necklace and quickly began to explain, telling her time was of the essence. Of course, she had asked me if it was real, making me tell her,

"Look outside and take a look at what car I just arrived in and you tell me if its real or not."

"Okay, good point," had been her short answer. After that she didn't take much convincing to swap clothes, even though I first had to convince her it was red paint on them not the dried blood it looked to be. Although to be fair, her wide eyes were more focused on the necklace anyway, so I think it was more a case of her *conveniently wanting* to believe me.

So, I handed over the diamonds and in return she handed me her purse that she admitted only had a credit card with a $1500 limit that half of which had been spent and a current account that held another $756 and $245.61 in cash. Which meant she just got the bargain of the century seeing as the necklace she now wore underneath the sweater was worth at a guess well over a hundred thousand dollars. She did at least offer me her overnight bag, that she explained had a change of clothes and some toiletries in it, meaning that she felt bad enough to add a little extra onto my side of the deal.

Then, after giving me her details for accessing her money, I thanked her and ran back to the car with what I could only assume was minutes to spare. I knew this as I had already been told upon my arrival how the plane was being 'delayed' for some bogus reason or another. This then meant that my dad had been told and was trying to get them to stall for time until one of his men or even he himself could get here.

Either way, my time was short, so I had dropped my new cabin sized luggage in the seat beside me, unsure whether it would fit in the trunk space or not. Then I made for the highway, but an hour later, I found that couldn't stand it any longer,

I had to call home.

So, I pulled into a rest stop, happy that it was pretty much empty that time of night. Then, after dashing inside, I found an ATM and drained as much as I could get out of the flight attendant's accounts before I ran back to the car. After which I took a deep breath and made the decision who was safe to call at Afterlife.

In the end, there was only one.

"Hey, it's me," I said the second he answered.

"Gods, Fae! Where the Hell are you!?" Theo asked before anything else, telling me that they were most definitely still looking for me.

"That's not important right now," I told him making Theo scoff,

"The fuck it isn't! Look, just tell me and I will come and pick you up...Hell, I will even drive you to an airport and get on a fucking flight with you, just don't do this alone...come on, don't be a pain in my ass, sis." The sound of his pleading tone made me wince a second, bunching my shoulders before forcing my muscles to relax with the release of a sigh.

"Well, you are always calling me little lost girl, so..." I said trying to sound a lot more lighthearted than I felt.

"Yeah, and it's so *not* the time to give that nickname new meaning," he responded dryly.

"Look, I appreciate it, Theo, but really, this is just something I have to do alone...yeah.?

"Fuck no, but do I get a choice here?" he asked sounding frustrated and I could understand why, seeing as Theo would most definitely be struggling with this. I remembered the day we first met. The way he had wanted to help me even then, even before he knew who I was to him. But that was Theo, he was everyone's hero and no matter how much I loved him for it, simply put…

Now was not my time for heroes.

"Not really, no…I just rang to…well, I just need to know how bad it is there?" I asked wincing before pushing through and just getting it out by asking.

"Well, Lucius is still alive, if that is what you mean?" he said sarcastically.

"Not really what I meant, no."

"Fuck, I don't know…what do you want me to say, Fae? The library looks like a war zone and mum hasn't stopped crying since you left." I tensed at that, holding myself rigid and closing my eyes against the pain.

"And dad?" I asked before the question got too hard to ask thanks to the heavy emotions I could feel trying to drown me under the weight of my heartbreak. But then he delivered a shocking blow,

"Well, that's the kicker, as soon as they realised you were gone they both left together."

"What!?" I shouted in utter shock at even the thought of it. For one why would Lucius even bother now that the pretense was over and secondly, why would my father even allow him to tag along? None of it made sense.

"They are both on their way back from the airport now, which I can guess they won't be too pleased about seeing as you weren't there…were you?"

"That's not a bad assumption to have there, Thor," I replied making him scoff.

"I can't believe they are together after what he did," I muttered mainly to myself.

"Yeah, well, it's true dad lost his shit after learning about you and Luc…" Theo started to say making me shout out, interrupting him,

"He knows that?!"

"Wait, Fae, why do I feel like I am missing a big piece of what is really going on here?" he asked making me realise that my time was up and now was the time to end the call. I had involved him too much as it was.

"Theo, I am sorry, I have to go, just do me a favour and tell dad that I am sorry...okay."

"No wait! Look, please just let me help you...you don't have to do this alone... fuck Fae, you don't need to do this at all! If you need a place to crash, then come stay with me. I will protect you, I will keep that shit stain away from you and..." I closed my eyes against just how tempting it was not to have to do this on my own, but then I knew that it wouldn't be me running, it would just be me hiding from the inevitable life I would have to go back to.

"Thanks, but I...*I can't.*"

"Why the fuck not?" he snapped.

"Because I can't involve you in my problems and besides, I am pretty sure after this I will be the black sheep of the family even more than I already was," I told him with a shrug of my shoulders he couldn't see.

"Don't say that! Shit Fae, I don't know what has happened here other than dad finding out about you two, but surely running is not the answer, not when there is a fucking threat out there and..." I cut him off once more,

"I dealt with that...look, I will be fine, don't worry okay and..." I froze the second I heard the other voice in the room, making me tense all over.

"Is that her...is that Faith?!" My mum's desperate voice invaded the conversation and it nearly broke me.

"Look, I have to..." I started to say when suddenly she was there.

"Faith...oh, thank God you're okay! Sweetheart please, you

need to listen to me." I closed my eyes once more and held them tight as tears started to seep from beneath them, telling her in a hard tone I felt cracking,

"No mum, that's where you're wrong, I don't need to listen to anything…"

"It's not what you think, you've got it all wrong. Me and Luc aren't or never have been anything more than just friends… please believe me, I don't know what you heard but it wasn't what you…" This was when I hit my breaking point and snapped,

"I can't listen to this! I have to go… just tell dad I am sorry. Goodbye Mum," I said quickly hanging up just as she shouted on the end for me to listen and before she could say anything more. Because I didn't want to listen to it right then. Maybe one day I would ring and listen to what she had to say, but I knew what I had seen. I knew what I had heard. They had kissed, they had shared a moment, spoken the words.

What else could it have been?

There was no other explanation than the one I had witnessed.

The reasons behind my breaking heart…

The confessions of their affair.

CHAPTER FIVE

BAD ASS AND BATS

After ending the call to my Mum, I found myself shaking as I didn't know what I wanted to do first, scream in anger or agony. Because I didn't want to allow her words to create doubt in my mind. I didn't want that poisonous and lying emotion called hope clouding my decision to leave.

No, she was just saying all of those things to try and get me to go back there. Because she loved me still, like a mother would. She cared for my safety. She would say anything. I swallowed hard and folded my arms across the steering wheel before burying my head there and sobbing, letting it all go. The sound of someone calling becoming nothing but a theme song for my pain and I looked side on at the screen through my tears, cancelling it with a stab of my finger and all those after it.

Then, I took a deep shuddering breath and started the car ready to follow through with the rest of my getaway. Which meant that I continued to drive, all the while asking myself what on earth Luc had said for both him and my father to be driving to the plane together?

It was the only part of this that made no sense. I knew my dad and if he believed Luc had been having an affair with his wife then other than outright killing him, which he couldn't do, the very last thing he would do was spend time with him in a fucking car!

But then again, when did any of this day make sense?

When did the sense part come into it, as everything in your life starts to unravel?

Never. *That's when.*

I looked at the clock and seeing that the longer I gave them, the more chance they had to issue their orders, it meant that it was time to put the next part of my plan into action. And well, for that I needed to speak to the only person in my life I felt I could trust. The only person who wouldn't try and convince me to go home or 'do what *they* thought was best'. I thought about Auntie Pip, but then I knew she would never go against my mum and she was clearly emotional after what had happened. So, as much as it pained me, I knew that I couldn't count on her.

No, there was only Wendy left in my life. And luckily for me I had memorized her number a while ago, which meant that I could tap it in to the car's inbuilt phone using its Wi-Fi and ring my last lifeline.

"Err...Hello?" Wendy answered in the way most people would when they didn't recognise the number calling them.

"Kirky, it's me," I said, unable to prevent my emotions from pouring out in those three words. Because that was the effect of a true friend, one you needed in moments of desperate need for comfort. I had missed my friend and had barely had the chance to speak to her during all that had been going on. But, before leaving for Afterlife, Lucius had given me his phone so I could call her, finally able to update her with the status of my relationship. News that seemed pointless now.

"Emmie! Oh my God, Jesus, I have been so worried!" The second her panicked voice said this I knew that she had already been contacted.

"I'm fine, honey."

"Yeah, well, that boy of yours doesn't seem to think so, as let's just say that he put the fear of God in me!" she said, making me tense.

"What do you mean…Lucius called you?" I asked with a shake of my head knowing that this didn't sound right.

"Oh yeah, he called me alright and your father, oh and then Dante, the asshole," she said in a tone that was incredulous and ended on a growl of words obviously disliking the last one, something I knew I would have to ask her about when the time was right. I had tried the last time I spoke to her, but it had been obvious she hadn't been ready. Something, that unfortunately in this moment I could relate to, so I hadn't pushed.

"What did he say?"

"I would ask which one, but I gather with the sound of heartbreak in your voice you only mean one…oh and also I have someone's skull to crack should I ever meet the asshole!"

"Yeah, well I will hand you the bat, but for now…" I said, leaving out the part that he would just catch it on the downward blow and snap it in two. However, my comment made her chuckle before telling me,

"Only that you had done another runner and that it was basically a life and death situation that you were found and that if I wanted to be any help to you, I would call him the second you called and tell him everything you told me."

"Gods, why would he do that?" I muttered in disbelief.

"My guess, because he cares and is freaking out that you

left him," she answered making me frown at the dashboard with a shake of my head. Then I found myself asking,

"Are you going to?"

"Fuck no! You're my girl, he can eat shit and die if he hurt you, which I am guessing he did." I snorted a laugh and wiped the tears that had escaped with the back of my hand telling her,

"Yeah...*he did.*"

"Oh Smock, I am so sorry, honey. Men are shits, what can I say?" I scoffed at that and said,

"You can say that again."

"Alright, men are shits, now you say it with me." I laughed and did as she asked,

"Men are shits...*you got that right.*" I said lacking her enthusiasm for it and making her whisper,

"Oh, honey...do you wanna talk about it?" I sniffed back my tears and told her,

"Maybe one day but right now it's just too painful, you know," I told her and right in that moment I wished I was back there. I wished I was about to knock on her door, ready to throw myself in her arms and pour my heart out. But then again...

I wished for so many things.

"I understand, honey. I wish I didn't but like I said, men are shits so what are you gonna do other than invest in a bat thing." I snorted a laugh at this, smiling through my tears before she then asked,

"So, what can I do, you coming home, need a plane ticket, whatever you need, I'm your Trekkie." I smiled, sniffing back the tears that threatened again, this time from the love I had for this woman...this wonderful friend of mine. As we may not have spoken much these last few weeks, what with all the craziness that was happening in my life, but it didn't matter. Because this was what real friends were, the ones who were there for you no matter how much time had passed.

They weren't the ones who got shitty with you for what you had or had not done. They understood the situation and gave you the space you needed, being ready at the first moment you needed it, surrounding you with their comfort. It made me long for my life back. It made me wish that I could just go home and camp out in my living room in my PJs with Kirky by my side making me laugh or holding me through my tears.

But I couldn't.

Because right now, my life wasn't my own. Lucius' phone call to my best friend was proof enough of that. Besides, I still had a job to do. Which is what I told her,

"I can't. I have something important I need to see through to the end before I can get my life back on track."

"Alright, now I feel the need to say this just because if anything ever happened to you and I hadn't, then I would never forgive myself…you know," she said in a serious tone that told me she was worried.

"Yeah, I know."

"So, here it is, the friend lecture part of the call." I laughed and said,

"Okay, go for it."

"This thing you need to do…is it dangerous?" I released a sigh before telling her,

"I am not going to lie to you because you're my best friend, which is why I am telling you, that yes, it could be."

"Smock…I don't…" she started to say, and I could almost see her shaking her head, wondering if her 50's pinned barrel curls were lasting through it. So, I cut her off,

"Okay, so before you say anything, there is something I need you to know about me."

"Which is?" she asked in a naturally suspicious tone. I took a deep breath and told her,

"I am kick ass." She burst out laughing and said,

"Yeah right, pull the other one," she said referring to her leg, one that was most likely attached to some quirky mad shoe of hers.

"No, I am serious and shit you not, my friend. I am a total bad ass", I said trying again.

"Seriously, this coming from the girl who makes painting her toenails look dangerous?" I laughed and I had to say, it felt damn good.

"Oi, I said I was bad ass not a gazelle…besides, as it turns out, you can totally beat the crap out of guys and still be clumsy enough to trip over standing still."

"Ha, who knew," she replied before adding,

"So, being serious for a moment, exactly how bad ass are we talking here, like John McLane or John Wick?"

"I would like to lean further towards the Wick but without his extensive knowledge of guns," I told her with a smirk.

"Holy shit! Are you serious?!" she shouted after first sounding like she might have spat out her drink.

"Deadly." I giggled happily in that blissful moment, ignoring the past and painful hours this day had granted me.

"So, like when…when did this happen, I mean what exactly have you been doing these past few weeks, training with the Marines?" she asked clearly surprised, as anyone would be.

"I wish… no, it's just something I have always done."

"Ermm…back up a sec, like why is this something I am only now hearing about?"

"Well, it never came up," I argued lamely.

"Okay, just so you know for future potential friend making, that granted, will never be as awesome as me but nevertheless, it should always come up… for example, like when we first met, you should have introduced yourself as, 'hello, I am Emmie, kick ass extraordinaire, my hobbies include collecting Lego, lame T shirts and putting men on their ass when they get too grabby…plus, I just bought a bat." I burst out laughing at that before agreeing,

"Right, I must really remember that for next time," I said with a smirk.

"I can't believe you didn't tell me! I could have been making money with you in underground fight clubs!" she said in a high-pitched way, again making me giggle.

"And just how many of those do you know about, huh?"

"Admittedly not one, but hey if I ever find a Brad Pitt look alike then I will follow him and see where he goes."

"Oh sure, that's why you would follow him," I said in a knowing tone making her laugh this time.

"And besides, don't you mean Ed Norton, as I believe…"

"Yeah, yeah alright smarty kick ass pants. So, back to this plan of yours, what do you need?" she said getting back down to business.

"Do you still have your connections in New York?" I asked, knowing she was right. Because as much as I needed this conversation for my sanity at the moment, I also had a time restriction set against me.

"Yeah…whyyy?" she said in a way that extended the word and I could just tell it was one of those, 'I have a bad feeling' type of why.

"Because I have a plan, but first I need money."

"Well, why not just…wait, you're not just running from the hot Ex are you? That's why I got a call from hot daddy too." I groaned and told her,

"Please, don't call him that and yes, I am running from everyone."

"But why?" she asked clearly confused, which became just one more thing to add to the long list of shit I couldn't tell her fully.

"It's hard to explain right now, but I promise you, Kirky,

one day I will explain everything…off the record of course, I said knowing this was only a half promise and feeling bad about it, but then again, I also knew it was a truth that I was forever forbidden to tell.

"Alright, but I am trusting you here not to get yourself killed…don't disappoint me…yeah?"

"I promise and if it helps, I really don't want to get killed either," I admitted.

"Good to know and just for the record…you are officially one of the coolest and most mysterious people I know, especially when I just thought you were a geek in PJs." I laughed at this and said,

"Oh Kirky, *you have no idea.*"

CHAPTER SIX

CHOP SHOP SHOWDOWN

Driving through the clearly dodgy areas of New York wasn't exactly my idea of fun, but neither was driving five hours straight to get here all the way from Portland, Maine. But then Wendy had come good on her promise to help and found me the guy I needed.

He was someone who worked at the New York Times and he had written a few articles on the Iron Triangle. This had basically once been a place where stolen cars went to die. It was a place in Corona Queens where the METS played baseball and where people used to turn their heads away from the slum across the street. A place that once looked more like an apocalyptic version of New York than what it did today, now that the city had finally stepped in and reclaimed the land after years of promising to do so. Hence why the flooded, pothole heaven was no more.

But before the high rise complex had been built, it had been Willets Point, a place known for its auto repair shops, scrap yards, waste processing sites, and similar small businesses that consisted of people all trying any way they could to make a dollar. It was a place where junkies slept in broken, rusting cars and only came out at night. It was a place where the smell of garbage had once been a scent people became used to. And where sights like a van's back doors being held together by three rolls of duct tape was considered the norm. Where graffiti on the walls and burnt out cars became the only flashes of colour in this typically grey part of the world.

But like I said, a world that no longer existed thanks to the city finally intervening. However, this merely meant that a lot more chop shops ended up opening around different areas of the city, as stealing cars and stripping them down for parts was still a business many didn't feel like giving up on. Which was where Wendy's contact came in.

See, after he had followed the wastelands of the Iron Triangle, he had ended up meeting quite a few people and only one name continued to pop up among the drunken chatter of small shop owners during that time. He was the one who dealt with the more, should we say, wealthy side of things, and movies like Gone in 60 Seconds became the documentary of life for this gangster.

They called him Big B, which from what I gathered could mean anything from boss, boulder, berserker and bone breaker. In other words, he was known as a ruthless, hard bastard that took no shit and was one scary motherfucker. This being the word on the street.

Big B was also the one who dealt with cars that weren't easy to come by or easy to steal for that matter, as it wasn't as if you could just jimmy a window of a Ferrari and hot wire one. Meaning that he had a syndicate of experienced and highly talented thieves working for him. He was also the one who had them stolen and on a container heading off to his clients before the owner even knew their prized possession had even been stolen.

He was in the big leagues.

And, as insane as it was, he was exactly who I needed right now.

So, I arranged to meet her contact, a guy called Micky and was just pulling up to Central Avenue after Wendy had arranged the meeting place. And well, seeing as I was the one currently sat in a Ferrari, then I wasn't exactly hard to spot. Which meant the second some skinny white guy with a baseball cap and a hood over the top approached my door and knocked on the window, I lowered it and asked,

"You Micky?"

"Bitch, I will be whoever the fuck you want me to be, now get the fuck outta the car!" he said pulling out a gun and pointing it at me through the window. It was at this point that I rubbed the top of my nose in frustration and said,

"I guess that's how you people say hi in New York then, huh?" He snapped,

"Bitch you fucking wacked or…AAHHH!" This ended in a scream of pain the second I grabbed his wrist and bent it back on itself making him drop the gun in my lap.

"Tut, tut, Micky, you don't think I would be stupid enough to drive my nice expensive car around here if I couldn't take care of myself, now would you?"

"Bitch, my name ain't…Ahhh, okay, okay." I cut him off by applying some more of that handy, agonizing pressure before giving him some advice,

"Tip for you Micky, never start off an answer with Bitch, especially if that bitch in question is the one who's had a bad fucking day and might just snap your wrist for the sheer fucking fun of it…now let's start again should we?"

"Yeah, yeah, okay cool…shit Bitc…I mean lady, you got

it!" he said quickly singing a different tune and wincing through the pain I caused.

"Good, now there is a place I am looking for around here that is owned by a guy known as Big B and well, seeing as you were intent on stealing my car, I will assume you know who I am talking about and where it is."

"Nah, nah, I was just gonna take it for a spin is all." I flattened my lips and cleared my throat before bending his wrist back a little more and making him scream again.

"Let's try that once again, should we Micky?" I said in a calm tone that was the total opposite to his. His fearful eyes scanned left and right making me add,

"Okay, let me put it this way, just how many cars do you hope to jack after I have broken your arm in three places… huh?" I asked adding even more pressure at the end to make my point and making him scream out louder this time.

"AHHH, Fuck! Fuck, Jesus Christ! Okay, okay, shit yeah it's over on Washington Avenue, just a couple streets down!"

"And this fine establishment, what does it look like?" I asked next and this time, he didn't hold back.

"Two double doors, blue, windows above…fuck oww, okay, just ease up, it looks like a shithole but it's a front," he said and like they say in the movies, he was singing like a canary.

"That's good. Right, now here is what's gonna happen. I am going to let you go, and I want you to remember that I have your gun, so no funny shit, Micky," I warned making him nod fast, obviously desperate for me to let him go and relieve the pain I knew my hold on him had inflicted. So, I picked up his gun with my free hand and pointed it at him making him back up the second I let go.

Then I opened the car door which shot up into the sky just like on a Lambo, giving it the appearance as if it had wings. After this I unfolded myself from the car and kept the gun on him, which was when he started to get braver, putting more space between us as he told me,

"Bitch, the joke is on you! Fucking wacked piece of shit… and my name isn't fucking Micky!" he said as he started running off, trying to get away from me as quickly as he could, cradling his abused wrist to his chest.

"I know, asshole," I muttered just as another car pulled up and from the looks of the family man saloon, it was safe to say that this was the real Micky. Mr family man got out of the car dressed like he had just thrown on whatever was to hand first, as the milky stain on his shoulder told me that it was more than likely he had a newborn at home. The stick family stickers on the car's window also told me he had three other children and a wife at home that was mostly likely wondering what her husband was doing leaving in the middle of the night. But then he had a kind, honest face with tired eyes that told me he needed at least five more hours of sleep at night. This also told me that the favour he owed Wendy must have been a big one.

"Wow, so Wendy wasn't kidding…hey, nice to meet you, I'm…"

"Micky, yeah… *I know,"* I said but then he spotted the gun and lifted his hands and looked freaked.

"Shit, whoa…okay, not sure what you are…" I quickly cut him off and said,

"Oh this, ah don't worry, I just pulled it off some punk who tried to steal my car, that was also my first indication that I was in the right place…although, I have to confess, I have no clue whether this thing is even loaded or not. The last gun I fired ended up being…well, should we say, under slightly unusual circumstances and let's leave it at that." He gave me a wary look, obviously wondering why his now 'not so good friend Wendy' had missed out the part where I was clearly bat shit crazy. Which I wasn't, I was just stepping firmly into the pissed off, woman scorned stage of a breakup.

"Look, she didn't explain exactly all the details and seeing as you have just turned up in that car, then I am not sure I want to know?" This was definitely said as a question, making me tell him,

"Oh, trust me Micky… you really, *really* don't want to know."

"Right, well then I will just quickly give you the basics as a favour to Wendy and then I was never here, if you know what I mean."

"I sure do, the real Micky…I sure as shit do," I answered cryptically.

OKAY, so one look at what I was about to do, and I most definitely wished I had taken the time to change my outfit. As, let's just say that a tight pencil skirt, skintight shirt and little blue tie was not exactly the bad ass image I was hoping to go for here. But then again, maybe I was going about this all wrong. Maybe the whole sexy, unsuspecting act would be better? Now, if I could just pull it off without first falling on my ass as I got out of the car, then yeah, that would be swell.

"Well, here's hoping that these thugs think with their dicks first and their trigger-happy fingers second," I said to myself after rummaging through the overnight bag and finding what I was looking for…jeez, was this chick a party girl or what? Blood red lipstick, eyeliner, hairspray…okay, so who needed a glitter stick in their travel bag for work? Where was she expecting we were headed, Vegas?

I flipped open her compact mirror and went to work, starting with getting rid of any evidence of heartache. Like the black track lines running down my cheeks from the mascara I was never wearing ever again! But thankfully, heavy makeup most definitely helped in this and with the whole sultry look I was hoping to achieve I snapped the compact shut. I completed the look with twisting my hair up into a loose bun and holding it there with a pen I found in her purse. This was so I could do the whole, hair flicky thing the second I got out the car.

Then I sat across the street and waited. And fake Micky had been right, the place looked like a real shithole. Like a large house that had cracked windows on the top floor held together by a geometrical shape of tape. Faded, peeling paint from split wooden siding framed the two large, blue roller doors that were the only part of the building that didn't look close to giving up and buggering off to find a scrap yard themselves like the rest of the tired building did. Next to it was an empty lot that was fenced and filled with scrap cars piled up, telling me this was a way to hide the good stuff at the back. Because one look at those solid locked gates and it was easy to see where the money had been spent.

Meaning, I knew instantly that I was in the right place and all I had to wait for was one of the big roller doors to go up, so I could make my entrance. This was after first sticking the gun in the waistband of my skirt, hiding it with the fitted suit jacket that matched the navy skirt. Then slipping my heels back on and hoping I could drive the car the way I needed to with them on, I focused on getting my timing right.

In the end it was only about a fifteen minutes wait until up they went, and my opportunity presented itself.

"Here goes nothing, Fae…time not to get dead," I said starting the engine and the second the random car started to clear from the opening, I floored it, making the car roar like a fucking beast was coming out of the shadows of Hell!

Needless to say, I got myself noticed pretty damn quick as the second they saw me coming everyone jumped out of my way. And this was just as the roller doors were lowering, which meant that I was thanking my lucky stars that this car was as low to the floor as you could get! Because I only just made it inside, slamming on the brakes and barely stopping in time before I hit anything or anyone, for that matter as one guy obviously wasn't as quick as the rest. Which meant that he ended up closing his eyes instead just as the stallion looked close enough to make a permanent imprint on his legs. The cocktail stick he'd had in his mouth fell from his lips the second he realised he could have died by a Ferrari related injury.

"Phew," I said on a sigh, looking lower so he could see me and in doing so I could make my Aunty Pip proud and mouth at him,

'My bad.'

Then, I took in a quick scan of the space, seeing a large twin garage that housed at least twenty cars on one side and a workshop on the other. Naturally, as expected, there were also multiple cars in different stages of being fixed or stripped down for parts.

The side I had driven the Ferrari into was where the work was done as there was a lift, a pit, and the walls that were framed above by half naked chicks, auto part signs, and shelves of paint cans. Below this were benches, and heavy-duty tools that were used to get the illegal jobs done.

Five guys all stood around wearing pretty much the same expressions, which was my cue to get out and start my pitch, hoping it didn't include my gun. One that I found out after fake Micky told me that the joke was on me, was actually because it was minus any bullets and was pretty much useless. But hey, you couldn't tell that from looking at it right?

Thanks for that one, fake Micky. Jeez the guy couldn't even steal a car properly I thought as I raised the door and tried my hardest not to trip on my heels as I got up out of the car. Then, as I did, I plastered on a grin, even going so far as winking at one guy whose mouth actually dropped open as I pulled the pen from my hair and shook out my two-minute hairstyle.

"Well, hello boys," I said with a smirk as they scanned the length of me, having no clue what was about to go down if the shit hit the fan. Thankfully for me, I didn't see an arsenal of weaponry amongst the cans of oil, so I was taking this as a good sign. Otherwise, I would have been up shit creek with a bullet shot limb as my only paddle!

But this was when I noticed that there was also a mezzanine level right ahead of me at the end of the shop. One that seemed to be where the office was, if the sound of one pissed off male was any indication. I knew this as I heard a door slamming and an angry voice snarl,

"What the fuck is all the fucking noise and who do I have to fucking kill to shut them the fuck up?!" Sheesh, that guy needed to relax, or maybe a valium…I mean the guy said fuck more than a certain, shall forever now be known as, 'asshole Vampire' did.

The guys all looked up the second he appeared, as did I to see a large brute of a man appear, who kind of reminded me of the dude who played Drax in Guardians of the Galaxy. Only without all the grey and red skin and very literal sense of…well, pretty much everything.

Then again, this guy wasn't half naked, although he looked just as angry as Drax could get, especially in a fight. His dark hair was shaved short, with the hair on his lower face longer than the top. He had hard eyes that looked smaller due to the furious look he seemed to be holding onto and his large nose had clearly been broken more than once. It was also easy to see him as the boss, especially with all the muscle that looked as though it was worked at by tossing rival gang members in some car crusher on the weekends. That or he just bench-pressed auto parts giving new meaning to the term 'muscle cars'.

Oh, and my guess was that Big B didn't like getting disturbed much.

"And who the fuck are you, lady?!" he snapped making me really wish I had rethought this plan of mine. Maybe I should have tried getting my hands on an actual weapon that wasn't useless and its only use was as a gangster looking paperweight. Although, I had a pen, so that had to count for something after the night with the merc...right?

"Oh, don't mind me, I'm just here to browse, you know, thinking of getting an upgrade..." They all looked at me as if I had lost my damn mind, so I rolled my eyes and decided to cut through the bullshit and get right to it,

"You're an illegal chop shop that deals in stolen cars and I just drove in here with a Ferrari, what do you think I am fucking doing here...about to ask for an oil change?!" And this was when I dropped the bomb and the reaction was what I had been expecting, but not what I had been hoping for.

"Bitch, you should have just said you were in the wrong place...damn shame, you were one fine bitch," Big B said before nodding to one of his guys that was wearing oil stained coveralls. I released a sigh and shook my head a little, taking note of the confused glances from the others. They were no doubt asking themselves why I hadn't yet started to run away in a panicked, girly fashion.

Well, they were about to find out, as the second the first one reached out to grab me, obviously acting as if he was about to fight with a girl and outright punching me in the face obviously didn't sit well enough with him. But hey, reaching out to grab me by the hair was fair game I thought with a roll of my eyes... oh, but I didn't think so!

The second he did, I grabbed his arm, ducked under it and

took it back on itself before kicking out at the back of his knee so he went down, then I twisted his arm in such a way that it dislocated his shoulder with a sickening sound. Then I dropped the screaming man to the floor and calmly stepped over him.

"Right, so as I was saying…I am interested in a trade… *no?"* I said as another man in coveralls, suddenly stepped towards me, this time grabbing a knife that was amongst the tools and also…was that an apple he'd been cutting?

He then looked up at his boss who folded his arms and nodded, obviously giving him the go ahead to stab me, presumably to death. Well, this should be fun, I thought with another tiresome eyeroll.

"Well, whatcha gonna do with that, grease monkey, bore me to death whilst I wait for you to get permission from daddy up there?" I taunted knowing that this was also a technique to use, as anger often made people slip up and act sloppy.

Some of the guys grunted a laugh and muttered about how 'this bitch' was going down. But a quick glance up at the big boss man and he seemed somewhat intrigued as to how this would go. Well, maybe putting his boys on the floor would be the start of good business. I mean jeez, I worked in a freaking museum, so what did I know, maybe this was like the initiation process or something. I mean come on, what was next for me after this, watching Pink Panther movies and training to become an international jewel thief? Oh, how my resume was certainly looking more colourful by the day.

Grease Monkey came at me and I instantly grabbed his wrist, twisting slightly as I tugged it down against his torso, then as I turned the blade back on himself, I thrust up after stepping into him. This move ended how I'd anticipated as it stabbed up into his balls, making him actually scream like a little girl. I even heard the collective hisses of imagined pain from the other three as they watched their colleague drop to the floor and more than likely no longer be able to father children. Which from the looks of him, was me probably doing the world a favour by not allowing him to add anything to the gene pool of life. Dude could have eaten corn through a picket fence after first scaring away the sheep!

"Holy shit!" one guy muttered under his breath making me smirk as I winked at him. This was after I had pointed the end of my now bloody blade at him, scanning the tip down the length of him until it ended at his meat and two veg…my guess, they were now the size of sprouts after just witnessing what happened to his friend.

Hell, for all I knew they could have just jumped back up inside his body to hide until this shit was over with. And from the looks of things, shit was far from over as I was left with three guys who all looked like thug extras from some old James Bond movie…seriously, was that actually a black turtleneck I saw beneath the cheap leather jacket?

"Anyone else wanna go, or you done with me breaking people yet and finally want to do a deal?" I asked, only looking up at the boss at the end. But then he scoffed, snapping,

"Tommy, you're up!" The biggest guy at the back then came forward and looked ready to go as if he was going to enjoy trying to kill me. Especially as he picked up a heavy looking tyre iron and started testing its weight by letting it fall a few times in the palm of his free hand. I gave him a wry look, tilted my head and said,

"Really, is that supposed to intimidate me or something… you see that in a movie, sweetheart?" I mocked this last part in an overly girly voice making him sneer at me in anger now aiming it high and hoping to hit me over the head with it, using his added height to do so. Well, lucky for me, I still had my knife, however, *not so much for him.*

"Time to crack your skull, bitch!" he snarled.

"Seriously, do you guys not know anything else to call a woman kicking your ass?" I asked before I pivoted my body, minimizing the surface of my body as I was trained to do in case a blow managed to get through my defense. I also needed to put myself out of his reach in case he grabbed hold of me to try and keep me trapped to the oncoming blows.

It was strange, how the moves seemed ingrained in my brain. As if I didn't even need to think about it, almost like breathing, it just came natural to me. Which was good because in fluid movements that barely even registered to my attacker, I delivered what could easily be considered as one of my most brutal attacks yet…well, other than the pencil in the brain thing.

I stepped inside the arch of his longer weapon as the attack came down from above, to strike out first before he could hit me with it. I sliced my blade down the inside of his elbow against the muscle that effectively took away his ability to grip the tyre iron. Then, I instantly put my arm up to block, with my palm facing me, which was another instinct kicking in. One done to protect my own vital parts of my arm, like my arteries and veins on my wrist.

Blood burst all over the sleeve of my jacket, coming from the deep slice I made to the inside of his arm before I thrust up and stabbed the blade into his armpit. This was to hit at the nerves there that prevented his brain telling his arm what to do…now his limb was mine. Oh, and how he was about to know it.

But before he could even think too long on that particular ouchy, I turned my hand, putting my palm to his forearm. I did this so I could push his damaged arm down in front of his body and at the same time sliced up with my knife, cutting out from his armpit and straight through the top of his bicep with a sickening sound. This ended up severing his nerves completely, rendering his arm pretty much useless and in desperate need of medical attention before he bled to death.

"AAAHHHH!" he screamed after the mere seconds it took me to complete this brutal move as he dropped to the floor right after the tyre iron did, its clatter drowned out by the sound of sheer agony.

But after this I felt the gun being snatched from my waistband and held against my head.

"Drop the blade and turn around slowly!" he shouted making me stretch a hand out, making a point of dropping the blade with a clatter on the oil stained concrete floor. Then I turned around slowly and faced the last two guys.

"Try dodging this, bitch!" he said with a snicker that didn't last long as he pulled the trigger, no doubt wondering why he didn't see a bullet redecorating my face red. Instead, I cocked my head to the side and looked around the barrel of the gun and smiled.

"My turn, turtleneck…try dodging this!" I said before I kicked him straight on, getting him the nuts and making him fall to his knees. He did so cupping them, like this would somehow help. After which I grabbed the back of his head and brought it down on my knee, splitting my skirt at the side with the action. After this I let go, making him drop to the floor now unconscious and with a broken nose.

"No bullets, dickhead," I said in cocky tone that lasted about two seconds after it was said, as I heard the hammer cock back on another gun behind me and the threat from Big B was clear…

"No, but there is in this one."

CHAPTER SEVEN

BIG B AND LITTLE DODGE

I soon found myself turning around slowly once again, only this time knowing the threat was real. Then I started to act panicked, showing him the fear he expected and making the big guy smile because of it.

"I have to say I am fucking impressed. Never seen a chick with balls as big as yours, shame this wasn't an interview, or I would have had you on my crew in a heartbeat...of course, it helps that you're hot as fuck!" he said looking me up and down with that hungry look.

"Uh, thanks I guess...I don't suppose this is your way of asking me on a date is it?" I chuckled in a nervous way, making him grin.

"Well, if I didn't fear my dick from being ripped off, then I would be tempted to go a round with you in my bed instead of pulling the trigger...damn shame," he said with a shake of his head, adding,

"No hard feelings, yeah? This is just business, Doll."

"Please, don't do this...just hear me out before you...well, you know, shoot me in the head," I said as I raised my hands slowly making him think that I was doing so to get him not to shoot me. I also moved ever so slightly to one side as I did this before I made my move. One that quickly made him realise that my fear wasn't real.

This was because the moment I got my hands up to the level of the gun, I quickly crossed them over at the same time stepping sideways so if he managed to pull the trigger, my head was no longer in the line of fire. Then in a flash of movement, I had the back of my wrist against his own and I grabbed the barrel of the gun with my other hand so I could flip it, which ended with it now pointed at his head instead of my own. After this I stepped back with it in my hand, doing as he should have done by putting distance between us.

"Oh yeah, thanks for loading this one for me, I am hopeless with guns," I said with a wink, making him start to look pale.

"Jesus lady, just who the fuck are you?!" he said as I nodded for him to back up.

"Just call me a woman scorned who's having one bad fucking day," I told him making him frown before telling me,

"Well, I know I didn't fuck you, as trust me sweetheart, I would most definitely remember a sweet, crazy ass piece like you."

"Aww, you say the sweetest things, sugar," I replied blowing a kiss his way making him smirk back at me.

"I do you wrong in some way?" he asked crossing his arms over his chest making his muscles bulge in the black shirt he wore open over a dark grey T-shirt underneath.

"Nope, in fact, I'd never heard of you until this day." At this he raised a disbelieving brow.

"So why you here fucking up my guys?" At this I laughed once in a disbelieving way and told him,

"Hey, you started it, buddy, by setting your dogs on me,

what's a bitch to do?" This made him scoff with a nod of his head before he asked,

"Then what do you want?"

"Like I said, what I want is to make a deal," I told him making him frown in suspicion.

"Then, Bitch, you really are crazy, how'd I know you ain't no cop?" Now this did make me laugh,

"Are you serious, you really think I would drive in here like a crazy person in a half million-dollar car dressed as a damn flight attendant, if I was an undercover cop…Seriously, you're that paranoid?" I asked letting my tone do half my point making for me.

"Then what are you doing with that fucking car? 'Cause I doubt being a waitress in the sky is that good for tips…unless you offer a little summat, summat extra…"

"Eeew, no…jeez, can you just go back to calling me a bitch as I will take that over a mile-high whore any day of the week, thanks," I said after making a face that said it all, pushing my glasses up my nose in disgust.

"Oh sure, why fuck a guy for money when you can just beat his ass and take it…right?" he argued, back to crossing his arms over his chest and looking down at his guys on the floor still groaning in pain…the ones that hadn't already passed out of course.

"Huh, excuse me, but do you see me stealing their wallets and besides, don't you think it's about time you get them to a hospital or something."

"Oh, now she's concerned… I dunno, you gonna shoot me when my back's turned?" he said first talking to the room as though we had an audience.

"Now why would I do that when I am just starting to like you.?" I replied sweetly.

"Cute," he said with a smirk before nodding to the last

guy in the room not broken and nodding to the guys that obviously needed help. Then he pulled out his phone and started snapping out some orders, using words like, 'Call the Vet' and 'Clean-up crew'. After this he turned back to me and said,

"You never answered my question, Dollface." So, I told him,

"Let's just say that I didn't feel like being with my boyfriend anymore and decided he didn't need it."

"And now?" he asked with what I now noticed was with a scarred brow raised.

"Now I just wanna get the hell out of Dodge and in doing so, am about to offer you the deal of a lifetime," I said making him once again look sceptical, in that bad ass menacing way of his before saying dryly,

"Yeah, like what, damaging more of my guys when they show up?"

"Not unless PMS kicks in before they get here," I replied with a wink.

"Funny," he said with a sarcastic grunt.

"Look, this is the deal, you get a car worth half a mill for any car you got in this place that has a pink slip so I can sell it legit... capeesh?" I said lowering the gun in hopes of finally gaining his trust.

"Are you shitting me right now, did you just say capeesh?"

"Too much?" I asked with a wince.

"What do you think?" he asked in a knowing tone, so I looked off to one side and muttered,

"Damn, it felt like the right time too." His grin said it all and he ended up muttering his own,

"Damn girl, but your crazy is making me hard."

"Okay, so ignoring the obvious imprint of your cock against your jeans... Mazel tov by the way," I said nodding to the impressive length and making him smirk as he fought another big grin.

"Ask yourself, would a sane person have just pulled the shit that I did unless they were desperate."

"Your point being?" he asked, clearly enjoying this conversation, as now he couldn't stop from grinning at me.

"My point is that lucky for you my sanity isn't up for sale, my car however is and for one night only you get the chance to cash in on that desperation, because I know what she is worth and so do you," I told him making him mutter,

"Jesus, you are fucking insane…hot, but fucking insane."

"Tonight, then you can bet your ass I am, but I am also gonna bet that those bleeding guys of yours aren't looking too bad right now and a quick trip to the ER is all it will take for them to be right as rain and you, my friend, will be sitting pretty, all because some crazy chick drove in here after having the worst fucking day of her life and decided a nice vacation from life looked good right about now, starting with a car that can't be traced…so whatcha say…we got a deal?" I said holding my free hand out ready for him to shake and after giving me a probing look for a few seconds, he asked,

"You gonna give me back my gun?"

"I don't know, you gonna play nice with it or do I have to take it off you again, only this time accidentally on purpose snapping something important when I get it back?" I said, making my point and in turn making him grin huge this time.

"Mmm, fuck I knew I would like you," was his strange and obviously aroused reply.

"Feeling's mutual…of course, that will change the second you try and shoot me again." He gave me a toothy grin this time and nodded,

"I think we have an understanding, Doll." I gave him a head nod in return and handed him back the gun, hoping that my act of good faith would gain me respect instead of a bullet. But then I picked up the knife I had dropped close by, wiping the blood on the leg of the guy whose balls weren't gonna be working great for a while and told Big B with a grin,

"I'm keeping this though." He laughed and said,

"Sugar, I am thinking you could do more damage with that than I ever could with this, but I respect the trade," he said tucking his gun in the waistband of his belted jeans after first lifting up his t-shirt showing the hint of ripped abs. Doing it like a badass gangster and motioning with a nod of his head for me to follow him. I looked behind me as the men on the floor, that I had put there, started to come around. This was of course helped by Big B, after he had kicked a few out of the way, making them groan after he had grumbled,

"Useless fuckers." Then he held a hand out to me like a gentleman to help me over the pool of blood that came from the tyre iron man. Who, I should probably mention, was looking paler by the minute and was by far the worse off.

"Alright, ya sexy bitch, what is it you need?" he asked after leading me into the other part of the garage.

"Now that, Big B, you can call me," I told him before walking closer to the line of sweet rides and I felt his gaze on me as I did so.

"Fast and Furious fan, eh?" I asked referring to the mean glossy black 1970 Dodge Charger RT, that I recognised as being driven by Vin Diesel in the movie. Although this one was minus the shiny chrome supercharger raised from the hood. He winked at me and said,

"But of course."

"It's nice, but for me its Eleanor every time," I said walking over towards the utterly gorgeous 1967 Mustang Fastback Gt500.

"These are all the legit cars we have, and you can pick anyone but that one." I raised a brow at him and said,

"Gone in 60 seconds? A little cliché for you, don't you think?" He shrugged his shoulders and replied,

"If the shoe fits."

I smirked to myself as I turned back to the line of muscle cars and saw my choices were a 1969 Chevy Camero SS in candy apple red, an Orange and Black 1969 Barracuda and a beautiful 1960 GTO Pontiac in midnight blue. But for me right now there was only one that seemed to fit, so I told him with my mind firmly set,

"Alright, in that case then I will take the Dodge."

"Fuck, I knew you were gonna say that! You sure, Dollface? I've got a sexy 1967 Chevy Impala Sport out back?" he asked showing the mask of a true wheeler dealer.

"I'll pass," I said giving him a knowing look after already running my fingers along the hood of the sleek and sexy looking Dodge.

"Not a Supernatural fan, huh?" I smirked back at him over my shoulder and replied cryptically,

"Oh, Big B, *if only you knew."*

A SHORT TIME later I was handing him the keys to my dad's Ferrari, knowing that it would cost him a car, but hoping all the same that one day he would get it back. Because you didn't dissect a car like this. No, this one would be in a container within the hour, I could bet my life on it.

I felt bad that I had stolen it from dad and hated that I was given no choice, but I was on a mission and one day when this was all over…he would understand that. After all, lives were at stake, my mum's included. And despite the ruins of our relationship, her life and even Lucius' still meant something to me. Even if I had absolutely no intention of being a part of them again.

"So, what's the plan here, Sugar, you going on the run or what?" Big B asked when there was nothing left but for me to say goodbye.

"What gave it away?" I asked as I pulled my case from the passenger's side and carried it over to the Dodge that he'd had one of his guys (not a broken one, but recently arrived) drive out of the shop for me. He gave me a wry look in return and said,

"Wow, that guy must have really done a number on you." His comment made me wince as the raw and recent memory assaulted me, one I had been purposely trying to hold back until I could afford the time allocated for such a mental breakdown. Which was why what I said next, I did so in a stone-cold way,

"Yeah, well I caught him kissing my mother so...what do you think?" His eyes got wide and hissed through his teeth before saying,

"Fuck, yeah, that would do it."

I put the bag in the trunk and took off my bloodstained jacket, throwing it in there before pulling my shirt out of the tight waistband of my skirt. I swear, I nearly moaned aloud just thinking about the shower I would have the second I found a motel for the night.

"Look, I know that after what you did to my guys...well, I should tell you to..."

"Fuck off and go to Hell?" I finished for him with a knowing grin, one that died the second he said,

"Yeah, but seeing as I reckon you're halfway there already with the shit you got going on, I gotta ask, do you even know where you're headed?" I released a heavy sigh and slammed the trunk shut before telling him,

"Probably best you don't know." He accepted this knowledge with a head nod, knowing it was meant in case someone came looking for me, which I had a feeling would happen.

"Well, if you're serious about disappearing then I know a guy," he said making me frown in confusion before he pulled out his phone and rang someone,

"Jimmy, it's Big B, yeah I got a job for you. I'm sending you this chick who needs a new ID…yeah man, the works, put it on my tab…yeah, fuck she's hot but I wouldn't try touching her, this bitch will break your fucking arm and bite your dick off at the same time!" I raised a brow at the same time putting my hands on my hips and making him chuckle with my sass. Then he hung up the phone and told me an address of where to find Jimmy.

"Why did you do that?" I asked in shock.

"Because you got balls and in my line of work, I respect anyone with the balls to do what you did and survive it… besides, I've been to that same Hell myself when I caught my bitch fucking my brother, so we got shit in common." I winced at the pain that would cause him also, not really thinking it a good idea to point out that he might not have been cheated on had he not referred to his woman as 'my bitch'. But then the bad guy was being nice to me, so I didn't think it wise to push my luck.

"That sucks and sorry she did that to you."

"Nah, it's all good, I got myself a good woman now, can't cook for shit but she's a dynamite in bed, so…"

"…You just order takeout." He burst out laughing and said,

"I knew I liked you."

"And dare I ask what happened to the brother and the ex bitch?" He grinned in a dangerous way and told me,

"She's still a bitch breathing if that's what you mean."

"And the asshole brother?" I enquired although I had no clue why or if I really wanted to know.

"And the brother's breathing but not walking so straight after I broke both his kneecaps." I looked back at the broken guys that were left and who were now either shaking it off or being put in a car and driven to what I assumed was a 'Vet', who took human jobs on the side. Then I lifted my hands up and said,

"Hey, I am clearly not one to judge here." He grunted a laugh and said,

"Shit, no you ain't." I winked and opened the door to my new car before sliding in behind the wheel. Then I wound down the window and nodded to the Ferrari and said,

"Nice doing business with you, Big B."

"Painful doing business with you too…hey, but you got a name, Dollface?" I put the key in the ignition and started her up. Then I revved the black beast until she roared and said,

"Big B, you can call me…"

"Little Dodge."

CHAPTER EIGHT

HEARTBREAK HOTEL

After this I sped off into the night, drowning out the sound of my heart breaking as I thought about Lucius, doing so with the roaring sounds of a V8 engine as I floored it along the highway. My new identity now sat in the glovebox along with a new license and passport. When Big B had said to give me the works, he hadn't been kidding as I even had the car 'registered' in my new name. His guy, Jimmy, had come through in a big way and it had to be said that he had been a master at his craft.

Although, finding out that Jimmy was in fact seventeen years old, lived in his mother's basement and was clearly a computer hacker on the side, wasn't exactly what I had been expecting. But then I also hadn't expected to be shown in by his sweet wholesome looking mother or finding myself stepping over empty pop tart boxes as I navigated the steps down to his 'apartment'. Something the skinny seventeen-year-old obviously thought was a nutritional staple in life, that and power drinks. The pyramid of pop tart boxes in the corner and the four toasters sat on top of a large glass cooler filled with cans, being the biggest indicator.

Then again, the freshly baked cookies his mother brought down for us was a nice touch, even though I did kind of want to ask her if she believed her son had made good life choices… you know, considering that her son worked for the bad guys.

However, when she mentioned that her Jimmy would help get me a good grade on my paper, I took a few things from this. One, she either had some major denial going on that may have been aided by drugs or I looked a lot younger than I was in what she must have thought was me wearing a school uniform.

Either way, neither of these things explained why I was in her basement at three in the morning and she thought it a good time to make cookies. Needless to say, the drugs theory won over my youthful looks…besides, I had seen myself in the mirror lately and knew that after the day I'd just had, then let's just say that cracks were starting to show.

Not that Jimmy would have noticed. In fact, the kid barely even acknowledged me as a new presence in his life…*period*. In fact, I think that I would have received more of a reaction out of him had I been dressed as a giant pop tart doing a sexy dance and juggling soda cans, than the tired, slightly slutty looking flight attendant I looked. Clearly this kid wasn't being ruled by his hormones, that was for damn sure. Nope, it was nothing but sugar and binary code running through this kid's veins. Although, why he had asked Big B if I had been hot was anyone's guess. Maybe he had been too scared off by the bitten dick comment to even acknowledge me.

Whatever the reason, other than looking at me long enough to flash a quick picture and ask me what I wanted my new name to be, that was pretty much the extent of my stay. Meaning that I had been back in my car in no time at all with a new life in my hands and a free cookie.

"Seriously, could this night get anymore fucked up?" I asked myself out loud, allowing the sound of my car starting up to be my only answer. Because after this, I had driven for another hour before I found that I could keep going no longer. Which was why I pulled off the 85 after seeing signs for Bluestone Wild Forest and forgoing the Best Western for something cheaper. For starters, I didn't know how long my money would last, so knew I needed to be conservative with my funds. Which meant that the end of my night was signaled by the rumbling burble of the exhaust as I pulled into the free space at the cheap hotel passing a sign for the Kingston Plaza.

"Great, just had to be a King in there somewhere," I muttered to myself after getting out of the car and stretching before shivering in the freezing early morning air. After this I grabbed my bag and got myself a room, ignoring the questioning looks I received from the receptionist, that clearly spoke of how much I needed caffeine almost as much as I needed a bed. I knew this when she gave me one of those judging looks up and down, so I couldn't help myself after I too looked down at myself, seeing what she saw, which admittedly was a mess. That's when I told her,

"It was a Hell of a flight." Then with a shrug of my shoulders I grabbed my keycard and pulled my case along, fully intent on getting my tired ass to my room as quickly as possible. Once inside I spent all of about thirty seconds taking in the blue carpet, basic furniture and bedding that had large bright blue circles over it that gave me a headache after only five of those seconds allocated. Then I dropped my bag, took a deep shuddering breath, knowing I had finally made it and quickly ran to the toilet so I could throw up nothing but bile.

After this I let my emotional wall come crashing down all around me, starting with vomiting and ending with me slumped down against the wall sobbing uncontrollably. I knew I was being too loud, so raised my hand to put a fist in my mouth when I suddenly spotted the blood on my fingers. This was such a sobering sight that suddenly I burst into hysterical laughter that I knew marked the sign for both exhaustion and stress.

Which was when I found myself stood at the sink, first looking down at my hands and then back up at my face. Now seeing the tear tracks were back, and although they were clear this time, they were still far too visible as they continued to run down my face, dripping to the sink from my chin.

So, I calmly removed my glasses, folding them gently before placing them on the counter. Then I first scrubbed at my hands before I went about washing my face. And I did this quietly, even methodically, all the while the tears didn't stop, but they just continued to run down my cheeks, silently continuing despite how many times I tried to wash them away.

In the end I gave up trying what seemed like a hopeless endeavor. No, instead I cupped my hands, drank down as much as I could to rid myself the bitter taste of bile and undressed. I decided it wasn't a good idea to shower for fear I would fall asleep, slip and crack my head open. And seriously, after everything I had survived over the last few weeks, then dying in a two-star hotel from being clumsy wasn't exactly how I would have imagined going out.

When I was down to my underwear, I walked over to the bed, briefly glancing at the window and seeing nothing but that damn sign.

Kingston Plaza…like the bloody land of Kings or something!

Fucking typical!

I tore my face from it, not even bothering with the curtains before I crawled beneath the sheets and turned out the light, closing my sore, tired eyes on everything that was now wrong with my life. And like all those nights before Lucius had become a fixture in my life…

I dreamt of a Vampire King.

"AMELIA…*MY AMELIA…MY KHUBA.*" The moment I heard this being whispered in my ear, every muscle in my body tensed before I heard that consuming voice of his cooing down at me,

"Be easy, sweetheart…calm for me," he told me, and I found I could do little else but obey, relaxing back as if feeling myself sinking under. Which was when I finally opened my eyes and saw Lucius leaning down over me in the bed. He was dressed how he usually was, in some dark suit only without the jacket. A tight fitted waistcoat that was a dark red this time and the black shirt underneath was rolled at the sleeves, showing his thick leather glove. But despite how sexy he looked, there was a haunted look to his features.

He looked…*worried?*

Actually, he looked as if there was a pain behind his eyes and it was one I couldn't understand. Did he feel guilty that I had discovered his secret? But surely, for that to happen he would first have to have felt something for me. Could it be possible that he had fallen for us both?

No! I was not doing that! I was not going to that dark place.

Which was when I started to mutter,

"This isn't real." And I knew it wasn't because there was no way he could have found me. At least not this quickly. I had left no traces since leaving behind the Ferrari. There was also no reason why he would come looking for me, unless he had been ordered to do so…had my mother put him up to this? Gods, the idea was sickening.

"It's as real as it needs to be," he told me cryptically,

making me frown and turn my head away, which was when the bed started to shift beneath me. I felt strange…as though it was made of a liquid I couldn't yet feel soaking into my skin. But then I looked down at myself and saw that I was back to wearing what I had been before I had changed, swapping clothes with the flight attendant.

It was the last thing that Lucius had remembered me wearing and that's when I realised this was his doing, not my own. This was Lucius' control, something that was confirmed when he rose from the bed and without touching me, he beckoned me closer with his hand. I felt myself floating up, being pushed from behind by the body of vapour that the sheets had turned into, before then evaporating from my skin. One I knew that in reality was naked, as I had stripped off when I had collapsed into bed at close to five in the morning.

But still, I rose up without commanding my own body to do so and soon stood facing Lucius in a shadowed room, that barely allowed anything to be seen other than Lucius and myself. Which was when I realised what this was.

"Am I in the Void?" I asked knowing this was a state of mind that was like a blank space the Supernatural beings of the world could access and bring others into if they chose. From what I understood about it, this was a part of the mind that could be used for communication or allowing another to access memories, visions or even a method of control. It was usually a protected place, but that protection only relied on how strong the person was at blocking others out or how strong the person was that was trying to get in. Now, from what I gathered, you could allow this connection if you chose to do so. But for Lucius, well he was the master of commanding the will of others, meaning that there was no one strong enough to block him. Well, no one other than the witch and well…me and before she became one of his Vampires, *my mother.*

But then it also made sense why he was here now. As it was becoming obvious that during the times I slept my mind was left vulnerable to a certain extent. No doubt added by the emotional state I was in. Which also made sense as to how the witch had been able to access that part of my mind. And right now, it was how Lucius was breaking into my Void against my will. Something I could tell was taking its toll, as Lucius looked strained, telling me this was taking a lot of his energy. But then…*he wasn't the only one.*

I knew this when he ignored my question and I found it near impossible to resist as he commanded in a stern tone,

"Come here." So, I stepped towards him, looking at my feet disappearing in the grey fog that surrounded us.

"We are in *your Void,*" he told me, being honest despite the fact I already had gathered as much. I looked around at the black open space around us that looked like an endless room.

"Why?" I asked wondering why it was I hadn't yet slapped him or screamed at him for breaking my heart. Or was keeping me calm all part of it?

"You will know soon enough, now turn around," he commanded making me do as I was told, and it felt strangely as if I had become a puppet in the hands of a master manipulator, being forever pulled the way he wanted me to go by invisible strings. It was as if my body belonged to him and my mind was nothing more than the remote he used to get me to do as he wanted. He almost seemed matter of fact, or was he just trying to get the job done quickly?

"Now, I want you to look inside this mirror and focus on the last time you saw your face." I frowned wondering why he wanted me to do this and was about to tell him no. Especially when remembering now when it was but before I could stop my foolish self, it started to appear. The mirror above the sink in the hotel room. It was all starting to appear in front of me, only now there was a dark shadow behind me. I even raised my hand to wipe away what seemed like the never-ending tears on my face. I also saw that I was wearing what I had been, the untucked shirt over the tight, ripped pencil skirt.

I looked down at the dried blood on my hands and found myself tightening my fists.

"Tell me who fucking hurt you?!" he snapped seeing for himself and the moment he did, I plunged my hands into the water, telling him in a tone void of emotion,

"You did."

Then the tap came on and I grabbed handfuls, splashing it all over my face scrubbing away the tears that continued to fall. I glanced to Lucius to see him snarl to his side, tearing his eyes from the view of what he had done to me.

"What comes next, show me!" he snapped, clearly struggling with the reality of what he was demanding of me. I pulled the plug letting the water drain, watching it in slow motion as if the water symbolized my life. I then started to drag the shirt over my head, and unzip the back of my skirt, before letting it slip to the floor. There should have been a bruise on my knee from using it to break that guy's face, but I knew that, like my hand and my head, I had healed already. Thanks to Lucius' blood in my system, I couldn't help but wonder how long that piece of him would last within me? Days, weeks… maybe a month or two?

Maybe if I just started running…maybe if I just ran and ran and ran until I could run no more, maybe then I could get him out of my system? I looked behind me around the incessant space and asked myself if I started now, would I ever find the end, or would I die long before?

"Back to the room," Lucius said in a strained clipped tone that told me he was losing his hold on controlling this Void of mine. But even so, I couldn't hold myself back from doing as

I was told. Which meant that the moment I turned around, he stepped back so I could take a step forward, and in doing so my surroundings changed. The Void morphed into the room I was staying in and like I had done before passing out, I walked towards the bed in just my underwear. Then just before I was about to get into bed, mimicking reality, he spoke.

"Stop. Now take a good look around."

"Why?"

"Look around the room, Amelia," he said but this time the whispered voice was one of seduction in my ear and I looked down to see his arm held at the front of me, a palm to my naked belly. But it was one that didn't make contact, just one acting as though it wanted to. So, I looked up and as I did the pieces of the room started to emerge from the shadows as my mind brought each piece of it forward into the light. It was like accessing a memory…or should I say, Lucius was.

Which was when something started to niggle at the back of my mind. It was that small voice of doubt asking myself why? Asking myself why he would want this…why he was here now, asking to see the room?

"Focus, Amelia…focus solely on my voice."

"But I…" I tried to argue, bringing back my own voice of doubt.

"No! Only on my voice…now walk over to the desk." I frowned as I did as he asked, but the moment I started to waver he growled angrily,

"Fuck! You didn't even look at it," he hissed irritably to himself.

"Alright, now walk over to the window," he ordered next and again I wanted to hold back, seeing it now as it started to emerge, beginning with the edges. Pieces of it started to knit together, like time was merely a thread that could be woven just as easily as it could be unraveled. The blue curtains, ones that matched the carpet beneath my feet started to come into focus.

"Go on...a little closer...a little bit more..." he urged, and his voice was becoming so strained, it was almost too painful to hear.

"Quickly now...quickly Amelia, run towards it now!" he said panicked and I did, I ran and the second I saw what he wanted me to see I screamed, now knowing that it was all a plot to find me! I knew it the second I saw that sign and felt the promised threat whispered in my ear,

"Finally... *I've got you now!*"

AFTER THIS I woke up and screamed one name,

"Kingston plaza!" I bolted upright and before even giving it thought I jumped out of bed, tripping up over the bedding that tumbled out with me. I grabbed a hand to my pounding chest and tried to breathe through my panic. The sun was blaring through the window telling me it was some point during the day, and I bent forward to try and ward off the nausea I felt starting to rise. I also found myself stumbling towards the wall so I could hold myself up against the light-headedness. One I knew was from lack of food and water and no doubt the remnants of the dream.

I found my way to the bathroom and without looking at anything else found myself bent over the sink so I could take large gulps of water from the tap, drinking it down before splashing water on my face. But it was only on straightening up, that the true nature of that dream started to seep back in and with it the dangers I now faced.

Lucius had found me!

"Shit!" I shouted before I was quickly running into action. I grabbed the bag I was yet to open and found a few spare outfits, so picked the most casual. This turned out to be a pair of dark denim leggings that actually fit me pretty good and a plain white t shirt, that was a bit snug over my larger breasts, which meant it ended up showing a line of skin at my belly. To this I also unrolled a khaki light-weight jacket that was an open draped front, parker style. One that told me the flight attendant chick didn't exactly pack for the weather.

I had also grabbed an insanely quick shower after finding a well-stocked vanity bag that had pretty much everything I needed and lots, lots more. The only items that I was left wearing that actually belonged to me were my glasses and my bra because there was no way I was getting into her B cups.

In total, it took me a record breaking fifteen minutes to get ready and out the door just as the phone started ringing. I froze with my hand glued on the handle as I looked back at the phone, doing so now as if it was a bomb about to go off. I held my breath as it rang and rang and rang some more before it finally stopped. This blessed silence then had the power to release me as I snapped out of it.

"Screw you!" I ground out bitterly before letting the door slam behind me, and quickly getting to the reception so I could check out. But then I found a different receptionist on the phone, saying in irritation,

"I am sorry, Sir, but it is like I said, I cannot force a guest to…oh wait, here she is," she quickly added the moment she saw me coming and I released a deep tired sigh before asking her,

"I am sorry, but do you mind giving us a minute?" She obviously grasped the situation pretty quickly and said,

"Sure, I will just be in the back room, take as long as you need." Then I took in a deep breath and put the phone to my ear, bracing myself for the sound of his voice.

"What do you want, Lucius?" I asked and his reply hit me like a punch to the chest.

"What do I want…? What the fuck do you think I want, Amelia…? Get your ass back home now!" he snapped sounding furious and this only managed to ignite my own rage, only mine was displayed with deadly calm,

"I am not a child, Luc, and I can do whatever the Hell I want with my life," I said making a point of calling him a name I had never done before, and he knew it, as I could hear the faint rumbling of a growl from his end.

"Yeah, and just how long is that life going to last out there unprotected?!"

"I think I have proven enough times how capable I am at surviving on my own, so if you don't mind, I have shit to do, so I will…" I started to say when he quickly interrupted me on an angry growl of words,

"Don't you dare hang up! So help me by the Gods, I will…"

"You will what, Luc, huh…because last time I checked you already ripped out my fucking heart and stepped on it, so what…you wanna see what more damage you can do?!" I snapped feeling the Gods' forsaken tears start to rise.

"You have this completely wrong and if you had just waited for five fucking minutes before running off, then you would have given me the time to explain that!" he argued making me frown so hard it ached.

"I know what I saw! And I know what I heard! Which means that I don't need your interpretation of events to clarify shit! We are done, we are over and the quicker you get that through your stubborn royal ass head the better this will be! So, you can just quit pretending to give a shit and run back off to mummy dearest and tell her that you tried your best!" I told him, now gripping the phone so hard my knuckles were white and I added something else to that list of things that ached, the main one being that of my fucking heart!

But Lucius wasn't done…*not by a long shot.*

"Now you listen to me, my girl and you listen well, you and I will *never be done, we will never be over*, which means I will *NEVER* stop looking for you. I will fucking hunt you down to the ends of the Earth and beyond…so unless you want a hard time running, then I suggest you keep your ass there and be ready for me because… I. Am. Coming. For. You!" he snarled dangerously, emphasizing each word and I swallowed hard after first closing my eyes against the sound of his threatening promise.

Then I placed a fist to the chasm sized hole in my chest and took a deep breath. One I needed if I was ever to say my Goodbye.

"Then to the ends of the Earth is where it will be…"

"Amelia…"

"Goodbye Luc. Have a nice eternity with…*with someone else's Chosen One,"* I said interrupting the threatening way he snarled my name, before I dropped the phone on the counter, along with my keycard and walked out the door to the sound of him calling my name before he then cursed it to the Gods.

Cursed it to the Gods that had long ago cursed me with broken fate.

Then I left this…

Heartbreak Hotel.

CHAPTER NINE

LUCIUS

OBLIVION

The very moment she fought my control over her Void and realised what it was I was doing, was the same moment when I finally discovered the limits to my power. It was as if the cord had been severed completely and I woke up with a roar of rage unlike any other!

It was like waking up in some kind of Hellish oblivion that was trying to drown me in pain and blind me with the darkness of her Void. Getting inside her mind had been a battle in itself. But staying there as long as I had was the reason I actually took one step and found myself falling to my knees. My strength was trying to fail me as I had never once felt so drained of power before in my eternal life. It was when I realised two things, both of which sent me hurtling into panic and rage. One was how strong Amelia was against me and secondly, in reference to the first, it just proved how strong this fucking witch was!

And now Amelia, my Chosen One, was out there and vulnerable in the world, stupidly leaving herself wide open! Gods, I was fucking furious with her, even more so than I was with myself for letting this happen! Gods, but she should fucking know better!

A thought that forced me to find my footing so I could stagger to where my phone lay on the table next to the bed I had slept in. Doing so with rest as the very last thing on my mind. No, I had only needed to do so in order to slip into her Void and take control. Usually, with most beings, I could do this whilst still awake but with Amelia this was not the case. I had needed to focus my mind solely on getting into hers, casting everything else out and doing so in the hope that all it would need was a quick view of her surroundings.

But the pain she had showed me she was in, was like being accused all over again. For if she believed herself to be the only one in pain, then she was utterly and foolishly mistaken.

Gods, but I could barely think and actually found myself holding my phone for a full thirty seconds before I knew what to do with it!

"Fuck!" I snarled before getting my ass into action, starting with barking orders at those I knew would get shit done!

"What do you need?" The gruff, deep voice asked at the other end.

"I need to know where in the US Kingston Plaza is and what hotel faces a sign for it, and I need this two minutes ago!" I snapped quickly.

"Gotcha," Dante said before cutting the call and at the same time I was out of the door and heading to Dom's office. This was where I knew he would be, seeing as he had his own people to organise and had many looking into the leads he thought he had…leads which I knew he hadn't. Because no one knew Amelia like me, not even her parents, but there had been little point highlighting this fact, not when it would merely antagonize the situation between us. For Dom may have had no choice but to accept my claim, but that didn't mean things between us wouldn't remain tense for a while.

Which was why the moment every fucking lead ran cold, I'd had no choice but to enter her Void. The part of a mind that enabled me to control a person and it was one that I had refrained from entering in a very long time.

However, years ago, I would do this by simply whispering the scenes I wanted her to see, not needing even half the amount of energy to do so. For in the early days, I had done this to ensure that she would dream of me. That I would remain a permanent figure in her mind. It may have been a cruelty, teasing her with thoughts that she believed she could never have, but at the time it was a necessary evil. For I needed to continue to be a constant in her life and this was the safest way I could think to do that. At least until I could finally become a constant in the physical sense.

But during the time I had been absent from her dreams, it seemed as though she had grown in her strength in shutting me out. I could quite honestly say that I had never struggled to control anyone before as I did only minutes ago, for even her mother's mind had been easier to access in her dreams all that time ago. Making me question if this gift had been passed down from her mother?

Even with the witch, there was nothing there but an impenetrable wall facing me. There had been nothing for me to access, telling me it was a spell that was hiding the Voids of both herself and that of her growing army. But with Amelia, there were holes in her defenses, ones only there as she slept.

Now the getting in had been the easy part. No, it had been remaining there that had been the real battle facing me and giving me no other option but to fight for the right. But then, whilst I was there, I knew all I needed was a single clue. *Just one.* Which had me hoping for a hotel logo on top of stationery, a welcome pack or Hell, a chocolate on her pillow would have been enough, just so long as it had the name of the place she was staying on it. But then when that came up empty, I knew I had to push her to the window so I could see for myself if there was a sign or anything. And that was where I had hit my jackpot.

Which was why I walked right inside his office without knocking and demanded,

"I need a helicopter here and ready to go as soon as possible." Dom heard this and he was out of his chair in a heartbeat. Keira, who looked as if she was being torn apart emotionally, also now stood from the sofa she had been dozing on.

"You have found her?!" she asked quickly, at the same time her husband growled,

"Where?" Which was the only question that mattered to him. This was naturally because he feared for her safety nearly as much as I did, something we had both discussed at length. Especially after seeing for ourselves that the witch was obviously still not done with her.

"I am waiting on the details, but she is near a place called Kingston Plaza."

"How do you know this?" Keira asked me with a questioning frown, but I didn't have time for a lecture on moral code so told her,

"I have my ways."

"It matters not, only that we get our daughter back," Dom said having my back as we had come to an understanding, he and I. Our priority was solely to get Amelia back. Now, as to our own personal issues, well they would have to take a backseat.

"You need to make her listen, you need to make her understand…maybe I would be better…"

"No!" I snapped before Keira could try and convince me that she was better at handling this.

"You've already spoken to her and it achieved nothing," I reminded her, unable to keep the annoyance that knowledge brought me after the conversation they'd had with her finally came to light.

"But…"

"No buts, Keira, Luc is right and as her Chosen, then it is his decision." At this Keira wasn't the only one to look at him as if he had been taken over by another entity. Hell, even I was questioning who the Hell he was!

"Oh, don't fucking look at me like that, I may not like this fucking reality, Luc, but I think we both know where fighting against the Fates has gotten me in the past," Dom snapped making me reply,

"I think you will find that I am the very last person who will disagree with you here. Besides, you couldn't stop me even if you tried and you know this." I replied because it was true, making him grit his teeth as he was forced to admit,

"Yes, that as well."

"So, you see, little Keira girl, *better the Devil you know,*" I said before my phone started ringing.

"Tell me you have an address." I barely refrained from snarling this demand, only taking a breath when he replied,

"And a number. I have just sent you the details," Dante informed me.

"I need that…"

"On it." Dom said before picking up his own phone and demanding the helicopter to get here asap.

"Anything else?" Dante asked, already fully aware of the situation.

"Yes, question Wendy again."

"Luc, I don't think…" I quickly cut him off and this time gave into my demon's urge to snarl at him,

"I don't want to fucking hear it! Now, I want it done and Dante…"

"Yeah?" he asked in a deflated tone.

"If she doesn't tell you anything, then I will be the next one questioning her and I don't need to tell you…"

"Yeah, yeah, that would be bad. I will use force this time," he admitted making me nod despite him being unable to see it.

"Good. Report back to me when it is done," I said knowing that this time he would get his answers, even if the Drude needed to bend a few rules to get them. Which meant invading more than one mind in search of my missing Chosen, something I had not one fucking problem with!

I hung up and got the information I needed before calling the hotel demanding that I be put through to her room immediately. Hoping now that I wasn't too late before she was on the run again. But even if this was so, I was hoping at the very least it meant that the net was closing in around her, as I would finally have a radius of time around a centre point I could work with. And after all, a Ferrari wasn't hard to spot in the daylight. Meaning that finally the cops may have more luck picking her up.

But in the meantime, I pressed in the number and started walking out the door as this was one conversation that was between me and my Chosen One only.

"Put me through to Miss Draven's room," I asked without bothering with any pleasantries.

"Let me just check the system for you, hold please." I had to hold back a growl of impatience.

"I am sorry, Sir, but we don't seem to have anyone by that

name." I gritted my teeth despite expecting this to be the case and said,

"Fine, then you may know what name she did give, for you can't have many slim, beautiful young women, staying there alone."

"Aww, that's sweet," the woman said making me grimace, for fucking sweet was as far from what I felt in this moment. No, murderous, furious, fucking mad was what I would have gone with and it was one that was quickly tipping over towards blind rage with every second wasted!

"Yes… quite," I gritted out before telling her,

"She's five foot five, black hair, naturally tanned, blue eyes, drives a Ferrari." She snorted a laugh and said,

"Are you sure you have the right hotel, Sir?" I held back the growl of frustration and gritted out my reply,

"Yes, I am sure, and I take it by that wry tone that your establishment is a shit hole?" I snapped making her backtrack,

"Well, no that is not what I am saying…"

"I don't care, just find the rooms where there are single female occupants!" I snapped,

"Oh, right…yes, I can do that," she mumbled and the sound of tapping on the computer didn't exactly fill me with confidence, but despite this and the fact that I nearly put another hole in the walls of Afterlife, a minute later she came back and said,

"There is only one and I will put you through."

"And the name?" I asked hoping it was one she would continue to use and would aid me for future enquiries if the unfortunate need arose after this phone call.

"Miss Eyre," she said making me roll my eyes,

"Jane Eyre?"

"Yes, that's right…oh wait, wasn't that a book or something?" she asked making me roll my eyes.

"Just patch me through!" I snapped before hearing it ring and ring and fucking ring until I was back with the receptionist.

"I am sorry Sir, but it seems…"

"Try again!" I snapped cutting her off and making her do just that. But once again it continued to ring, making me snarl,

"Pick up the phone, Gods be damned!"

"I am sorry, Sir, but perhaps you could try later?" The receptionist suggested making me want to throw the fucking phone against the wall as my answer.

"No, she is there!" I growled out.

"Then perhaps she doesn't want to…"

"Take this phone to her room!" I demanded.

"I am sorry, Sir, I can't do that," she told me, clearly shocked.

"Why the fuck not, is it attached to the fucking wall?"

"Well, no it's handsfree but I cannot exactly go harassing the guests," she argued back making me close to snapping and using mind control on this bitch despite the information I needed from her. Because the possibility of doing so might render her useless, depending on her state of mind…because honestly, I wasn't sure I wouldn't just go too far. I wasn't exactly what you could call in control and restraint was close to becoming just a fucking word that meant nothing but failure.

"Just fucking do it!" I snapped making her say more firmly this time,

"I am sorry, Sir, but it is like I said, I cannot force a guest to…oh wait, here she is," she said making me suddenly tense, my hand needing to find the wall to hold myself steady.

"Put her on the phone." I forced the command through my lips on a barely held back snarl. Then I heard her sweet voice and I swear I actually sighed in relief.

"I am sorry, but do you mind giving us a minute?" The

receptionist replied with some nonsense and I held my breath waiting for her.

"What do you want, Lucius?" she said in a tone that said it all, making me unable to stop myself from snapping,

"What do I want…? What the fuck do you think I want, Amelia…? Get your ass back home now!" Gods in fucking Hell, I was so angry!

"I am not a child, Luc, and I can do whatever the Hell I want with my life," she said calmly but the second she called me Luc, I knew what little patience I'd had before this phone call just evaporated. She never called me Luc and I hated hearing it coming from her lips. She wasn't Fae to me or even Faith, she was and always would be my Amelia and the same went for her.

I was her Lucius.

"Yeah and just how long is that life going to last out there unprotected?!" I threw back at her, wondering if she had even considered the dangers of being out there alone.

Her answer said it all,

"I think I have proven enough times how capable I am at surviving on my own, so if you don't mind, I have shit to do, so I will…" Once again this forced my hand to crush the nearest door frame as I threatened,

"Don't you dare hang up! So, help me, by the Gods, I will…"

"You will what, Luc, huh…because last time I checked you already ripped out my fucking heart and stepped on it, so what…you wanna see what more damage you can do?!" she threw back at me and I swear it was like receiving a verbal slap, one that continued to sting through my next set of words… words that were said in hopes of actually getting through to her.

"You have this completely wrong and if you had just waited

for five fucking minutes before running off then you would have given me the time to explain that!"

"I know what I saw, and I know what I heard, which means that I don't need your interpretation of events to clarify shit! We are done, we are over and the quicker you get that through your stubborn, royal ass head the better this will be! So, you can just quit pretending to give a shit and run back off to mummy dearest and tell her that you tried your best!" After this I was actually forced to take a step back as if she had been here in front of me. As if she had her hands to my chest and was now pushing me backwards with every word she threw at me. Which was when I officially lost my shit with her!

Now came the real truth behind my threat, one I would make good on if it was the last thing I ever fucking did in this world! Because convincing her was something her mother had failed at. But then, I was about to discover that I would be no better at this, for I also had my anger set out against me. Which meant that instead of trying to lure her in and convince her of the truth, I was left with nothing but letting bitterness coat my threat,

"Now you listen to me, my girl and you listen well, you and I will *never be done, we will never be over*, which means I will *NEVER* stop looking for you. I will fucking hunt you down to the ends of the Earth and beyond…so unless you want a hard time running then I suggest you keep your ass there and be ready for me because… I. Am. Coming. For. You!" Once I'd finished this dark and possessive promise, I found myself barely able to drag in enough air to keep breathing!

I was almost panting like a rabid beast and barely keeping a lid on the one that already consumed me. The one that wanted to break free and roar so loud down the fucking phone at her that it would shake the foundations of Afterlife.

But after last time and needing to be brought back from that

Hellish part of me, by none other than Dom, then I knew the importance right now in trying to keep my demon under my control. Not the other way around. Of course, the flaw in this plan was Amelia and her utter refusal to listen to reason. Now, on some level I was trying to put myself in her mind set, for I knew she was hurt and truly believed that what she had seen to be the truth. Mistaken roots grown from insecurities I myself had planted there seven years ago. But to know that in that one moment it eradicated everything I had tried to achieve these last few weeks was beyond my comprehension!

That my words meant nothing to her. That she obviously believed it all to have been an act, one played so well and all for what, so I could protect her just because her mother wished it?! It barely seemed plausible as far as reasons could go. But then, what else was her mind to conjure up, for the reasons she believed I would kiss her mother?

Fuck!

All I could hope for was that my threat was enough to ring true and she would give up this hope of running from me. I mean what chance did she really think she had. This was me we were talking about...*did she not know me?* I was a fucking hunter! I had been an assassin longer than I had ever been a King! Hunting people was what I had been given new life to do first...Hunt those who would not kneel.

And now it seemed as if history was repeating itself as I found myself hunting rogues. But before that, it was time to hunt something far more precious to me and when I finally captured her, Gods I wasn't going to make her kneel...

I was going to tie her to my fucking bed and this time, I wouldn't use silk, *I would use fucking chains!*

Then I wouldn't release her again until I had convinced her of the truth and until she agreed to marry me! To tie herself to me in every way possible!

In fact, I was just about to open my mouth after this thought had calmed me somewhat and try and reason with her some more, when she said something to me that cut me not just deep but to the fucking core…

"Then to the ends of the Earth is where it will be…"

"Amelia." I hissed her name in warning for her not to continue but it was one she ignored and did so anyway. Now giving me what she foolishly believed was her version of a goodbye, one that I would never allow to fucking happen!

"Goodbye Luc. Have a nice eternity with…*with someone else's Chosen One,*" she said before I heard the clatter of the phone and I was left roaring her name in anger before hammering a fist down on the nearest piece of furniture I could find.

After which I found myself once more drowning in my own pain. A darkness that consumed me as panic gripped my heart in its vice like grip. But this time it wasn't the deadly grip of the Devil with his hand inside my chest.

No, now it was Amelia's and she was pulling me under.

Under into a heartbreaking…

Oblivion.

CHAPTER TEN

ROYAL VOWS AND DELEGATION

"The helicopter is on its way." Dom informed me the second I made it back inside his office.

"I need a word alone," I said after taking the time needed to compose myself enough to form actual words, a skill I would be needing for the next part of my plan to be put into place. Because there was no denying what that phone call had done to me. Meaning that Keira took one look at me and then at Dom before deciding that it was best not to argue or be stubborn. Something she and her daughter clearly had in common. That and the habit of running from emotional difficulties, being something Keira had certainly done her fair share of in the past.

"I will go and make some calls, see if she has reached out to Ella or not," she said referring to Amelia's cousin, who I knew she was close to. I waited for her to leave, before coming right out and telling him,

"I need you to take the lead on hunting the rogues and finding the witch whilst I am looking for her."

"You didn't find her?" he asked in a strained voice that spoke of his disappointment and worry.

"No, I found her, but given the way in which I did it also caused her to run again." He raised a brow in question before surmising for himself,

"The Void."

"I will not apologize, Dom," I stated before he could say anything else but then he surprised me by releasing a sigh and deflating back into his chair,

"I would not expect you to, Luc." After this, it was my turn to grant him the questioning look.

"You know, when I first met Keira, I would find it near impossible to stay away from her. And just so I could do as I pleased, I would make her believe my appearance in the night was nothing more than a dream. I was no better than a fucking stalker," he admitted making me scoff,

"You're not telling me anything I didn't already know, my friend." After this he looked at me head on and shocked me when he came right out and said what he had been leading up to,

"I know you own her building, Luc, and I know you filled it with enough security to go unnoticed and you situated your own people to live there using your witch to hide the fact from Amelia. I also know about you hiring Dante to watch her, which I gather is more recent considering you most likely had your own people do this years before."

"I will not apologize for that either," I said in a firm tone, not even taking a second before answering.

"And once again, I don't expect you to, but what I want to know is how long?"

"How long what, Dom?" I snapped not having the patience for this fucking conversation right now.

"How long have *you* been *stalking* my daughter?" he asked

nodding to me and emphasising his own words, whilst giving me a knowing look. After all, he had admitted to being there once before. Either way, I told him frankly,

"What does it matter, the fact remains that it happened and I…"

"…And *you* were keeping her at arm's length for the very same reasons I did the same with Keira. It had fuck all to do with me or Keira deceiving me and asking you to." This was quite a deduction but then again, it came as little surprise considering he had been through this all once before.

"I also take it that you were the reason she went to Germany and you were also the reason she left and came back a broken version of her former self." At this I released a frustrated sigh that said it all.

"I don't see how this is fucking relevant now!" I snapped seeing little point in having this conversation now, of all times.

"And I don't give a fuck if you do or not, I deserve an answer, Luc!" He threw back at me and I decided that instead of telling him to go fuck himself like I wanted to, I knew that on some level he was right. After all that had been kept from him, then perhaps he did deserve an answer.

"Fine, yes it was fucking me! The time was not right…I was not, did not…*fuck.*" I hissed getting lost for words and hating that he was the one to witness it.

"And I also assume that this was where she first formed her belief of your attachment to…" At this my warning growl cut him off before I snarled,

"Yes…fuck, Dom, really… you want to do this now?!"

"You're waiting for the helicopter to arrive and can do little before it gets here, so yes …yes, we have to fucking do this now!" This last part was most definitely said as my own warning, and I tore my face to the side with a shake of my head.

"Then I think you already have a pretty clear concept of

what you have been missing these last years," I said pointing out the obvious, for it seemed since finding out about Amelia and I, then he had spent his time digging deep enough to know the true depth of my obsession for his daughter.

"That may be true, but what I would like to know is since when?"

"Since when?" I repeated his question wondering why the fuck it mattered.

"Since when did you discover who my daughter was to you?" I dragged a hand through my hair in frustration and snapped,

"It doesn't fucking matter!"

"It matters to me… now tell me when!?" I released a pent-up growl and came close to walking out the office telling him that I didn't owe him shit! I answered to no one, least of all him. But then it only took a single memory to infiltrate through my anger to prove that statement wasn't true…not anymore. It was the sight of him embracing his daughter outside the gates of Afterlife. Because Dom may no longer be classed as my King and the days had long passed since I called him my comrade, but I had to remember that he meant something to Amelia.

And for that reason alone, he deserved my respect. I released a sigh and looked back at him.

"Since the night I saved her life in London, the night of the tournament at the Devil's ring," I admitted in a strained tone making Dom close his eyes as he absorbed this information and tried not to give into the urge to try and kill me…*again.*

"So that is why it was like pulling Gorgon fangs to try and get you to come to council meetings" I shrugged my shoulders and said,

"What do you want from me, Dom…I may be considered a cruel bastard by most who know me, but I've always tried to do right by your daughter."

"And if I hadn't been the one to bring you together that night of the gala…what then?" he asked making me growl this time,

"Don't fucking go there, my friend, for I was nearing my limit as it was and needed little pushing on the matter. Amelia was always mine to claim, despite what you or any other fucker may think, so do not presume to think that you had a hand in this…she would have been mine soon enough." He growled back at me and again the limits of his patience on the matter were wearing as thin as mine were. Which was why I suggested,

"It is all of little consequence now, don't you think? Besides, we have more important aspects of the past to deal with…you know, like the fucking witch you failed to kill… don't think that I missed the part where Keira wasn't the only one keeping the true nature of things from the other," I reminded him this time making him look uncomfortable at the turn our conversation had taken.

"I hardly think one equates to the other, Luc, and besides, times were different back then. Keira is different now and knows the way of our world. Back then she was innocent, and she was…"

"Human. Yes, I remember," I finished for him dryly.

"She also needed to learn an important lesson that night and that was not trusting in what it is you *think* you see."

"Yes, and from the sounds of things, after this last twenty-four hours, then I would say that your daughter also needs to learn this lesson," I told him dryly.

"Well, at least we both agree on that…she should not have run from here...she shouldn't have run from you," Dom admitted surprising me, and my look must have said as much as he responded to it,

"I am aware of the irony here, Luc, as despite how much I

may not like it, I have no choice but to accept the claim. Besides, I think you have proven enough to me that we have a common goal here and that is her safety comes first." I nodded once and agreed in my usual way,

"Indeed."

"Then I will give you this time to do what it is I know you do best, hunting without the usual outcome of course." I smirked at this for we both knew that I spent more years being his personal assassin than that of a King.

"Naturally," I said in agreement.

"I also wish for an outcome that in time her anger is replaced with acceptance of the truth, as naturally Keira is beside herself with worry, and as you know, this is not a sight I relish seeing."

"I can see that, Dom, and that hope will turn into a certainty if I have anything to say about it," I told him, now getting to my feet as I could hear the helicopter in the distance. He granted me a knowing look before continuing,

"The guilt of this last twenty-four hours lies heavily on her. In other words, Luc, I ask you this, not only as a father, but also as a husband…find my daughter, protect her and please, for the love of the damn Gods…fix this." I released a deep weighted sigh and nodded, bowing slightly in respect. A respect that I thought in that moment he deserved in return. Because by asking me to do this for him, well I knew it had most likely been one of the hardest moments of his life. After all, I had once been granted the title of his greatest enemy and now here I was, being asked to hunt down his daughter. Even though he knew that by me doing so, it also meant he had no choice but to accept the outcome of such…that Amelia was mine to claim, announcing it to our world.

So, naturally, for that alone he deserved not only my respect but also my promised vow,

"I will stop at nothing in achieving all in which you ask, of this you have my word…"

"I will find her."

CHAPTER ELEVEN

BLOODY CRUMBS TO FOLLOW

"It's not here," I growled angrily in response to Zagan's comment on the missing Ferrari, one that was clearly not in the hotel parking lot as I had hoped for. Although, admittedly, I wasn't surprised that she was long gone, but finding myself furious all the same. But after the receptionist's comment about not seeing a Ferrari, something from the looks of the place that would have stood out, I now wondered at her still having the vehicle at all.

The moment the chopper was coming into land, doing so in the nearly empty parking lot of the hotel, I had the door open and was jumping the ten feet down not caring who the fuck saw me. I was then striding towards the entrance scowling at the cheap building with a curl of my lip.

I swear that it took all my strength not to rip the door off its hinges before I stepped up to the desk. A woman, whose features barely registered more than the artificial red colour of her hair and heavily made up face, looked up as I approached.

Her eyes widened at the sight of me and did a leisurely scan of my physique one that, in this moment, was tensed to the point that had I been just a man my muscles would have ached. But then I knew that until I got her back in my arms once again then my days of relaxing were over. Instead, my body was held taut and at the ready for anything.

"Good afternoon, do you have an...?"

"Silence!" I commanded, knowing that I didn't have time to waste so I took control of her mind now that I had regained my strength to do so without causing permanent damage. She naturally did as I ordered, becoming that of a willing servant with few thoughts of her own.

"Do you have security cameras?"

"Yes."

"Good, log in to the computer and bring up the guest information," I demanded of her, making her do so quickly and efficiently. Then, as Zagan and Takeshi who had been assigned to aid me, walked inside I issued my orders.

"Zagan, the security system should be in the back. Takeshi, re-trace any sense of her outside and see what you can find." Both nodded and went about their duties without a word.

"I have finished," the woman said stepping back. So, I walked to her side of the desk and turned the screen my way so I could look for myself, scanning a finger down the list of names.

"Room seven, has it been cleaned?" I asked the moment I saw the name 'Jane Eyre' on the system, seeing for myself that she had paid in cash. But of course, she didn't want to be traced. The question became where she got that money from to begin with. Had she really been reduced to stealing it? That certainly didn't sound like Amelia, but then again, I knew for myself what the depths of desperation would make a person do.

"No, but it will be shortly."

"Call the chambermaid and tell her to leave it. Then give me a key to the room," I told her making her pick up a radio and call the maid to relay my order. Then she picked up a blank card and assigned it a room after swiping it through a reader. I plucked it from her fingers the second it was free from the machine and was striding towards the rooms with determined steps, knowing that I had no time to waste. My only hope was that she had left some clue as to what she was planning next. Or at the very least, clues as to where it was she had come from, that way I may discover her intentions as to where she'd planned to be her destination.

Pip's earlier question had been what if she had no plans? What if she had simply got in the car and decided to keep going with no destination in mind? But at the time, both Dom and I had dismissed the idea. Because Amelia always had a plan. It was who she was. It was ingrained into the core of her. And I would bet my fangs on the fact that by the time she had made it outside the boundary of Afterlife that she had already started to formulate a plan in her mind.

It was what made her so dangerous. She was one of the smartest people I knew and for that reason alone I knew that hunting her down was going to be no easy feat. But everyone left something behind. And even the most insignificant thing could lead somewhere.

Especially in the age of technology. Everything had a digital fingerprint. Even the packet of a coffee cup could lead a person in the right direction, as everything had a code to chase back to the source. From manufacturer, to buyer, to distribution and then to consumer. It was all breadcrumbs to follow and as smart as my girl was, everyone at one time or another slipped up. Now, my only hope was that she slipped up this early on and behind the door I was now approaching was a slip up made sooner rather than later.

I opened the door and entered, taking a moment to breathe deep, taking in the lingering scent of my Chosen. But doing so ended by finding myself having to fight my demon as he rose to the surface. To the point that I could see the reflection of crimson eyes staring back at me through the mirror in the bathroom as I stepped inside.

I picked up the still damp towel that had been left on top of the counter and brought it to my face so I could take in the new soap she had used, familiarizing myself with it. Then I fisted it angrily, letting the water seep through my hand and drip down my leather glove. I threw it aside with a slap against the tiles and scanned the room for anything more.

Then I frowned as the faint smell of bile reached my nose and I walked closer to the toilet seeing now a tiny speck of vomit at the rim, telling me that she had been sick. I growled angrily as I turned away from the sight, before spinning and putting my fist straight through the glass above the sink, shattering the image of my anger.

I tore it from the mirror letting shards of glass clatter with the song of destruction raining down against the ceramic bowl, before looking down at the blood pooling around the shards that were still embedded in my skin. I calmly pulled them free and in doing so remembered the blood I had seen on her own hands, making me question where it had come from? Had it been left from the cuts I had seen there that I now knew was from her being fooled into opening the vault...or had something else happened to her?

Gods, but if something had then I knew that my vessel would never survive the rage of my demon without him tearing free! I snarled down at myself before I turned my back on the damage and left the bathroom. Instead, I walked back inside the room and took in the hurried array of her actions. I walked to the coffee tray and ran a finger along the selections of teas seeing that nothing looked missing. I looked down and located the trash bin, kicking it back under the desk when seeing it was empty. She hadn't even been here long enough to drink something.

There wasn't even a fucking a receipt or food wrapper, *nothing.* It was as though all she had come here for was nothing more than to stop for sleep and that was it. Gods, but the girl must be running on fumes by now and all I could hope for was that she was at least eating on the road. I hated to think of her not taking care of herself and I swore that when I finally found her, then it had better not be in anything less than the perfect condition I had become used to seeing her in before all this shit began!

And well, from the evidence I had found in the bathroom, then my hope for this outcome was looking less likely by the fucking second! I walked over to the pile of clothes she had left on the floor to see now that it was a uniform…the flight attendant's uniform to be exact. But of course, she had swapped clothes with her to keep up the ruse and not arouse suspicion when leaving the plane. However, this then made me question what if her clothes weren't the only thing she had swapped with her?

I knew that she had gone to her room before leaving but hadn't taken her purse, passport, phone, nothing that could be traced to her, but what if she had taken something after all…

A bargaining chip?

After all, she needed money somehow and I could not imagine that Amelia had just decided to leave it all up to chance. No, she would know that she needed money, if only to fill the tank of a very expensive car that didn't exactly get the best mileage. So, what if her reasons for arranging the jet weren't solely to fool us? After all, driving there first had been a risk in itself, for we must have only just missed her being there.

I pulled my phone from my back pocket and made the call.

"You found something?" Dom asked as way of answer.

"Perhaps," I told him, not surprised that he hadn't asked if I had found her. Because he knew as well as I did, that she would be long gone from here by the time we arrived.

"Then what do you need?"

"I want you to tell Keira to go to her room. Look again to see what is missing…it would have to be something of value," I told him, knowing that an explanation wouldn't be needed.

"You think she would pawn something to fund her escape?" he asked then relayed the message to Keira who didn't ask questions.

"I think she bribed the flight attendant for more than just the use of her clothes. I didn't think of it at the time, but her decoy told me she had been paid, yet Amelia's purse remained in her room. So, it stands to reason she must have paid her with something, and I think Amelia would have bargained for a lot more than just a uniform." He agreed before giving me what I wanted before needing to ask for it.

"I will have her account checked and have the girl questioned."

"Good, my only hope is that Amelia slipped up and is still using her card, but I doubt it," I told him making him agree once more.

"Knowing Fae, clearing her accounts would have been one of the first things she did, but it is worth looking into."

"Well, knowing how much cash she has will at least give me

an idea of the limits set against her...or should I say set against me. Let me know what you find," I told him.

"Of course." After his agreement, I hung up and went back to the uniform, hoping to find a receipt or something more in a pocket but what I didn't expect to find was blood.

Blood...

That wasn't hers.

CHAPTER TWELVE

DEVIL'S RIGHT HAND

I left the hotel with my hopes of being able to track her from the air crushed as it became clear, after speaking with witnesses, that it was as I suspected. No-one had remembered seeing a Ferrari of any kind in the parking lot. Meaning that my cunning girl had somehow managed to change her car. Now, how she had achieved that without having proof of ownership, I didn't yet know but at the very least I was close to finding out. And the key had been her friend Wendy.

Dante had come through, as I knew he would for it was clear that he didn't want me anywhere near her. So, with the ultimatum I had set against him, he had done the job. He had exercised that certain skill set he was known for and admittedly, was a master at. Doing what he did best, which was manipulating her dreams. Something I should have been able to do with just as much ease with Amelia, but something was changing in her.

She was getting stronger.

I'd never had a problem before entering her Void, especially while she slept. Which made me question now if my blood, my influence and essence in her was doing something more than just keeping her immortal? It made me begin to question the past and start asking myself if I had missed something?

Either way, it didn't change the fact that the timing couldn't have been worse, despite being at least assured that should she find herself injured in any way, that she would heal. But then I also knew that eventually my essence in her would run its course and when it did, then even in this way I could not protect her.

A fact I spent a great deal of time worrying about and ultimately dreading. But naturally I was hoping it wouldn't yet come to that. That time, even though it felt like it was slipping through my fingers the longer she was gone from me, would run out for her long before it did for me. However, despite feeling confident that I was tightening the net around her with every hour that passed, I also couldn't dispel the fabled tale of assumption biting me in the ass!

But as new information was coming in, I had to act accordingly, starting with the flight attendant. Dom had called me to let me know that my instincts had been right, the only thing missing from her room had been a diamond necklace that she had bargained with. Something I was happy to discover, he had retrieved. This was solely for Amelia's benefit, for I could have bought her all the diamonds she wanted, I was fucking rich enough!

But knowing Amelia the way I did, then I knew that she would already be trying to think of ways of getting it back one day. Little did she know was that it was worth over two hundred thousand dollars. Something we discovered she had traded for nothing more than a small overnight bag, a uniform and a total of $1751.61, that she had drawn out at ATM's on her way to New York.

Dom had been furious, doing little more than writing the girl a check for double that amount and telling her that she should count herself lucky that she received anything at all. If it had been me, she would have lost a lot more, not gained from it. For if it hadn't been for the woman's greed, then I would have most likely found her by now, seeing as she would have run out of gas and had no choice but to try and make it on foot.

However, this gave her enough money to make it to New York, which I discovered was her first destination after Dante had recovered a phone conversation Wendy had with her from her memories. He mentioned some cryptic shit about never giving Wendy access to any sporting goods, mainly the use of a bat and also the name of a friend of Wendy's who worked at the New York Times.

Which was exactly where I found myself now, stepping through the glass front of the Times' building on 620 Eighth Avenue, Manhattan. Doing so with the sole purpose of finding the next piece of the puzzle and discovering why the fuck she had wanted to meet with a reporter!

Thankfully, before Dante had given me this information, he also had the foresight to do a background check on the guy. I swear if he wasn't a royal in his own right then I would have been tempted to bargain with him into joining my people and letting me become his sire. But then the big bastard didn't exactly need an upgrade of power and nor was now the time to be making offers. As being tied to my life right now was looking more like a fucking death sentence than anything remotely close to personal gain.

He was most certainly efficient in what he did, that was for sure.

Like the information on the reporter, Micky Donnelly, who was nothing more than an unsuspecting family man who had on occasion rocked a few boats with some of the articles he'd had published in the paper. Granted, this was mainly with politicians and other businessmen in power, but as of yet nothing too bad that it had got him fired.

But my one and only question was why him? Something I was close to discovering as I made my way to his cubicle on the floor Dante had told me I would find him. I ignored all the looks I received, making it known I was interested in nothing but my destination. I swear, but I found myself cursing the use of elevators by the time I finally got there. Especially after one woman in a tight blue dress thought that by continuously 'accidentally' knocking into me, that this was going to make me suddenly look at her differently. That I would look at her with anything but the indifference I had been showing her. Meaning that by the time I reached my floor, I was close to snapping and baring my fangs at her! Especially when the doors finally opened and she handed me her card telling me,

"Call me and I will prove to you that I'm not that clumsy." I curled my lip in disgust, dropped the card to the floor and walked away telling her,

"I'll keep my clumsy, thanks." Then I found my intended target and got right to the point, leaving the outraged woman dumbstruck.

"You were asked to meet a girl with a Ferrari last night." I heard him release a sigh down at his keyboard before he finally turned around to look at me,

"Damn that Wendy! Look, I don't know who you…oh." The sight of me looming over him stopped him in his tracks and after taking a look at our very noticeable size difference, he visibly gulped and started to sweat. His heart rate also increased, and I followed his gaze to my clenched fists, one where the leather of my glove was cracking.

"What I mean is…ahem…what is it you would like to know?" he asked after first needing to clear his throat. So, I put a hand to the small partition wall of his booth, leaned closer and said in what I knew was an intimidating, and threatening way,

"Why Micky… *I want to know everything.*"

ONLY TEN MINUTES later I had my phone back in hand and was issuing my next order,

"Bring the car around, we are going back to the helipad," I said before stepping on the elevator, now having all the information I needed to continue my search. Which also meant it was time to inform Dom just what his precious little princess had been up to. Something that waited until I was once again folding myself inside the limo that had been organized to be waiting for me once the helicopter had landed.

I tapped on his name, wondering whilst waiting for him to answer if it meant that I now needed to change his contact name from asshole to something less derogatory, especially seeing as we seemed to be working together on this.

"Please fucking tell me that you have found something useful?" Dom snapped, obviously like me very near to the end of his patience and answering my internal musing I decided that asshole would stay for now.

"Well, I think I may have found your car, although I am pretty sure you're not going to like its destination," I told him.

"Just tell me, Luc, where is it?" His tone said it all and one that would soon turn from frustrated to furious in a heartbeat.

"In a chop shop in Albany," I told him making him growl low and menacing, gritting out the question,

"And what the fuck was my daughter doing at a fucking chop shop!?"

"That, my friend, is precisely what I am about to find out, but I think we both can guess, seeing as she wasn't driving your car when she arrived at the hotel," I said pointing out the obvious.

"Gods in fucking Heaven, Amelia!" He cursed under his breath and I didn't bother telling him that I had already uttered the same curse seconds after the reporter had told me who it was that Amelia had been trying to find.

"Let me know what you discover."

"And the car?" I asked making him groan,

"Use your imagination and if that doesn't work, write a fucking cheque, after all I know you're good for it." I scoffed a laugh before telling him,

"Fine but consider it a gift that I will be reminding you of when I am marrying your daughter." After this I ended the call to the sound of his growl and allowing my frustration a moment's reprieve after smirking at the thought of riling my former King. A sound that despite the circumstances still managed to amuse me.

However, that amusement died the moment I started issuing orders which included calling the helicopter pilot and telling him to get the bird ready as I wasn't wasting over two hours driving to Albany from the city. Which meant arranging yet another car to be waiting for me when I got to whichever pad was closest for us to land on. During which time I also called Dante, now with a new name for him to research,

A gangster by the name of Big B.

The moment the reporter had mentioned him an image of the blood on Amelia's hands instantly came to mind and I hated where those reasons took me to, having a bad feeling in my gut. But then again, I also didn't see any bruises on her in the image she portrayed back to me in the mirror and none were described when questioning the receptionist at the hotel.

Which was why, by the time I reached Washington Avenue and was sat across from the chop shop, I already had a pretty good idea of what I would find inside. Knowing Amelia, it would be broken bones and a red Ferrari.

"Do you have what I need?" I said as a way of answering the phone the moment Dante called me back.

"Oh yeah, I have what you need," was his amused answer.

"Good, time to go and introduce myself then."

"It would be rude not to," he agreed with what I knew was a smirk. And my answer was a simple and knowing one…

"Indeed."

NIGHT HAD STARTED to fall by the time I got out of the limo, telling the driver that I would no longer be needing the car and as I took one look at the double roller doors, I told him,

"I will shortly have alternative travel."

Then I slammed the door and walked across the street up to the doors that I knew were locked. I decided against knocking and instead got right to the point. Something I did by reaching down and forcing them to lift, snapping the locks with the resounding echo of cracking metal as the doors started to crumple upwards. I felt the anger rolling through my senses and rage fueling my blood as it pumped around my body at a greater speed. Now I know I could have just walked inside and commanded every mortal to their knees, at the same time draining them of every memory that contained my girl.

But really,

Where was the fun in that?

No, this way it gave me the rare opportunity to expel some

pent-up anger and frustrations. Which was why, when I walked through the now broken doors, I cracked my head to the side, relishing the snap of pain it rewarded. Gods, but I needed what felt like a whole day on the mats, fighting someone with skill. Because one look at the mortals in this garage and I almost wanted to roll my eyes. Although, the more I looked, taking in the details of each, I finally allowed myself a deadly grin.

My girl had done well.

Damn it, but I hated it when she was fucking right! She could take care of herself. Fuck, but just looking at these guys and now I was wondering if she couldn't be classed as a dangerous weapon on the streets of the mortal world. Of course, it wasn't the mortal world I was concerned about…*it was my own.*

"Who the fuck are you?!" Some guy shouted at me as he walked towards me in what he no doubt believed was a threatening way. So instead of answering him, I snapped out a fist quicker than he could react and broke his nose…*again.*

He dropped to the floor instantly and I hated the fact that I wasn't free to give more into the punch. For it wouldn't have just killed him, my fist would have most likely embedded itself inside his skull and that shit was one mess that even I didn't relish the idea of right now. I still had a lot of travelling to do and didn't foresee doing so with brain matter crusted on my knuckles as being exactly practical.

Amelia didn't realise it yet, but it was why I always forced myself to hold back when fighting her. Doing so more with the aim of teaching and well, the last time most certainly ended more to my advantage. Especially when it was becoming clear the addiction to tying her up that had manifested in our sex life very early on.

But this was unsurprising, as it was true that I was a dominant lover, even spanning throughout my long history. But since Amelia, naturally being the first mortal in my bed, well then there was no comparison. The urge to keep her in place and unable to take away my enjoyment as I made her mine and claimed her body, was just too tempting not to give in to. This was also helped by the fact that she also enjoyed it...*immensely,* for I always made sure of this fact before finding my own release.

But right now, it was time for a release of a very different, *violent* kind.

"Oh shit, not again." I heard one of them mutter and from the looks of the sling around his arm, then it wasn't surprising, nor was the fact that he started to back up.

"Let me guess, you're the motherfucker missing a Ferrari?" The question came from the mezzanine level above and from who I expected to find walking closer to the rebar railings. Of course, his choice of insults had me questioning exactly what Amelia had said, for however it had happened, she had somehow managed to do business with this asshole.

I replied with a deadly grin,

"No, I am the horror story your boys will tell others when asked how you lost your life, should you choose not to co-operate of course...now where is my woman, *Bryant?"* I told him making him sneer down at me at the sound of his own name from my lips.

"I don't know who the fuck you think you are or where the fuck you got that name but both just signed your fucking death warrant...'cause, unlike the last time someone walked in here and fucked with me, now we are all packing, asshole and from the looks of things, you look shit out of luck, as you should have brought a gun." I smirked at this and told him with a confidence that cracked the air around me along with my knuckles,

"I don't need luck, Bryant, just as...*I don't need a gun."* I let these last five words out with a demonic growl that made his eyes widen. Then I reached down and picked up an air line before ripping it from the air compressor it was attached to. As the first guy pulled a gun from the holster at his back, I swung the hose and hit him square in the chest with the impact gun that had been the tool the forced air had been used for.

He landed backwards into the tall red tool chest, knocking a set of wrenches off the top with a clatter of sound. By which time, I had started pulling the hose back to me, and was swinging the end of the tool ready for the next asshole. But then one came running at me from behind and I sidestepped with time to spare. This was so that when he passed me, I could then wrap the length of hose around his neck. After this I twisted my body downwards to one knee putting my back to his. The move took him with me and started to cut off his air supply.

It was only when I felt his body go limp that I let him go, just as the first rain of bullets started from both my level and the one above. So, I threw up a hand and stopped them in their path, making them drop to the floor like metal hailstones. And it was just as they were no doubt asking themselves how the fuck I had done it that I turned towards the closest car that they had been working on. It was one that was minus its wheels, hence the impact gun, and soon that wouldn't be all that was missing.

I grabbed the open door to what I could now see was a Mercedes, ripped it from its hinge arms before using it to throw at the men who were all foolishly stood close to each other, making them one big target for me. The impact rocketed into them, knocking each man back into the wall of tools, just like their fallen colleague before them.

This also caused their guns to scatter along the floor and neither one looked like they were getting up from the hit anytime soon. Or if they knew what was good for them, they would simply fake their injuries.

After this I focused my attention on my intended target seeing now that the big man had gone pale.

Good, it was time fear played a part and like I said, it was time for his own horror story.

One that featured…

The Devil's Right Hand.

CHAPTER THIRTEEN

BITTER IRONY

"Where is she?!" I snarled out the question dangerously, now focusing all my attention on who was known to the underground world of organized crime as Big B.

"I don't know what the fuck you mean, one of my guys jacked that Ferrari from some chick yesterday," he said obviously lying, as I granted him a knowing look before I told him,

"Now, I might have been inclined to believe you, however you've got two problems with that."

"Oh yeah, and what are those, dickhead?!" he shouted back down at me.

"One is that my girl would never allow someone to steal from her and secondly…" I paused to motion to his broken men now bleeding on the floor and said,

"...this looks like her handy work." And as if on cue one of them groaned in pain making Bryant sneer down at them before shaking his head as if they were all fucking useless.

"Now, unless you give me what I want, then you will join them and trust me when I tell you, asshole, you really don't want to see me painting your fucking floor crimson, as I promise you...you wouldn't like my idea of art," I told him before I disappeared from his view and calmly made my way to the staircase beneath where he was stood.

"You a fucking cop?!" he shouted, and I laughed once and told him,

"Do I look like any fucking cop to you?"

"You look fucking insane and someone who needs a taste of lead in their brain!" he said training the gun on me as I slowly walked up the metal staircase that led to what I assumed was his office. But from the look of the slight tremor in his hand, by now he knew that having his gun was pointless. Naturally the sight of his fear made me grin before warning him,

"Oh Bryant, I am not insane...No, I am so much more than merely insane, something you will get a taste of should you decide not to tell me what I want to know...*and fucking soon.*"

"Fuck, tell me that she didn't learn her fighting skills from you?" he shouted, finally admitting that he had seen her, which I knew was only the start.

"No, for if she had, then she would have slaughtered the lot of you."

"Look, I did the girl a solid, gave her the fucking car she wanted and that was it. It was business, you want the Ferrari for my life, then fucking take it!" he said quickly, thinking that I was there for metal over flesh.

"Oh, I am taking it, but I didn't come here for a fucking car...now, tell me where she is!" I roared this time after first snatching the gun, then throwing it so hard that it embedded in the wall. After that I grabbed the front of his jacket and yanked him hard into my fist held at his gut, so he doubled over with the pain.

"Fu...ck...I...fuck, I don't...don't fucking know, alright!" he said once he managed to get his breath back. I folded my arms and watched him as he struggled back to his feet, using the railings to aid him.

"Besides, if she is half as smart as I assume she is and seeing as it only took you a day to track her ass down, then you already know she would never tell me where she was headed." I growled in frustration, knowing the asshole was right! Amelia was too smart to slip up like that. But then, just as I took another step towards him, I saw something there. It was in his eyes.

He knew something.

So, I grabbed his collar and yanked him the rest of the way until I was in his face. Then I snarled at him, as I was done with wasting time! My demon growled angrily, and I couldn't fight it when my fangs started to grow and my eyes morphed into crimson death,

"Fuck! Jesus fucking Christ, what the fuck are you!" he stammered in fear, making me get drunk from the delicious scent of it.

"You're not telling me everything," I warned dangerously before snapping my fangs at him and I had to give it to him, this one managed to keep his bladder in check.

"Alright, fuck, okay she is not worth my life. I helped her out...more than I fucking should have...*clearly,*" he said, obviously knowing now the full depth of shit he was in.

"Helped her how?" I asked after letting him go and he straightened his jacket before telling me,

"I put her in contact with one of my guys, got her a new ID." I growled deeper at this and snarled in his face, making him tense and jump back as if ready for me to slash his throat.

"I should fucking kill you for the trouble you have caused me!" I threatened before turning my back on him with a frustrated growl, needing to take a breath to calm the rage of my demon and preventing him from coming through fully before going on a murderous rampage, starting with these pathetic shit stains on society!

"Then why aren't you?"

"You think I should?" I challenged back on a snarl over my shoulder, making him raise his hands and say,

"I ain't complaining."

I released a sound of frustration, pushed the rest of my demonic self down and told him the truth,

"You may have added to the challenge set against me in finding her, but the fact remains that you helped her when you didn't have to…that means something to me."

"Enough for you not to kill me?" he asked clearly needing confirmation of the facts.

"Precisely…besides, once I have her back, then to know that I had killed you would no doubt cause its own headache for she clearly liked you," I told him before I walked towards the staircase fully intent on getting the information I needed and getting back on the road.

"Yeah, how do you know that?" he asked following me. I waited until I had reached the bottom before answering.

"Because you don't have a scratch on you," I told him making him grunt a laugh before admitting,

"She was one hard bitc…lady of yours," he replied catching himself in time before he received death for a different reason, as disrespecting my girl was a sure way to end his day…*permanently.*

"That she is," I agreed with a smirk towards the whimpering men of his that were only now trying to pick themselves back up off the floor.

"Yeah, well she didn't exactly have nice things to say about you, or the reasons she was running." I tensed and felt my fists clench trying to remember the reasons I was leaving him in one piece. He had balls, I would give him that.

"A mistake I will shortly rectify, after I am given that name of course," I told him making him hiss,

"Fuck it, this is one relationship the Devil himself wouldn't want to get in between!" he said getting out his phone and making me smirk for he had no idea just how close to the mark he was with that one.

"Yeah Jimmy, it's me, that chick I sent you, well I need the new name you gave her," he nodded a few times and then a grin spread over his face before he responded,

"Good work, kid." Then he hung up and told me what new name she had picked,

"She only gave me a nickname, never gave me her real one but I am gonna take a guess here and say your girl's first name is Amelia?" I frowned in question before snapping,

"And just how the fuck do you know that?!"

"Because I think she is trying to send you a message," he commented with a brazen smirk.

"Yeah, and what is that?"

"I may not be a history buff, but even I know this chick is lost." I growled and ground out a warning,

"I have the patience of the Devil if you want to see it!"

"Lia Earhart, she changed her name to Lia Earhart," he told me and had I been told this under any other circumstances surrounding the reason I was here, then I would have laughed. But it was like Bryant had said, she was clearly trying to send a message. She now wanted me to think of her as a ghost. Well, little did she know that she was about to become resurrected, because a name was all I needed…that and the car she was now driving.

"What was the trade?" I asked nodding to the line of stolen goods on wheels.

"Dom's Dodge." I raised a brow in confusion…how the fuck did this guy know her father?

"Come again?"

"Not a Fast and Furious fan, eh? Well, your girl certainly seemed to be, of course she wanted Eleanor first but there was no way I was parting with her."

"Fucking get to the part where this is fucking important to me!" I snapped as he walked towards the other side of the garage, pulled a cover from the Ferrari and said,

"Dom is the main character in the movie that the black 1970 Dodge Charger RT belonged to, it made her smile when she picked it, so I gathered it meant something to her." I gave him a nod and answered with my usual dry,

"Indeed," as this was starting to sound like my fucking catchphrase these days! But she certainly had a sense of humour or a fancy for irony as Bryant went on to explain in the movie it was his dad's car. And seeing as she'd just stolen her father's car who was named Dom, well her choice was starting to make sense. Especially after I asked,

"I am curious, what did she tell you her nickname was?" He grinned at this and replied,

"Little Dodge."

"But of course," I muttered with a shake of my head.

"It's gotta be said, she definitely has a sense of humour, even told me her plan was to get the Hell out of Dodge and now she's in one." I ignored the next level of irony she obviously was making a statement with and instead found out all the details surrounding the car, like the all-important license plate. After this I plucked the images of my demonic self from his mind, as was law and then I demanded the keys to Dom's car.

"Aww, fuck man, come on, you gotta give me something," he complained as I got inside the half a million-dollar sportscar after first telling him,

"I have given you something." Then I started her up making her roar angrily as if desperate to get back to its owner and added,

"You fuck over people for a living, Bryant… so consider this the redemption of others, with the added bonus you get to keep your life…" Then I pulled down the door, watched the roller doors go up after doing so with my mind and muttered to myself this time,

"…not all of us can claim the same."

CHAPTER FOURTEEN

MISSING THE UNEXPECTED

Three days later I found myself back in the very last place I expected to be, but I had come full circle, finding myself at the very beginning! I swear, but I was starting to question the level of expertise Amelia had at evading capture or I was asking myself if I had lost my touch for hunting?

Either way, I was pissed about being back here but there was nothing more to be done. She had indeed become a fucking ghost and I was hoping that something new would come to light after I had delivered Dom's Ferrari back to him. Meaning that yet a-fucking-gain I was walking inside of Dom's office with fuck all to go on.

"Still nothing?" he asked in that same hopeful tone he always had whenever we spoke, as I had kept my word and continued to keep him in the know. I threw his keys at him and snapped,

"What do you fucking think!"

"Gods, what is she thinking?" he replied with a disappointed shake of his head.

"I can fully imagine exactly what she is thinking, Dom, and other than my head being on the end of a fucking spike at the gates of Afterlife, then I don't see your daughter returning home any time soon," I said kicking out the chair and gripping the back of it, feeling the wood soften under the grip I had on it.

"I take it you found the Dodge then?" he asked making me snarl at the fucking memory.

"Oh yeah, I found it alright," I said before releasing my death grip and deflating into the chair opposite his desk, now scrubbing a hand down my face with my own frustrations. Then, with my elbow to the armrest, I continued to rub my brow as if it would help alleviate the building pressure there.

"And?" His question caused me to take pause and raise the hand from my forehead in a gesture that said it all…*I was pissed off.*

"And… as suspected she sold it, that's what…"

"I get you're obviously not used to getting your ass handed to you when it comes to your intended target evading capture, but you've got to give me more than that!" Dom complained, making me growl at his words before releasing my anger on a sigh, knowing that he was right. I told him that I would keep him informed and I needed to remember that my own frustrations and worries were mirrored in her father's gaze.

"I had the Dodge traced and found it at a dealers in New Jersey." He raised a brow and commented,

"That close to New York?"

"Yeah, which means that she planned for me to find the chop shop and drove for as long as she thought was safe to do so before selling it."

"She didn't do a trade?" he asked making me shake my head, feeling fucking tired and old at that!

"No, they paid her cash, then called her a cab." Dom swore in Persian on a hiss and shook his own head, commenting,

"That girl is too smart for her own good."

"Yes, and the only comfort both you and I will get out of how intelligent she is, is that if I can't fucking find her then neither can the witch. But be sure, Dom, that comfort I find is fucking slim at best!" I snarled angrily with a clenched fist finding the desk to hammer down against.

"As it is with me…I take it you tracked the cab?"

"Yes, but little good it did me as it took her to Newark bus station," I told him remembering turning up there and being forced to watch my girl on a security screen as she bought her ticket and disappeared up the steps inside some Greyhound coach.

"So that's it… she's just gone?!" he shouted, now getting the full depth of my frustrations.

"Using the security footage, I was able to discover that she bought a ticket to Columbia, South Carolina," I told him knowing that it was pointless considering the outcome but doing so all the same.

"And?"

"And I had my people waiting for her there with instructions to contain her until I arrived but when the coach pulled into the station, she wasn't on it. We then discovered that a woman by her description got off at one of the stops in Winston Salem, North Carolina and never returned. After that the trail ran cold because the only camera footage, we have is of her walking away on foot. Where it is then believed she used a payphone to call another cab company to take her somewhere. But then she also could have caught another bus to somewhere else or bought a fucking car for all we know!" I added this last part with a growl of words, hating that I didn't fucking know!

"I take it you're having all bus stations monitored?"

"I am, but the challenge set against us is the small town stops that have no security footage, so there is little hope to track her movements, as it seems her plan is to continue this pattern of bus hopping until she gets to wherever it is she is going."

"And I take it there is still no signs of her trying to leave the country?" he asked once I had finished explaining the bus situation.

"No, her new passport has been flagged at all airports, but I think we can safely assume that if she is being this cautious when simply using the bus service, then she will make sure that she stays away from planes."

"Then what do we assume her next step to be, for she will have to settle at some point?" he asked making me release a sigh, then rubbing the back of my neck I told him,

"I agree, as at the very least she can't leave the country, so all that is left is for us to do is to be ready when she does settle, as gaining another ID won't be easy…not without her contacts."

"Ah yes, I remember meeting this Wendy," he said with a shake of his head as if the memory was an amusing one.

"Dante is having her watched and her calls are also being monitored, but I would be surprised if Amelia took the chance of involving her again," I said, knowing that the only reason she did so in the first place was that she knew it would take us the time she needed to get away, before we were able to start piecing all her steps together.

But the fact that she sold the car did now present a bigger problem for she had more money and enough to settle down somewhere as the Dodge hadn't been cheap. Meaning that it could be weeks before she slipped up again. Which was why I made the decision to keep invading her dreams until one of two things happened, she either slipped up and showed me something she didn't realise would lead me to her, or she became so strong at blocking me out that my chances of doing so again would become too limited.

Naturally, I was hoping for the first.

"So, what you're basically saying is that we have little choice but to wait, is that it?" His tone said it all.

"Hey, I don't fucking like it any more than you do, but if you have any better plans then please, fucking share away, Dom," I snapped making him release a heavy weighted sigh, a sound I had become used to hearing.

"Truth is, every way I look at this and trust me when I say, Dom, I have spent a long fucking time looking at this, but with every idea I have it is as if she is ten steps ahead of me and I just don't know how to get ahead…not without knowing her intended destination."

"And you have entered her Void again?" he asked, surprising me enough to show it.

"I am no fool, Luc, you may not have wanted to admit it to Keira how you found her hotel, but you're a fool if you think I haven't already tried myself." I raised a brow and asked a simple,

"And?

"And nothing! She is like her mother, a fucking wall the size of that monstrosity that surrounds Lucifer's palace. Besides, I am not the master of her will here, you are." I released a low growl of irritation before deciding to be honest with him, seeing as we were alone,

"I will admit, doing so isn't easy and I fear if she grows any stronger then I won't be able to access her mind at all." His eyes widened in surprise but thankfully he chose not to comment on what any King would feel was a weakness, which was why admitting such wasn't easy. He knew this, which is why he merely nodded for me to continue.

"But I will continue to try until I find something as,

unfortunately, for the moment, it is all we have left to go on." And this was true. Which was the only thing that prevented me from giving in to the rage I felt, one that grew from feeling both useless and beaten. But then with nothing left to go on, I was forced with no other choice but to put all my hopes of finding her in that of her own stubborn mind. One that I noticed lately had refused to sleep, no doubt in hopes of preventing me from gaining access once more.

I had been furious with her once realising this, but over the last few days every time I had tried, I had found no way of entering her Void. Meaning that if there were no cracks in her mental walls, then her mind was not at peace and she was not sleeping. Making me wonder when it was that she was getting rest?

Of course, I couldn't spend all of my time focusing on her mind for I would be no use to anyone by spending all my energy this way. And honestly, I wasn't even sure if I could manage it or not, for it wasn't as if I had ever tried.

No, my guess was that she was simply picking random times of the day to power nap, in hopes that I wouldn't have the time to break into her mind and take charge. But then, there was only so long she could keep this up. As she was mortal and unlike my own kind, as we didn't need even a quarter the amount of sleep they did.

Naturally, this also made me worry, especially if she had bought a car and was hoping to drive it to wherever it was she was hoping to get to. However, I thought it prudent for the time being to keep this from Dom, as he had enough on his hands to worry about And besides, I had to admit that having him on my side was easier and I worried that he would ask me to stop trying to discover her whereabouts through her Void if he knew it could offer potential risks.

No, only I would make that call and for now, I thought

finding her was more important than the sleep deprivation. Besides, I was also hoping that she was smart enough to know that her health came first.

So this was why I changed the subject and I did this by asking,

"Tell me about the situation with the rogues."

AFTER THIS CONVERSATION it was unfortunately another six days later that any new information came in and during this time I had gone from difficult to murderous. I had travelled to seven different states running after leads that never amounted to anything but lost time and pointless effort in the name of hope. And in all of that time the only pieces of information that had been of little value, had been four different cabs, three more buses and not even a single night in a hotel, motel or even some small- town bed and breakfast.

I had tried, albeit unsuccessfully, to enter her Void and the most I had seen was her sat asleep in a Greyhound seat on some coach. One I could only discover was on its way to Jacksonville, Florida. But naturally, when I had arrived there and was waiting for her, she had been a no show. Just like all the other stops along the planned route I had placed my people. Which meant that she had become wise to what I was doing and decided to change tactics.

I knew this after one witness' account said that a woman asked the bus driver to pull over in the next town, even though it was unplanned, because she wasn't feeling well. Naturally she was convincing enough for him to do this. So, she got off the bus and was last seen crossing the street and disappearing inside a coffee shop. It was also said that she looked exhausted, which meant that since then, I hadn't tried to access her mind again. This was after seeing for myself the damage I was doing. As she no doubt woke in panic, desperate to get off the bus and knowing her, hadn't slept since.

To say that I was worried about her was a fucking huge understatement and I was therefore forced to give it some time. This was in hopes of at least letting her get to where it was she was determined to travel to. And the hardest part was that I couldn't be sure that she even had a plan to speak of! It just all seemed so random but for all any of us knew, Pip had been right from the start, that she could have just been closing her eyes and sticking her finger on a map.

However, after the mention of Jacksonville, then she was singing a slightly less random tune and one more, should we say...out there.

"Why Florida, what is she planning, a trip to Disney World, or hey, maybe a nice relaxing cruise?" To which both me and Dom commented that it was hardly likely, especially seeing as Amelia got seasick and hated boats.

Of course, before this Dom hadn't exactly been impressed to discover just how many of his own family knew of mine and Amelia's relationship long before he did. A list that it would seem looked longer than those who didn't know. Making Pip comment at the time cryptically,

"Hey, it's starting to feel like that Friends episode, you know the one where everyone knows about Monica and Chandler, but Ross and it all started with Joey, only Dom is Ross and Keira you're Joey... only without the whole 'how you doin' thing going on...what?" Everyone in the room had looked at her in the usual, questioning way. With the exception of Keira, as her giggle told us that she knew exactly what this had obviously been in reference to.

Needless to say, that Dom didn't exactly take kindly to this. Especially not when finding out that that not only his own son knew, but his brother as well. In fact, the only one who seemed not to know was Sophia, who at that point, received a harsh and questioning look from Dom making her snap,

"Don't look at me like that, I am as pissed off as you for being the only one other than you in this family who didn't know! And besides, I think we are all missing the biggest plot hole here!"

"And that is?" Dom snapped,

"How the Hades in Hell did Pip keep it a secret all this time!"

"Hey! I will have you know...oh, what am I saying, she's right, I have no clue either," Pip admitted with a shrug of her shoulders, looking to Adam and mouthing another, 'no clue, do you?'

But despite this personal set back against Dom, his main focus had remained on aiding me in trying to find his daughter. However, after exhausting every mortal resource we both had, along with trying to free up that of supernatural means also, it still gave us nothing. Because it had to be said that the capturing of the rogues had also taken a lot of our combined manpower and wasn't a problem either of us, as Kings, could simply ignore until Amelia had been found.

Which meant that in total I had been without my Chosen One for a total of eleven days and the knowledge of such was taking its toll in a way that it had me questioning how I had ever been able to function without her before. Before I had finally allowed myself to claim her.

But since then I knew what it was to have her in my life and not just as a spectator of her life from afar. I had slept with her in my arms. I knew the touch of her face, the smile in her eyes and the comforting weight of her body next to mine. I had thought it would have been the absence of her blood, of her essence or even the shallower reason of missing the sexual gratification claiming her brought me. But then the most surprising revelation was it was the little things that I found myself missing the most.

Her laugh, the way she bit her fingertips, the push of her glasses when deep in thought. It was her witty humour or our lively verbal battles. It was watching her cook and boasting at how masterful it was. The way she would become animated when explaining something she was obviously passionate about, like explaining storylines to things she wanted me to watch. And during these times, the way she unknowingly would nod or smile at the TV when she agreed or sweetly found something touching on the screen.

It was all of these things that finally made me understand the full depth of my love for her. For it wasn't the things that I would have believed most important in claiming a Chosen One. Like the way she ignited for me in the bedroom, or the addictive taste of her blood, a flavour granted by the Gods and labelled my own personal flavour. It was all the things I never would have believed could be important to me.

And Gods, I missed every single fucking one of them and I wanted them back!

I wanted her back.

And I was starting to believe that she wouldn't be going through the same longing as I was. Well, that was until on the twelfth day, I finally received word and this time it wasn't from one of my contacts.

No, it was from her.

Her drunken phone call.

CHAPTER FIFTEEN

THE CHASM OF HEARTS

The moment my phone started ringing I pulled it from my jacket pocket and not recognizing the number I answered it, expecting it to be one of my contacts on the road.

"What have you got for me?" I asked, which these days was the usual way I answered most calls. I had been on my way to Dom's office, where he seemed to spend most of his time. Although, I had been informed that he had some new evidence that she had been seen on some security footage at a shopping mall in Jacksonville where she had been spotted.

So naturally, I had been on my way there as he told me the footage was being sent to him. It was our joint hope that whatever it was she was seen purchasing might then lead us to the next clue to follow. Although, granted I didn't see what it was that she could have bought from a shopping mall that would give us much to go on. Unless it was a ticket to a destination, road map or better still a travel guide on that particular area. Naturally, I didn't hold out much hope for either of these things.

No, instead my hope came, unbeknown at the time, in the form of answering my phone on the way there and finally, after nearly two weeks without it, I heard her voice.

"Nothing but hello, I guess," she said softly, referring to the way I answered the phone. I swear in that moment I had to question whether I was fucking dreaming or not, for my steps faltered until I found myself struck frozen in the middle of the hallway.

"Amelia?" I said her name in question, doing so now in a hushed tone, as if testing my own sanity.

"Hey, yeah it's me," she said sounding strange and I was soon to find out why.

"I know, sweetheart, and I am..."

"I am so tired, Lucius," she said interrupting me, her words mirroring the sound of her voice. However, I couldn't help but take pleasure in the fact that she was back to calling me Lucius.

"Then stop running and come home to me," I told her softly, trying to keep my voice steady, even though to do so wasn't easy as my body was anything but relaxed. I wanted to say so many things in that moment, but I also didn't want to push her too soon, too quickly. Just the fact that she was reaching out to me was a huge step, not one I wanted to squander by making demands I knew she wouldn't like.

"Or you could just give up and let me go," she suggested making me close my eyes against the very idea of it.

"That is never going to happen," I told her, still keeping my tone as calm as I was physically capable.

"But I am so tired, I just need to sleep, and you won't let me," she said in such a small voice that my heart ached for her. She sounded so alone, so lost and even a little scared that it made me question what had happened.

"You can sleep, sweetheart, in fact you need to," I said in an urging tone.

"No, but that's the thing, I can't because you won't let me and I know you won't because every time I do, I feel you there or I wake up scared that you're trying, so I am just getting these useless power naps which is starting to make my brain useless and like mush."

"Amelia?" I said her name in question as it was clear something wasn't right.

"No, seriously, some old guy asked my name today and I told him it was cornflake, because that was what I was eating at the time," she said on a rush of words and I knew then the reason she had been brave enough to make this call.

"Amelia, have you been drinking?"

"Yes, I have recently developed a taste for cocktails, but there is this one that's called a long island iced tea and it's yummy but so very dangerous, as I spent a while looking for my room and I was at the wrong side of the, let's call it a place, 'cause I am being sneaky remember…Ssshh," she said in an endearing way that made my chest ache because all I wanted was to be there with her. To scoop her up in my arms and take care of her.

As what if being drunk could make her vulnerable? It could put her in a dangerous situation, like if she was unable to fight? Gods, I hated that I was forced to think this way, but without knowing where she was, then being paranoid had become an everyday occurrence. One only fueled now by the sound of her being inebriated.

But then I also knew I couldn't scold her for it, as she would most likely hang up and I would have lost my opportunity. No, I needed to keep her talking. Besides, it looked like she might be in a hotel because she mentioned looking for a room.

So in hopes of it sounding like an innocent enough question, I asked,

"Did you find it?"

"Find what?" she asked, ending it with a little hiccup that again, made me ache for her sweetness.

"Your room, sweetheart, did you find your room?"

"Oh that, yeah I am here now. Why, do you want my pillow chocolates?" she giggled making me swallow hard through the sound and tell her softly,

"You keep them for me." I then held back from adding, 'for when I get there' knowing that it would only remind her that she was being hunted. Something her drunken mind had chosen not to focus on if the lighthearted part of this phone call was anything to go by.

"Then why did you ask?"

"Because I want to imagine where it is you are, whilst I am speaking to you," I told her in a subtle way.

"Ha! So, I can give you a clue as to where to find me... nope, nope, I don't think so," she said in a playful tone and I could hear her shaking her head, which must have made her burp, as she giggled again at the sound. So much for her mind not being focused, I thought wryly.

"I think you're safe by telling me if you are sat on the bed or on a chair," I pointed out.

"Bed and it's comfy," she said, obviously giving it a little bounce as I could hear the slight squeak. I dragged a hand through my hair in frustration and, forcing my tone to continue to be calm, I asked,

"And do you still have a drink in hand, or did you leave your last cocktail at the bar?"

"Nope, I left it at my table, although I should probably drink some water, they say that's good, right?" she asked making me sigh,

"Yes, that is probably best, do you have any or do you need to call room service?" I asked, all the while trying to discover little bits of information. For I knew if it had a bar and room service then I could cross all motels and bed and breakfasts off my list.

"I have some in the fridge," she told me, and I heard the sound of her getting up and opening a door. Then I heard the sound of a bottle cap twisting telling me she was doing as suggested.

"Is there anything else in there, like food to soak up the alcohol, as that will help also?" I asked at the same mentally wondering how many hotels could be crossed off a list due to the contents offered in a minibar.

"Oh, Gods, I couldn't eat another bite! There is a lot of food here, like they are constantly feeding you!" she said laughing and taking another sip of her water, telling me that would most definitely help in narrowing my search as it was starting to sound as if she were at an all-inclusive resort of some kind, perhaps in Florida as Pip suggested.

"That's good," I commented trying not to let on where my thoughts were.

"It is? Why, because I think if I keep eating like this, then I will be the size of a house by the time I get there…I've been living on junk food, and I can't decide which was my favorite," she said rambling and not realising that she was giving me more and more information, so I decided to push a little.

"No, you won't, maybe a cute little hippo, but not a house." She giggled at that and Gods, how I had missed the sound.

"Unless, of course, you are planning on writing a book on the junk food of the States?" I said making her laugh, at the same time I was holding myself rigid, as if waiting any moment for a single place name.

"Umm, now why didn't I think about that?"

"I will let you have the idea, at a price of course." She made a huh, huh sound and after another little burp slipped out, she asked in a sceptical tone,

"And what would that price be exactly?" This told me that I needed to continue to be cautious here, so decided to change my answer,

"I will only ask for fifty percent of the cut and a place on the book tour." She laughed again,

"Great, I will see you in Milwaukee then." My heart started pounding and I asked in a feigned amused tone,

"Why, is that where you are?" However, the hope in my tone was easy to hear because she released a deep sigh and said,

"No, I am not in Milwaukee, Lucius." I closed my eyes against the disappointment and forced myself to say,

"That's a shame, I hear they have good beer there."

"Really?" she sounded genuinely interested so I kept the conversation going and told her what I knew of the place,

"It's known for its breweries, also your uncle would like it."

"Yeah, how come?"

"It has the Harley Davidson museum there." At this she laughed.

"Oooh, I wonder if they have a job going," she teased, making me reply,

"Well, it is said to have Elvis Presley's bike there, so how is your knowledge of the King of Rock and Roll?" I teased back.

"The King of Blood Rock, pretty good, the King of the famous hip roll…not so much." This time I was the one to laugh and tried once again,

"Then may I be so bold as to suggest that be your next destination… better yet, let me meet you there and I can be your guide."

"Nice try, as I think that would defeat what I am trying to achieve here." I gritted my teeth at her reply.

"Which is?" I braved to ask, knowing that I was pushing this.

"I may be drunk, Lucius, but I am not stupid…you won't find me, you know, she added in a sad tone and I swallowed hard, making a fist with my hand and pressing it against the top of a sideboard I was stood next to.

"Then why did you call me…why chance it?" I decided to come right out and ask.

"For two reasons, the first being I wanted to ask you a favour," she said making me raise a brow intrigued, telling her,

"If it's for me to stop looking for you, then I am sorry, but I can't do that, sweetheart."

"No, I don't suppose you will, but can you at least let me sleep?" I hated that she was right to blame me in this, despite telling her,

"I am not stopping you from sleeping, in fact, I encourage it."

"Yeah, so you can sneak into my mind and try and get me to show you…"

"Sleep, Amelia," I interrupted her in a tender tone.

"Yeah, so you can…" I swiftly cut her off again and added my reasons why she should sleep,

"I won't risk your health for the sake of finding you. If you are asking me to let you sleep, then I will honour your wishes and grant you a promise that after tonight I will leave your mind in peace." She released a deep and weary sigh before she muttered a small and sweet,

"Thank you." I nodded, despite her being too far from me to know, instead forcing out,

"You're welcome, Amelia."

"You know you don't need to do this, you don't owe them anything," she said making me frown, hating what reasons her mind had warped reality to be. Which was precisely why I told her,

"Despite what you think, I am not searching for you for any other gain but my own." I heard her swallowing down her emotions and I knew in that moment that she was crying, and my back hit the wall at the faint sound of her trying to hide it from me.

"I wish I could believe that, *you have no idea how much I do,*" she told me, and the wood crumbled in between my fingers.

"You are the only one who has the power to change that, my girl." At this she cleared her throat and I could almost see her shaking her head, so before she had the chance to back track, I asked her,

"Tell me the second reason."

"Second reason?" she asked as she'd obviously forgotten her own words.

"The reasons you called, you said there were two, so I am asking what was the other?"

"Oh that," she said in a small voice that only made me want to hold her.

"It doesn't really matter now, does it," she told me, making me silently utter her name before I could speak again.

"It matters to me…*it always will,*" I told her making her sigh,

"And if I tell you, you swear to keep your promise, you won't try and get in my head again…right?" I hated doing it, knowing what it could end up costing me, but I said it anyway,

"I am usually known to be a man of my word, yes," I said unable to keep the strain from my voice.

"Then I will tell you." She took a deep breath, muttered a whispered, 'what am I doing?' before she did it anyway and told me,

"I was watching a couple dancing tonight. They couldn't stop smiling at each other. It was like the whole world didn't exist, as if not a single person was there watching them… like they were the only two people in the room. It was so beautiful, like they had spent their entire lives dancing to that same song…*you know?"* At this I took a deep breath and closed my eyes, seeing it for myself and feeling the same pain that she had felt watching it.

For then she confessed,

"I called because…*I miss dancing with you."* The moment the words finally were allowed to flow over me, I lost my stance allowing my body to slide down the wall until I was sat on the floor leaning against it. An elbow to my bent knee was when I rested a heavy mind in my hand, holding it there as if it was suddenly too much to ask my body to support it.

Gods, how much I wanted her back!

"Then choose not to miss it and come back to me, for I can only promise you a dance when you're back in my arms," I told her, making her suck back a sob.

"I…*I can't."* This was when I couldn't help but lose the fake persona of patience with her,

"So that's it then, you truly believe that we will never see each other again!?"

"The world's a big place, Lucius, but who knows, maybe one day I will be ready to come home and maybe then I will be able to look at you again without it being too damn painful. Without this feeling, without this fucking agony that is tearing me in two…without remembering…"

"Without remembering what…*tell me?"* I asked forcing my hand to ease the pressure on the damn device that I wanted to crush in my anger, in my frustration and in the drowning reality that my own fucking heart was breaking!

But then she whispered her answer before hanging up the

phone and I swear that crack in my heart became a fucking chasm,

"Without remembering…"

"…the days you loved me."

CHAPTER SIXTEEN

AFTER THE NIGHT'S PROMISE

After she hung up the phone my head dropped, and I must have looked like a man broken. In fact, the only reason my phone survived was in the hope that she would call me back. I was also damning not having my people monitoring my phone for calls to be traced, thinking the very last thing she would have done was call me.

But she had.

She missed me.

The knowledge was like a bitter scented balm that soothed the doubts of her actions in leaving me. I was furious that she had left, of course I was. And knowing that she was somewhere in the world hurting did little to relieve the ache. What did relieve it, however, was knowing that her heart was still mine and it gave me hope that not all was lost between us. That the fight I thought I would have on my hands once I did finally find her, no longer looked like an impossible win.

But the true pain came from not knowing when that battle would be. I had tried to get what information I could from her.

But I swear the moment I heard her voice again it became harder to focus on the mission. Of course, knowing she was drunk had been an advantage I wanted to exploit, which was why my promise made was only one for after tonight. Because I knew if she had been drinking then the barricades on her mind wouldn't be there and the best part about it was, *she wouldn't even realise that I was there.*

But first I needed to pick myself off the floor and in this moment, I will be honest, that in itself seemed like an immeasurable task.

"Now, that looks like a place I have been before," Dom said making me barely even acknowledge him by anything more than a shrug of my shoulders. But then, as the silence between us grew, I found myself asking,

"And did you also curse the Gods, as I do now?"

"Every damn day me and Keira were apart," he replied honestly. Then I saw a movement in front of me, making me look up to find his hand was held out for me to take. So, I took the moment between us for what it was…

A show of kinship.

I rose to my feet with his help and shook his hand in silent thanks before letting go.

"I take it she called?" he asked nodding to the phone in my hand with the now cracked screen.

"What gave it away?" I asked dryly.

"Other than often looking down at a broken phone being a place I have also lived through, then it is the look of someone who's just had their chest ripped open and their heart handed to them." I scoffed at that and said,

"And I take it this is also something…"

"I have experienced…let's just say that my daughter shares many traits with those of her mother. Give it time, Luc, she will see sense."

"Yes, well just as long as that sense doesn't include a French prick with daddy issues." At this he growled at the memory before grumbling,

"Don't fucking remind me of that poisonous heartbeat with a death wish."

"Yeah, well lucky for you, you're not reminded of the shit stain every time you clench your fist and hear leather groan." At this Dom laughed as we started walking towards his office,

"All in the name of saving the world, Luc."

"That's easy for you to say, you didn't get ten years of Michael Jackson jokes from Pip." At this he actually threw his head back and laughed, so loud in fact that as we walked into the office Keira was startled by the sound.

"Alright, you two walking into a room both laughing tells me that I have reason enough to be concerned," she stated with a frown. Then Dom walked up to her, tipped her head back before telling her,

"Nothing to concern yourself with, but how do you think Amelia would feel about changing her name to Billy Jean?" At this I growled,

"Not fucking funny." To which he ignored me and told her,

"Amelia rang Luc." Her eyes grew wide before looking to me with hope blooming quickly.

"She did?!" I nodded and before I had the chance to explain the extent of it, Pip and Adam chose that moment to walk in, with her asking,

"Someone was talking about me, I know because my third and favorite toe was itchingalingalo." Keira laughed and muttered,

"Oh Gods, not this again."

"Well, am I wrongalingalo?" she asked with her hands on her hips above what looked like a fucking red and white polka dot tutu.

"Wrongalingalo?" Keira dared to ask.

"She is trying out this new thing where the last word in every sentence ends in an alingalo sound and if you could find any way to get her to stop this, then I would be in your debt," Adam replied making her smack him and complain,

"You said it was cutealingalo?"

"That was before I realised the level of your commitment to doing so, my little peach," he replied flicking her nose playfully.

"Ha, well that's what you get for being a Mr Doubty Pantalingalo!" He groaned and muttered,

"No that is what I get for having an insanely cute wife...any news?" Adam asked after making this comment, no doubt hoping to end the discussion with a certain colourful aspect in his life.

"I just received a call from her," I informed him, unsurprisingly, making Pip the first to comment.

"Holy shitalingalo," she uttered gripping onto Adam's arm as I knew that Amelia leaving the way she did, hadn't only affected me or her parents, but it had shaken everyone who cared deeply for her. It was also the reason why most of Dom's council were still out there looking for her, using what resources they had to do so.

But no resource would be enough and not like the one I would be using against her one last time. However, before that, I explained what had been said, making Keira get teary once more before she started blaming herself... and cryptically, damning the Fates. But before I could ask why, Pip suddenly shouted,

"Oh my good Gods given me a giddy Auntyalingalo!" I frowned down at her and before I had chance to bark at her to talk fucking properly, Adam intervened.

"Perhaps it is a good time to take a break from your

personal quest and just speak your mind…doing so quickly," he added when nodding back to me to see for herself how close to the edge I was. Of course, reliving through the painful call hadn't helped matters. Which was when she shouted,

"I knew it, she is on a fucking cruise!" Everyone groaned in exasperation.

"But we already told you, she gets seasick, Fae hates boats," Keira argued whilst Adam, mouthed a 'Sorry' at me, excusing his wife, which she saw and hit him on the arm for.

"I am being serious!" she argued making me fold my arms, barely having enough restraint left to force out a clipped,

"Explain."

"Think about it, what did she say, she mentioned loads of food, check, she mentioned a couple dancing, uh yeah, check, and she mentioned old people, check, check and triple check, because there are loads of them… *the oldies just love their cruises,*" she said this behind her hand aimed at Dom who, as usual, didn't look as though he had a clue how to deal with her.

"I hardly think just because she mentioned food, old people and dancing that it is enough to assume…" Dom started to say, until his wife interrupted him.

"Actually, I think she is right," Keira said after looking deep in thought.

"Told you, it's the oldies, it's common knowledge," Pip commented with a wink at me.

"Plus, why now, eh?" Pip asked,

"Why now, what?" I asked in irritation.

"Yeah, I mean there must have been a reason she felt safe enough to call you," Keira pointed out, obviously agreeing with her friend.

"And safe enough to get blotto drunkalingalo…what, still no?" Pip said adding this last part when Adam cleared his throat and shook his head down at her, telling her silently to still keep her crazy at bay.

"I have to go," I said quickly, making the four of them stop to look at me as I walked towards the door.

"Where?"

"Where do you think...*to find out if you're right?*"

AS EXPECTED, the moment I linked my mind with hers I felt little resistance unlike all the other times before. It reminded me of the past when I was free to plant dreams in her mind. Something at the time that had been easily achieved. Which was why, when I stepped into her Void, I wasn't surprised to find I did so in the middle of a heavy dream she was having. This had been precisely what I had been hoping for, as when she woke, she would do so believing it was a dream she had created and nothing more.

As this time, I was here merely to observe, not make demands of her mind. I wasn't forcing her to look around or access any memories. I was simply a spectator hoping that her dreams would feature where she was and what she had seen recently. Simply put, she would just think that she had dreamt of me by her own doing.

Because even though I wasn't breaking my promise, I knew she wouldn't have seen it that way. Besides, she had sounded tired and I didn't want to do any more damage than I already had done. I wanted her to sleep and do so peacefully, something I knew she hadn't been able to do since she started running.

That being said, I still had to know. I had to know if there was any truth to Pip's theory. Because as much as I wanted to deny it even being possible, the fact remained that the idea of her taking a ship hadn't even occurred to me, nor had it to anyone else. Which was why I foolishly hadn't thought to have her passport flagged at any ports. Meaning that she had conquered her dislike of sailing just to get away.

Naturally, the thought didn't sit well with me but then again, just because I hoped for something not to be true, it wouldn't make it so. Which was why I felt as though I had no choice but to invade her mind once more and for what I knew would be the last time…for I would not reward her for trusting to call me by breaking my promise to her.

However, the moment that I stepped through the dark edges of her mind was when the room around me transformed into that of a small dance floor. It was one surrounded by empty tables and chairs…well, almost empty. As now it held only one occupant sat at a table facing the empty floor head on…

Amelia.

It was as if she was waiting for something and the moment the music started to play, I knew what. Seconds after this, an image emerged in the centre of the dance floor, a lone couple dancing who looked to be in their seventies. And Amelia had been right, the sight was a startlingly symbolic one.

I walked slowly towards her as she immersed herself in the sight of the couple, telling me that she was replaying parts of the evening. She even had the tall cocktail glass in front of her half consumed and the five empty glasses also there keeping count.

"I told you it was a beautiful sight," she told me without taking her eyes off the two.

"That you did, my Khuba, that you did," I told her, barely even acknowledging the sight, for I was too mesmerized by the sight of her. She was wearing a black lace, cocktail dress with her hair swept elegantly off to one side. But it was her haunted eyes that concerned me, the way they watched the couple with lost hope in their depths.

Then she said softly,

"The dance ended." I looked towards the couple and saw them suddenly begin to float away. It was as if their image was caught on the wind and the painting of life had started to fade into the darkness after being dragged away by the elements against them.

"Then dance with me," I said holding out a hand for her to take, knowing that now it was safe for me to touch her, for it was a dream she controlled. She finally looked up at me and I found myself taken aback by the slight spark of hope I saw there. Then she looked down at my offered hand and took her time in deciding, telling me,

"Can you forgive me for dreaming of you." I frowned first at her question, wondering in fact if this question wasn't aimed at herself.

"There is nothing to forgive, for I always want you dreaming of me," I told her, and it was something in my response that made her place her hand in my own and tell me,

"Then I will forgive myself instead."

I didn't like the sound of that but instead of telling her so, I walked her to the centre of the dance floor. After which, the same song the older couple had been dancing to started to sing out around the room. It was our turn.

"Why do you feel like you need to forgive yourself?" I finally asked after a few silent minutes of leading her around the room, to which she answered,

"Because I will suffer for the memory of it tomorrow." I tensed at this, something she could feel as it seemed to resonate down from my frame and into hers.

"Then why think of me at all?" I snapped making her swallow hard and tell me,

"Maybe I am just addicted to the pain of you." I tore my face from hers at the agony this brought me and swung her around and then back to me, catching her and holding her against my chest. We seemed lost in the moment and just as I wished to kiss her, she closed her eyes and said,

"Maybe I always have been." This stopped me in my tracks, and I straightened, before telling her,

"You're not addicted to pain, Amelia, you're just running scared from being forced to face the possibility of it finding you." At this her eyes widened before narrowing as my words obviously started to hit home. Then I swung her around, letting her spin out to the side and as she was held there at the stretched length of our hands holding each other, she looked back at me and said,

"You mean of *you* finding me." At this I yanked her hard once more, making her spin back into my chest before gripping a hand at her hip. Then I looked down at her and issued her a promise,

"Oh, make no mistake, my beauty, I will find you and when I do, I won't bring you pain, I will only bring you truth, one that will make you sorry that you ever ran from me." At this she yanked herself from my hold and told me,

"I don't think I like this dream anymore." I frowned back at her, crossed my arms, and told her,

"Then run from it, after all, it's clearly what you do best." At this she looked as if I had slapped her and I nearly cursed my anger. Especially when I was here for the sole purpose of discovering where she was. Instead I was pushing her to do as I expected she would, which was start running from me again. So, the second she turned around and ran towards the door, I growled in frustration, cursing before going after her.

"Fuck! Amelia, wait!" I shouted before running through the vision of the room she had been in and the second I got through the door, it all started to change. Soon I found myself running down a narrow corridor filled with doors, one that continued to branch off, causing me to get lost in the maze. Yet I could hear her softly crying and I tried to follow the sound, making me wonder if this was the part of the night where she explained that she couldn't find her room.

Then finally, when I turned a corner, I saw her at the end. She was staggering down the narrow aisle with her shoes dangling from her fingers. She was also swaying slightly, before she steadied herself on someone else's door, apologizing to no one before she continued on. I muttered a curse again and made off running down the length of the corridor after her, hoping to catch her just before she got to her room so I could see for myself.

However, the second I saw her disappearing around yet another corner I snarled in anger, hitting out against one of the doors as I passed. I rounded the same corner, only I was too late as I wasn't met with a door like I had hoped to be. No, instead I was suddenly inside her room. And that was when I saw her.

The image of her as I knew she was now. Curled up on the bed, still wearing her dress, one that had bunched around the tops of her sun kissed thighs. Her shoes remained at the side of the bed where she had obviously dropped them and next to her, was a half-consumed bottle of water. But it wasn't the water that took my interest, no it was the room's phone that she was clutching to her chest, the receiver off the hook and in her hand, as if it brought her some comfort.

The sight caused me to stop dead in my tracks and all earlier anger fled me. She looked so lost. So lonely and vulnerable, that all I wanted to do was scoop her up in my arms and hold her through the night. To whisper in her ear that I would take care of her and to beg her to stop running from me. But two things stopped this and the first was when she whispered my name in her sleep,

"Lucius, you promised." After this I was about to ease her

mind and tell her to go back to sleep, when something else caught my eyes. So, I glanced from her sleeping form and found,

Another window.

It was small for a hotel room and as it started to come more into focus, rising from the shadows, the size wasn't the only thing I noticed. It was the view beyond that had me transfixed. The seemingly endless abyss, that this time wasn't just part of her Void.

Nor was it a sight that had been conjured up from the random access of memories.

No, this time her dream had quickly become my nightmare, as the reality of where she was had finally come to light.

Because Pip had been right…

My heart was at sea.

CHAPTER SEVENTEEN

AMELIA

LONELY LIFE AT SEA

I woke the next day and wasn't surprised when I discovered I'd slept most of the day away. Not that I had anywhere I needed to be or really anything to do on this floating hotel. I mean, I had spent the first few days trying to get over being seasick, something that finally calmed once I got used to the movement. I knew most of it was mind over matter as I didn't like boats, something I discovered after taking the one and only trip on my father's yacht, that he had naturally named The Catherine. This was actually my mum's first name, but she always went by Keira, her middle name.

Well, needless to say that after spending the week throwing up, I think it was safe to say that I wasn't a natural seafaring girl by any means. In the end, my dad had arranged travel for me to get back home after realising that my green skin wasn't going to change anytime soon. It was also one of the reasons I had chosen to get to Europe this way. I knew it would be the last journey anyone who knew me would think I would take. Besides, everyone always goes straight for the airports and no one ever thinks about cruise liners.

Granted, this particular way of escaping was a little out there, especially as it would take me twenty-one days, eight of which were spent at sea. But I also had to say that the second I stepped on board and we finally left the port in Miami, I could finally breathe. I made myself relax, taking a breath and all with the knowledge that I had made it.

This was all made possible the day after I had left the hotel in my new Dodge, after Lucius had found me. I had driven just under two hours and sold my car to the first dodgy dealer I had come across. I accepted his deal, just because I needed whatever cash I could get my hands on without any questions asked. Of course, it also helped having the car in my new name to convince the guy that I hadn't stolen it. Not like the first I had, stopping myself from saying so just in time.

After this it was days of bus hopping, knowing that Lucius wasn't far behind and if I could just get to Miami, then I had a shot at getting out of the States. The flaw in all of this had been my new fear of sleep, which resulted in power naps, asking people sat near me if they could set an alarm on their phones to wake me up. I also made sure never to sleep at night, knowing this was when Lucius would be waiting for me, expecting it.

Hence my drunken phone call and one that even the memory of it made me rub my temple and groan out loud. Gods, but I had even slept with the phone next to me and why? It wasn't as though I could have expected his call back. He couldn't trace me here, I made sure of that.

I had just been glad for the opportunity to finally sleep, something only possible as Lucius had given me his word that he wouldn't try again. And well, as sneaky as the bastard could be, he wasn't the type to break a vow...

No, just hearts, I thought with a grimace.

But the phone call last night had lasted longer than I told myself I would allow. Something that just couldn't be helped as the temptation of his voice was just too much to fight against. Gods, how I hated myself for missing him the way I did. Which unfortunately became the worst part about my decision to take a cruise, it was the time it gave me to think.

When I had been on the road all my mind had focused on was the next part of the plan. The next safe place to stop, picking the small towns that would be less likely to have security cameras or other ways that might be enough to track me.

The hardest one had been in Jacksonville when I had no choice but to buy supplies, as I knew it would look a little odd getting on a cruise for a holiday with nothing but the dirty clothes on my back and half empty hand luggage.

So, after the first thing I bought being a baseball cap and new jacket, I kept my head down and bought what I needed, which had basically been everything. Then I dumped the flight attendant's clothes and bag, now having new luggage of my own. The cocktail dress I had bought onboard after realising that if I wanted to leave my room at night and do so without sticking out like a sore thumb, then I needed to buy a dress.

Because as great as camping out in my room feeling sorry for myself for twenty-one days sounded, I had lasted about two days before that shit got old. So, instead I had fallen into a rhythm of life on board, which started with a morning art class. This was something I sucked at despite the sweet encouragement I would get from the retired ladies I had in my group.

Then after some failed art, I would go for a swim and dry on the sunbeds with a book from the library. After this the rest of my day pretty much centered around food, getting ready for the evening and planning what live show there was to watch or what new movies were scheduled. To be honest, as holidays went, then yeah, I could totally see the appeal. But for someone trying to get over heartbreak, then spending all this time by myself wasn't ideal. Every fucking thing reminded me of him. The evenings were the worst, for every time I saw a blonde male in a suit from behind, I thought of Lucius.

I had even been hit on whilst at the bar, and the conversations always started the same way. What did I do for a living and what was I doing on the cruise alone? And let's just say that telling them I was on the run from my Vampire ex-boyfriend who I caught kissing my mum, wasn't exactly the most convincing of stories. Hence, why I had come up with my cover story long before getting on board. Telling people that I wrote articles for a travel magazine and next month's issue was a feature all about life on board. I even had a catchy title for it, just to add weight to my backstory, it was going to be called,

'Lonely or Lively Life at Sea.'

Of course, I think some of the ladies at my craft table got the wrong impression to this as I ended up with a different grandson's phone number or email address every day, and I was gaining quite a collection. Enough at least to have my own black book half filled, should I feel the need to become a sexed-up floozy during this next stage of my life.

But through all the smiles and jokes told, I always ended the day stood in front of the mirror, removing my make-up and asking myself what the fuck it was that I was doing? I wanted to call home every damn day! I wanted to talk to my mum and hope that if I absorbed the lies enough, then I had the power to turn them into truth.

I wanted to speak to my dad and ask him how he was after what I had forced him to discover, feeling guilty of the fact every day since it happened. I also wanted to call Wendy, or even Ben, who admittedly I hadn't spoken to since the day I left London...since I discovered he had been planted in the building and ordered to become my friend.

I wanted to connect with those I loved and cared about, but I knew that with everyone, there was a chance of a slip up. A chance that something could be discovered from the conversations we would have. I already knew that they had most likely got to Wendy, as I suspected they would. No doubt Dante would have been in charge of that one. Gods, I even felt guilty for that, wondering what I might have put her through.

But no matter how tempted I was and how alone I felt, I just couldn't chance it. So, I would just have to wait. Because really, just how long was Lucius willing to hunt me down for my parents' sake? Because he felt responsible?

I mean, it was clear that Lucius obviously cared for me on some level as I would be an idiot to believe anything else. But I also knew that he wasn't above trying to lure me back by any means necessary. And it had become obvious that lying was already a skill of his that I had been a victim of far too many times before.

But what hurt the most was that I missed it. I missed the lie so fucking much that behind this closed door and in this small cabin, I couldn't hide it. Not even from myself. Because the tears in my eyes that stared back at me every night wouldn't go away. They just wouldn't leave me. The pain wouldn't go away.

Not even for a second.

No, all that would happen was that numbness you relied on to make it through the day and function. The cloak you wrapped around yourself whilst you smiled at others and made polite conversation. The cloak that made your heartbreak invisible to everyone around you. But it was a cloak that you had no choice but to remove at the end of the day, hanging it up by the door at the ready to use the moment you had to leave and face the world again.

Then there had been the couple dancing and something in me crumbled. I had watched that couple dance and the sight of their love for each other had set my cloak of fake smiles alight. Burning it to ashes at my feet as if I had just stabbed a rogue. I had tears streaming down my eyes and found myself stumbling back to my room after the wrong man had asked me to dance. After the wrong man's hand was offered and I looked up to see it attached to the wrong man. That's when my illusion to the world on board had shattered and six strong cocktails and the offer of a dance had been all it had taken for me to break.

To call him.

Oh sure, I had convinced myself it had all been solely for the promise of sleep, but it was a lie. I just needed to hear his voice. That beautiful voice that I just wanted to hear whispering sweet words of seduction in my ear as I slept in his arms. I wanted his teasing, his comfort, and his strength. I wanted his dark promises of pleasure and the stern command of his dominant sexual tendencies. But I also wanted his laughter to be the answer to my jokes and the sound of his amused responses to the silly things I said. Gods, but even his growls of anger and frustration were on the list of sounds I missed.

But most of all I missed the way he loved me…even if it was for a short time and wasn't real, I still missed it.

I missed it all.

And by the end of it all, twenty-six days since first running, I ended my journey on the last night at the very back of the ship, looking out to sea with a glass in hand. With what I hoped was the last of my tears streaming down my face, knowing that I had done it…

I had really run from the only man that I'd ever loved. All because he could never fully love me back. Maybe the Fates had got it all wrong or maybe it was just me that had? Maybe there was no such thing for me as a Chosen One or maybe it was just all bullshit and the fucking Fates didn't mean anything.

Which was why I had lifted my glass, toasted the moon, and said,

"Fuck the Fates and fuck love…*I'm done."*

Then I downed the rest of my champagne, calmly placed my glass on the deck and walked away with what felt like the whole world at my back.

That was the first night I went to bed and didn't cry into the mirror before it. My tears had finally stopped. Because now, the moment I walked off this ship I had a plan.

And like all the ones before it, this time I knew nothing was going to get in my way.

The real journey had just begun.

CHAPTER EIGHTEEN

LUCIUS

MAP OF THEIVES

"Amelia!" I bolted upright with her name being once more cursed from my lips as I called out for her in my sleep. Then I reacted as I did every time I woke after yet another fucking dream of her, I bent my knees, hung my head, and dragged both hands through my hair in frustration as I hissed a curse in at least ten different languages. Then I looked up at the room that no longer felt like my own, but more like a fucking shrine to the girl. All her stuff remained around me, untouched and waiting for what felt like the ghost of her to come back and walk into the stack of empty shoe boxes in my closet.

I was back at Blood Rock, for there had been no reason for me to stay at Afterlife any longer. Not when I finally discovered what cruise liner she had boarded, and that the ship's destination had been Europe. Genoa to be exact and unfortunately it came to light why she had chosen such travel.

Because even after I had discovered that Pip had been right, it had taken far too long to find the fucking ship she had taken. This was thanks to PortMiami holding the title, 'cruise capital of the world' for a reason, seeing as it was classed as the busiest cruise/passenger port in the world. And with over 5.5 million cruise passengers passing through the port a year, even in the space of a week, well it was a fuck load of people and cruise companies to check through. And by the time she was finally found, it had been too late... *by one fucking day!*

One fucking day and I had lost her again, knowing nothing more than she had arrived in the MSC Cruise Terminal at Genoa after stepping off the ship named the MSC Seaside.

So naturally, I had flown to Italy and the search began all over again and just like all the other times, it had gone cold almost as quickly as it had begun. Which meant that after a week of nothing, I returned to Germany, hoping that her passport would be flagged should she try and leave the Schengen area. Airports and all ports had also been flagged, so it was believed that she had either disappeared in Italy somewhere or she had bought herself a car and was determined to settle somewhere in Europe.

My first thought had been that she was trying to get back to the UK. But after discovering that her options when purchasing her cruise ticket included one to travel to the UK, it told me that she had picked Italy for a reason...I just didn't know what.

Because if there was something that I knew about Amelia, it was that she had a plan for everything she did. Every step of this had been well thought out. Which meant that Amelia had a destination in mind and therefore I knew that the key to finding her was first discovering *the why*.

But it had been seven weeks since she first left, and I was

still trying to find out that damn 'why'! Which also accounted for why I was permanently pissed off and if I had a reputation for being an asshole before, then now, I had turned into a fucking tyrant! Which, given the circumstances, was of little surprise. Especially considering I had started every day for the past seven years with a report on my desk explaining the most minute aspects of her life and now... well, now I didn't even have that.

I had fucking nothing!

Which meant that the moment I had finished getting ready for whatever fucking day this was going to turn out to be, I stopped dead the moment I found Dom stood waiting for me in my living space. I didn't bother with the steps but instead released my wings and was down there facing him, sparing myself the extra seconds it would have taken my legs to do so. But then he raised a hand and said,

"I am not here to give false hope, Luc." I released a grumbled sigh and snarled,

"Then what the fuck do you want, Dom?"

"I take it there is still no news?" he asked, and I was tempted for my demon to be the one to answer this time. Instead I raised my arms to the sides, looked down at myself and snapped sarcastically,

"Take a fucking look, Dom, and tell me, do I look like I have any fucking news, or do I look like a violent King on the edge of insanity?!" This response made him release a sigh and admit,

"Point made."

Then he turned slowly, taking in the living space, and seeing for himself that his daughter was all around us. This was by the way of all of her possessions that were exactly where she'd left them and were naturally forbidden to be touched. In fact, other than Dom, then no fucker dared come down here. It was an insanely possessive reaction to have but I didn't care. I didn't want to share my piece of her with anyone else.

Which was only one of the reasons that I didn't like that her father was here now and walking around the space as if he were taking a mental note of everything.

"Fuck me, but you really do love her, don't you?"

"What gave it away, the fact that I am going out of my mind with fucking worry or her Star Wars collection on my shelf?" I asked with a sarcastic growl of words, a tone he ignored as he walked over to the glass case with her Lego model of our home inside it. My whole body tensed, and my fingers curled into fists. I had to force myself not to tell him to get the fuck away from it.

"A love I can see most definitely goes both ways." he said nodding down to my prized possession.

Her second gift.

Her first had been that of her heart when she first told me that she loved me.

"Yes, well last time I checked, Dom, that love you speak of stole a car and fucking left me, so I wouldn't go making wedding plans just yet," I reminded him with a barely held back snarl of words.

"She spoke to Keira," he told me, now gaining my interest back, but the fucker held up a hand and said,

"I stand by my earlier comment and am not here to grant false hope as she gave nothing away." I growled in frustration slashing a hand through the air and cursing,

"Fuck, will this woman ever give me a fucking break!" Dom chuckled and said,

"Not fucking likely but gain comfort in the knowledge at least that she is safe and well." I scoffed a grunt of acknowledgment despite feeling that same comfort. My girl was safe. That was something at least.

"What did she say?"

"Keira tried to explain once more but was mostly shot down by her saying quickly that she didn't want to hear it but was just ringing to inform us that she was fine and living life. That she was happy and that she didn't want us to worry any more than we have been," he said with the hint of purple coming through his gaze telling me this had been difficult for him to hear, prompting me to ask,

"And?"

"And I grabbed the fucking phone and demanded that she stop being damn foolish and come home!" I laughed once and commented wryly,

"I bet that went down well."

"Well, she hung up the phone shortly after that, which didn't exactly make me very popular."

"Ah, so that's what you're doing here, hiding out from your wife, eh Dom?" I commented with a smirk and the first one I had felt there in weeks.

"Fuck off, you cocky bastard," he growled making me laugh this time. Then I couldn't help but be the pathetic asshole I didn't give a shit about appearing when I asked,

"At least put me out of my fucking misery and tell me, did she at least mention my fucking name?" At this he granted me a look that said it all, even if his words followed suit,

"No, Luc, she didn't mention you." I felt his words fuel my pain and anger, wishing in that moment I had the freedom to just start smashing up the room. But then, one look at my girl's personality that coated every surface and well, I quickly swallowed down that urge.

"But I think that the fact she even called at all is a good sign, that she is settled and feeling more comfortable to reach out. After all, we have a better chance of finding her once she'd stopped running." He said everything that I had already heard before and it brought little comfort after seven fucking weeks!

Which is why I snapped,

"Good, now we can move on to the part where you tell me what the fuck it is you are really doing here? As I know you didn't just drop by, not when you could have called to tell me this seemingly shit and utterly useless piece of information," I said letting my anger be known and having fucking zero patience for having my hopes heightened with the sight of him, before they were annihilated by the knowledge, she hadn't even mentioned my fucking name!

Dom released a sigh and looked like the reply he wanted to give he refrained in doing so, obviously knowing that I was a King on the edge and thought to give me a reprieve.

"I wanted your permission to have the map copied once more." I frowned back at him and commented,

"I am surprised that you would even need to as I believe I made enough copies for all of the Kings, something that was agreed between us would be the only copies made...although, that seems pointless now seeing as the Witch made off with the fucking original," I added but still, I wondered at his request.

"I gave my personal copy to Vincent before he left to conduct his own investigation, as there wasn't a spare for him the day we had the meeting of the Kings, as I was under the impression one was made for Amelia, which she left, did she not?" I frowned as I started to work through that meeting. Had Vincent not taken one that day?

"Yes, I had one made for her, which she left and is now in my possession," I told him but still a nagging feeling started to rise.

"And you're sure that Vincent didn't take one?" I asked again.

"He simply believed that due to his absence at the beginning of the meeting that his copy was held back, but I take it from the looks of things that this wasn't the case." I didn't answer him, but instead I started to work through my memories and then yes, I saw it. I saw the way he had taken the map from Theo at one point to look at it, before he then gave it back to him.

But Amelia had taken one. I remember seeing her eagerly grabbing one and being forced to hide my smirk at the sight. And this was the one I had assumed she had left in her room. I'd thought by doing this she was making a point to show that she no longer cared to pursue the answers. I had picked it up and kept it with me. Which now had me questioning, what if she had fooled me yet again?

"Luc, what are you thinking?" I looked back up at Dom to find his arms folded, a questioning look on his face, as he tried to follow my racing thoughts.

"I am thinking that our little lost princess might not be quite as lost as she has allowed us all to think," I told him before holding out my hand and requesting,

"Give me your phone." My demand made him pull it from his suit jacket, unlock the security feature with his thumbprint and hand it to me. I scoffed at the picture of Keira and himself on the front making me roll my eyes without comment, making him mutter,

"Just you wait, asshole."

I ignored him, mainly because he was right. Amelia and I didn't have a single photograph together and the ones I had of her were all from afar and taken without her knowledge. Making me envious that he had that and what I wouldn't have given to have been granted a picture of her smile to obsess over.

"Adam, no it's me Luc, listen I need to know, exactly how many copies of the map did you find on my desk before we left for Afterlife?" I asked knowing that if anyone would remember it would be Adam, he was meticulous about the details.

"Six, why?" I looked up at Dom as I answered Adam's question,

"Because I had seven copies made." Dom raised a brow understanding where my thoughts were headed.

"So, you're sure?" I had to ask.

"I think you get that I don't make mistakes, Luc," Adam responded making me reply with a grin,

"Oh, I know you don't."

"You think someone stole one when they were still in your office?" he asked slamming me back to a memory. It had been shortly after our argument, Amelia and me. It was also one she had sheepishly come to my office to apologize for, after once again taking my meaning and twisting it into something dark and untrue. A common trait with my girl, so it would seem.

But then after that, Amelia had made a note of seeing them on the desk. She asked me about them, making some funny comment about planning a lame treasure hunt or something to that effect. Then, after spending time going over the map together, there had been a phone call from Dom demanding once more to speak with his daughter.

Shortly after which, we had left my office only when doing so, we had barely rounded a corner when she told me she'd forgotten her sweater, running back for it.

The seven copies of the map had still been on my desk waiting for Adam to retrieve.

"Oh, we had a thief alright, and I think I have a pretty good idea who," I told Adam who laughed once and said,

"And let me guess, a troublesome little princess now going by the name Lia Earhart." I didn't answer him, as I didn't need to. No, instead he added,

"Keep us posted." Then I ended the call.

"I must say, Dom, but that daughter of yours is becoming quite the thief these days."

"You think she stole a copy of the map from you?" My look echoed the words that followed,

"No, *I know she did*, which means that she left a copy in her room on purpose to throw us off the fact that she was still pursuing it," I said leaving now to go to my office to retrieve that same copy. Dom followed and quickly made the point,

"But even if she did, we all agreed the maps are useless, so how would she know where to go?" I stopped in my tracks, giving thought to his comment before I then turned back to face him.

"What if she found a way?" I asked.

"Luc, I am fully aware of my daughter's intelligence, and speak very highly of it in fact, despite where it has gotten her right now…that being said, we have had all our people working on cracking that fucking map, all of the Kings have also had their own people on it and nothing!" I dragged a hand at the back of my neck thinking about all he'd said and knowing it to be true.

But then, this was Amelia we were talking about, which meant I knew anything was possible.

"I think you're forgetting that she was the one who cracked the box and discovered how to open it."

"Yes, but are you really telling me that my daughter has somehow now deciphered what seems to be the biggest fucking puzzle on Earth right now and maybe as we speak is at its destination?" I gave a him a knowing grin just thinking about my girl and said firmly,

"Yes, Dom, that is what I am fucking telling you."

"But that is…" I quickly ended up cutting him off,

"Fuck! Gods be damned!" I suddenly shouted stopping once

more and raking a hand through my hair near yanking it from my scalp for being so clueless!

"What! What is it?"

"I have been so fucking blind, that's what!" I snapped.

"Luc, I have little patience for this."

"That day in the library, she had the box with her…" I reminded him.

"Yes, we know, the witch lured her to my vault, we discovered that, what is your point?"

"Yes, we did, but after she discovered what she thought had happened between Keira and me she gave me the box back, made a point of it actually by forcing it into my chest," I told him but he still didn't see the connection I was trying to make to the big bastard.

"And?"

"And ask yourself, why would she do that? Why, if she already knew that she would take her secret copy of the map and go on the run to try and discover its secrets…especially knowing that she may need the box to do so. Why not take it with her?" I pointed out making him now see where my train of thoughts were headed.

"Because she didn't need it," he said in a tone that spoke more to himself.

"Exactly, because she didn't need it," I repeated.

"What if something happened in that vault that showed her the way to discovering the map's secrets. What if it had something to do with the box and she discovered how to use it to discover the destination before giving it back to me, counting on the fact that its secret wouldn't be discovered by our people," I continued, not only laying all the pieces of it out for him, but for my mind also.

"So, what you're saying is…"

"That if we decipher the map, then we find out where our girl is hiding," I finished making him agree.

Then he placed a hand on my shoulder and said,

"Then I'd better leave you to your work and your own journey of discovery."

"And I will keep you informed of any progress made," I told him making him nod in thanks and then as he started to walk away, he turned back to me and said,

"Go bring our girl home, Luc."

Oh, but I would do much more than that, for I had a princess to reclaim, meaning only one thing…

The hunt was back on.

CHAPTER NINETEEN

HIDING IN BLOOD

After hours spent looking at the box and pouring over every fucking report I had received on it, I wanted to throw the fucking thing out of the nearest window and let its new home become a frozen lake. I was starting to believe that one of two things must have happened. One was that Amelia had officially hit genius status or the God of dumb fucking luck had struck a deal with the Fates and decided to give her a healthy dose of it!

Honestly, I wouldn't have been surprised at either, but knowing how smart she was for this ancient crap, then I would put my money on it being mostly her doing and a bit of the other. Now, if the Fates would just be so fucking kind and grant me the same courtesy, then I could swiftly move on to the part where my ass was on a plane and heading to wherever the Hell it was in the world she had been hiding.

I pulled the map from beneath the papers it had got buried under and placed it angrily on top, putting the box next to it, expecting it to do something…fucking anything! Hell, I would take the fucking Devil's hand reaching out of it and slapping me three ways from Limbo, just as long as what followed was the fucking answer!

"AAHH FUCKING THING!" I suddenly roared after grabbing it and throwing it at the wall. An action that ended with a small explosion of glass from the frame I had hanging there, with the picture I had taken of the lake now floating to the floor.

I raked a frustrated hand through my hair and held it at the base of my neck before releasing the strands on another growl. Then I got up with a sigh and went to retrieve it, first having to brush off the shards of glass and not giving a shit that doing so ended with a bloodied hand. Well, at least it was from something other than putting a fist through a wall, which was novel for a change, I thought sarcastically. To be honest, it was of little wonder why no one wanted to be near me these days.

But with my council spread out around the world dealing with the crisis the rogues had presented, then for once I found my castle near empty. At first I had been tempted by Adam's offer in accompanying me in my decision to return here. But then, with Adam came Pip, and I knew that in this current state of misery I was in, then I wasn't sure Pip's personality would survive it.

Even having the new work being done on the club hadn't been enough to keep me occupied. Surprisingly, of all people I had given Sophia, Dom's sister, free rein to arrange this shit for me. This was after Dom's recommendation as she too was worried for her niece's safety and clearly needed something to take her mind off that worry. I had accepted the offer with only one rule put into place…

Not a single shade of purple.

This, Dom had found most amusing. On the other hand, I

had walked out of the room, stopping long enough to warn Sophia,

"I am not fucking joking." Then I had handed her a limitless credit card and left.

Well, it had to be said that she was good, for the club was nearly finished despite the fortune spent on overtime alone. But from what I had seen from some pictures, it was looking good. However, not good enough to tempt me into travelling back there to see it firsthand. At this rate I wouldn't even be at the fucking reopening of it, as I refused to do so without Amelia by my side.

Speaking of which, I placed the box back down on my desk and sat staring at it as if this would help, before looking down at the blood pooling in the hand I had kept away from it. I snarled down at the sight, feeling as if my fucking blood was the cause of all of this. My blood and the tainted hand of a fucking Titan tyrant!

I fisted my hand, letting the thick crimson rivulets rain down through my fingers, before I hammered it down on the desk next to the box in my anger. It split the wood from the force, making the box tip into the bloody print of the side of my fist. The second it did, it vibrated before unlocking as it had done many times before. I decided I needed to do something. Maybe there would be some sort of specialist out there that I didn't yet know about.

As much as I hated to admit it, one thing was for sure and that was I was out of my depth here. Which also meant that I was simply wasting time by sitting here staring at the fucking thing!

So, I decided to fold up the only copy of the map with my gloved hand being careful not to get blood on it. I intended to put it back in the box for safe keeping.

At the very least I knew that I didn't need the original which

I had intended to keep. This was before the Witch had got her hands on it, of course. Because somewhere between Dom's vault and the portal door back into Afterlife, Amelia had opened the box. Fucking typical, seeing as that had been the only place a seeker couldn't fucking seek!

Had Takeshi accomplished this, he would have been able to see how Amelia had unlocked the map's secrets. That way she wouldn't have stood a chance at being gone so long, as I would have discovered her destination from the start.

But yet again, it just felt like another barrier set against me by the fucking Fates themselves! I grabbed my phone off the desk and rang Adam, thankful that he answered on the second ring, well at least I thought he did,

"I'm sorry but Mr Ambrogetti can't come to the phone right now, this is due to an unfortunate accident that we are calling The Great Inflatable Butt Plug incident of two thousand and... Ooops, no sugar belly, I most definitely did not, slash *did*... answer your phone again...eeek!" I groaned aloud and started to rub my forehead, knowing now how I'd made the right decision in not taking Adam up on his offer. Thankfully, Adam's voice came on the other end after the sound of slapping naked skin was heard. This and demonic growls and giggles after it.

*"Now sit still before I tie you over my knee again...*Hello?" Adam muttered what everyone would have known was a pointless threat seeing as this was most likely her aim in the first place.

"Adam, its me."

"My Lo..."

"Drop the shit, Adam, no one is fucking here!" I snapped making him release a sigh before muttering down at Pip,

"Time to get up, little one."

"Aww, but you promised you would be the teacher this time

and I stole your phone and everything!" I heard her say and knew she was pouting, even from here.

"We will play later, Peaches, now go do your homework ready for me." At this she shouted,

"Yey! Hell yeah, I will, just you wait and see, those equations are gonna look the shit, we are talking hearts, kisses and little cupid cocks in the margins and everything!"

"Good girl," he responded on a chuckle, making me regret the call and wished I had just sent him a fucking text!

"Alright Luc, go for it."

"Are you sure, 'cause you could just go ahead and rub salt in the wound and fuck whilst I wait?" I snarled making him laugh instead of taking me seriously.

"Don't give her ideas, Luc, it's the last thing she needs… now I take it you needed something…other than some alone time and a porno of course." he added because the bastard knew he could.

"Asshole," was my muttered response and again he laughed.

"I need to know if there is anyone else out there who can look at this map, anyone we haven't thought of."

"Luc, come on, we have been through this, we have had every geographical expert looking at it and half the idiots believed it was the lost city of Atlantis!" Adam certainly had a point and he would know being the poor bastard that had been charged with meeting with them.

"I take it this has something to do with Amelia taking an extra copy of the map?" he asked getting to the point.

"Stealing an extra copy of the map, yes," I corrected before adding the real reason for my call,

"She found a way to decipher it, Adam."

"Whoa, okay so that's new…how do you know that?" he asked after first expressing his surprise.

"Because she purposely left a copy in her room and gave me back the box, now why would she do that?"

"Because she didn't need it anymore…alright, point taken, and you officially have my attention," he replied making me raise a brow,

"And I didn't before?"

"Luc, I have my wife here dressed in a naughty schoolgirl outfit, bent over my desk and leaving very little to the imagination other than the fucking pencil she has been sucking on this whole time…yes, only now do you have my attention." I scoffed before being the one to mutter this time,

"Point taken."

The amusing part about this comment was that most people who knew Adam, had never heard him speak this way. But seeing as we had that kind of friendship, then unless anyone was around, this was the natural way of things. And in truth, it was that kind of honesty I needed right now.

"Okay, so what do you need?"

"I want you to put together a team, anyone from experts in the geographical field, to Philologists, to the study of fucking ancient map reading…Hell, get me a fucking Scribe for all I care!" Adam laughed and made another point as was his way,

"Unless you're referring to the Jewish recordkeeper variety, then I think we are all out of luck at finding an ancient Egyptian who documents the life of a pharaoh."

"Adam." I growled his name as a warning of my dark mood.

"Alright Luc, I will see what I can do…where do you want to meet?"

"I will come to you, as I think you have more chance of finding the people we need in the States…fuck, but it's not like it's lacking in the amount of Universities."

"That's true…and the map?" he asked.

"I am putting it in the box as we speak and will bring

both…wait…what the…?" My voice trailed off the second I opened the box further thanks to the blood I had already spilled for it. But the moment a drop of my blood dripped inside the box, it started to do more than just vibrate this time. No, now it started to open at the seams before it suddenly stopped.

"Luc? What is it?" I didn't tell him, wanting to find out for myself first.

"Go, enjoy your wife, I will call you back later," I said hanging up to the sound of him cursing me, no doubt for leaving him in the dark. Adam loved a good puzzle as much as the next geek. Hell, but from what I had been told, he and Amelia would often be found hunched over a crossword or some new challenge bought for them in the way of some plastic, multicolored puzzle cube.

But as for me, well this was challenge enough and it just looked to be one I had just cracked…*finally.* So, after throwing my phone down on the table, I shifted the box closer to me. Then I lifted my right hand to my mouth, one that had already started to heal. After this I let my fangs extend and bit hard into my own flesh, deep enough to make it bleed thoroughly. Then I removed the map and allowed my blood to pour down into the box.

In seconds it started to unfold before my eyes making me curse,

"Fuck me…it worked."

That was when it all started to make sense, as seeing her hand bleeding had obviously been when she had discovered the box's secret just as I had. Because once the box was flat, it was easy to see the channels of blood that had started to fill. Channels that were there for a reason.

But for me that reason became something else entirety as I placed the map over the now flat piece of wood, watching as its destination started to seep through the paper.

One that included a name.

One I knew all too well.

"Gods, can it be?" I muttered in astonishment as I looked up at the painting above my fireplace. And for the first time in a long time, a real grin emerged as that reason became one that mirrored both my past and my future.

After this there was only one thing left to say,

"I've got you now, my little Šemšā…"

"I've got you now."

CHAPTER TWENTY

AMELIA

NOW AND FOREVER

The second the song came over the radio, I cursed that my hands were full and was therefore unable to turn off the beautiful notes of Lady Antebellum's, 'I run to you' quickly enough. It had been nearly two months of banned love songs and as the lyrics seemed to tell my life's story it was of little wonder why…

'I run from hate, I run from prejudice, I run from pessimists, but I run too late…I run my life, or is it running me?'

And wasn't that just the question right now I thought as I struggled to the table with yet another armful of research papers my friend Yosef had given me. Damn my Spotify account recommending songs!

I quickly got to the table only dropping a few scrolls and one book, doing so just as the lyrics continued with...

'Run from my past, I run too fast, or too slow it seems... when lies become the truth...'

"Yeah you can say that again!" I said picking up my fallen articles with annoyance and slapping them back on the counter just before grabbing my tablet and turning it off just as the beat kicked up with,

'That's when I run to you... this world keeps spinning faster, into a new disaster so I run to you...I run to you baby'

"Nope, not now and not ever," I commented as I killed the music and the second I did, that was when I felt it. Like a presence so powerful it sucked all the energy from the room and left me near gasping for breath. And that difficulty in breathing wasn't just from the moment you realised that you were no longer alone, but it was more when you realised *who* it was that stole that solitude from you. Because when you were on the run there was only one being out there you hoped not to find in the room with you...

The hunter.

And I knew my time was up when the first words spoken in that smooth hypnotic voice of his told me,

"Now that is a shame."

I sucked in a deep breath, placed my hands on the table just to steady myself as his name slipped from my lips,

"Lucius."

Then I felt him stepping up behind me and I tensed as I heard those forbidden words whispered in my ear at the same moment he took possession of my body. He did this by gripping my arms and pulling me back against the strength of him,

"Found at last, my Khuba."

I gasped and started to struggle in his hold, making him grip me tighter before banding an arm across my torso, telling me softly,

"Ssshh, be still now…*I won't hurt you."* I tensed, closed my eyes as the tears started to rise as I told him fiercely,

"And I told you once before…*you already have*…now let go of me!" At this I felt his arm turn to steel and the rumbling vibrations at my back matched that of his low growl of frustration. But he had no clue as to what he was doing to me right now. How much pain he caused me by being back in his arms once more.

Gods, but how I just wanted to relax back against him. How I wanted to let him hold me and say to hell with my strength. One that seemed to be sucked right out of me, especially when he suddenly turned me to face him and snarled angrily,

"And I told you, *that I never would!"* Then, before I could stop myself, I slapped him across the face as hard as I could, until the pain lashed across my own skin. Then, before he could react in any way, I lost every good sense I had and grabbed him by the shirt, yanking him into me. After this I reached up and crushed my lips to his the second I pulled him down to meet me! Doing so with so much passion, it felt as though it had the power to burn us both to Hell for our sins!

His own reaction only managed to fuel my own into holding onto him tighter. This was because he had one hand fisted in my hair at the back of my neck and the other fisted in the material of my shirt at the base of my spine. There he held me to him as if he feared that I would suddenly disappear through his fingers. As if he was doing everything in his power to prevent that.

Somewhere in the back of my mind I had that nagging voice

telling me that this was wrong. That I shouldn't be doing this, that he was no longer mine and I didn't belong to him. That I was angry and upset. But above all else, it was questioning why he was even here and why was he kissing me so desperately, it felt as if he needed me like he needed his next breath? None of it made sense, least of all the way my hands curled around his neck as if to anchor him to me, never wanting to let go.

But then I started to think of everything I had been through these last two months. I thought of all the pain and suffering he had caused me. I thought about what seemed like the endless tears and cursing his name as I woke from my nightmares. And then after all of this my mind forced me to ask myself...*what was I doing?*

So, I let my fingers uncurl from his hair, and just as they started to lower, he knew. He knew that he was losing me because he pulled his lips back enough to tell me on a dangerous promise,

"No, I am not fucking letting you go!" Then he pushed me back until I was trapped between him and the table. So this time I had no chance of escaping him as he really kissed me. And foolishly, I opened up once more, doing so on a whimpered moan, as he plundered my mouth, tasting me, drinking me in and consuming me whole. He ravished me just with his kiss, and I swear it felt powerful enough to brand the memory to my damaged, fragile soul.

And I wasn't the only one who was affected in this way, as when he finally released my lips, doing so now, as we were both panting, he placed his forehead to mine and told me,

"By the Gods, how I've missed you." I swallowed hard, so hard that he could hear it, that along with the feel of my emotions getting too much to hold back as I shuddered in his arms. Which was why this time, instead of simply pulling away, something I knew Lucius would react to in a negative way, I

tried a different tactic. Because I couldn't let him kiss me like that again…I just wouldn't survive it.

"Please, Lucius…please."

"What is it, my Khuba?" he whispered down at me, as his hand cupped my face before caressing a thumb across the apple of my cheek. His beautiful eyes scanned my face, my hair, even down to my neck as if needing to take in every inch of me. Gods, but just with that look alone he made me feel so treasured.

"Please, give me time… this…this is all too much to take in," I whispered, finally braving to look up at him, meeting his eyes as his gaze came back to mine. He released a heavy sigh before placing his forehead to mine once more, a rumbled sound of frustration coming from him before he lifted his head so he could kiss me there.

"Alright Amelia, I will give you this time…"

"Thank y…"

"But it is time that will be spent by my side," he said cutting me off and giving me little choice in the matter. I looked away from him, knowing that right now I didn't have it in me to argue. No, I just couldn't think much more past the realisation that he was here with me now. So, I nodded without looking at him, simply waiting for him to step away and finally give me that space I felt desperate for. It was as though I couldn't breathe. As if I had forgotten the process or something.

But then he grasped my chin and turned my face back to his, giving me little option than to do as he wanted. However, despite his dominant grip, his eyes softened in a way I used to love.

"Don't shut me out," he whispered gently and this time I couldn't help but close my eyes, needing to rid myself of the sight of what was happening. Then finally I could breathe again when I felt him stepping away, cursing under his breath in a

language I didn't know. That was when I finally opened my eyes and turned my back on him. Finding myself once more holding onto the table top and grasping at the papers there, as if the feel of the pages beneath my fingers would help take me back to what had once been my reality. The one I had built up without Lucius.

Not here. Not back here in this dream world that I had been stumbling blindly through the whole time Lucius had pretended to want me. Back to the place he seemed to want to force me back to. Which made me hiss,

"Why?"

"You know why, you are just too blinded by what you think you saw to see the truth behind the veil of pain," he told me making a breath get stuck in my throat on a gasp.

"I won't go back there…I won't go back to Afterlife. You can't make me," I told him, turning back around to tell him the last part of this vow, which was when he surprised me.

"I have no intention of trying to force you to," he told me with a fold of his arms across that wide chest of his. Gods be damned, but why did he have to look even better than I remembered. In fact, my memories hadn't done his image justice and even then, he had been the one to feature in every one of my fantasies. Also, I had never seen him dressed in anything other than a suit or jeans and a t shirt. But right now, he was dressed for summer and I hated to say it, but Gods, he looked hot and that had nothing to do with the temperature.

He wore a worn denim shirt open and rolled at the sleeves with a white t-shirt underneath. He had dark grey cargo shorts that reached his knees and had multiple pockets, that looked to have a pair of aviator sunglasses hooked in one. I knew that most likely a phone and wallet would be in the others. A pair of black sandals that looked like the kind wore for hiking and a black glove that looked like strapping you would have on for a boxing match, completed the look. Who knew that Lucius had a glove for every season, I thought with a concealed snigger.

But it made me wonder what he thought when seeing me now after all this time. My denim shorts, striped red and white vest top and white sneakers weren't exactly anything to write home about.

Besides, my mind was kind of stuck on the part when he said that he had no intention of forcing me to go back to Afterlife.

What the Hell?

I turned back to the table and started to pile up the books just for something to do other than look at him…it was too painful, knowing that perfection wasn't mine anymore. I wasn't free to touch it, to own it and drink it in wherever I wanted to. I swallowed down the hard lump of my reality and tried to get my hands to stop shaking.

"If that is true, then I still fail to see what it is you're doing here," I said trying to keep my tone steady, which helped without looking at him. But when he started laughing, I shot him a dumbfounded look over my shoulder.

"Seriously?" he asked, making me frown in answer.

"You just slapped me, kissed me and then I kissed you back, *only better…* and you're asking me what it is I am doing here?" he said making me slam a book down and snap,

"Your kiss wasn't better!" At this he folded his arms over his chest making the denim at his arms tighten around the biceps in that delicious way that made it really, really hard not to look at.

"It was," he stated condescendingly.

"Gods, you're so arrogant! No, it wasn't!" I told him making him smirk in that cocky way before he leant his body forward at the waist slightly so he could tell me,

"Yeah… *it fucking was."* I shook my head and rolled my

eyes at him making his own widen before a full-on grin arose, making me hold up a finger and snap,

"Oh no, don't you even fucking think of it!" Of course this was referring to his spanking rule as punishment for what he deemed a 'disrespectful gesture'.

"Trust me, sweetheart, since you ran from me, then I can assure you that I have thought of little else but *doing it* and it has not one fucking thing to do with you rolling your eyes at me." At this my mouth dropped open in surprise and he nodded to my face and said,

"Actually, you can include that expression on the list as well." At this I snapped my mouth shut and narrowed my eyes at him.

"You're unbelievable!" I snapped making him tell me in a firm and pissed off tone,

"No, what is unbelievable is that you made it this far and this long alone…I have to say, you broke all records with that one, Princess."

"Oh, I was waiting for how long it would be before you went back to calling me Princess," I threw back at him.

"I believe I used the term Khuba and sweetheart first, or didn't you notice and was too busy waiting for one that suits your pissed off mood?" Grrr I hated it when the asshole made a point!

"Ahhh, Gods, you're intolerable!" I snapped with a throw of my arms making him nod my way and tell me,

"Yes, and for these last two months, then the feeling is mutual, although I would have chosen impossible, stubborn, reckless, obstinate, and tenacious…oh, and of course, infuckingsane! But hey, you go ahead and pick one," he snapped making me reply in a mocking tone,

"Oh right, just because I chose to leave you, eh…? Because

that could never happen to the mighty Lucius without being insane...*clearly."*

"Ahh, so you picked one...good choice, as it was the one I was leaning heavily towards myself." I growled at him and turned back to the table and then spun around, opened my mouth to say something that never came. Damn it, but it left me at just the sight of him raising a brow in question before I huffed and turned back to the table again now looking like an idiot.

Then I took a deep breath, found my words, and turned to face him one last time.

"And she's back again," he muttered the moment I knew what I wanted to say, ignoring his sarcasm, and telling him,

"I was insane for..." suddenly I was stopped dead, losing my train of thought and the ability to speak when a hand covered my mouth and he was inches from me.

"I am going to stop you there, Princess, before the humour of this moment runs dry and the memory of your kiss is replaced by the bitter bite of your tongue lashed my way," he warned making me look up at him with wide eyes before I mumbled against his hand,

"I thout you sid your kiss wass bett...er?" At this he grinned down at me and, keeping his hand in place, he leaned closer and whispered,

"It was but yours was a good contender for first." I swallowed hard and his eyes flashed a shade of amber at the sight. Gods, but I had missed that sight, so much so that it made my chest ache. I would see it sometimes in my dreams. Those eyes watching me through the darkness, as if watching over me, guiding me to the safety away from my nightmares.

"But then, it is unsurprising, seeing as you are out of practice," he told me in a playful tone that made me growl behind his palm before I gripped onto his wrist and bit into the soft fleshy part near his thumb. However, this didn't exactly have the desired effect, as he just grinned down at me, before taunting me,

"Harder, sweetheart, for it tickles." I growled and yanked it down with a hard tug forcing him to release me. Then I snapped,

"Oh, but I don't want another mental image of you 'practicing' thanks." At this his playful humour was gone in an instant and darkness took over it before he got closer to my face and snarled,

"Reel in your claws and tone down the bitch act princess, for it doesn't fucking suit you!"

"Oh my Gods, you utter asshole!" I shouted pushing on his chest, happy that he stepped back so I could escape his hold.

"I can't believe all this time I have been spending it miss...I mean thanking that I...uh...left." I trailed off my sentence not knowing what to say to cover up the mistake I'd made, as I knew he heard it when he shot me a look of shock before his angry features softened. I turned my back to him and started to walk away when he grabbed my hand and tugged me back to him.

"Spending it?" he asked, making me clear my throat first before answering,

"I just told you."

"No, what you just told me was a lie to cover up the truth," he argued, making me swallow down about half of the things I really wanted to say to that. And he knew it. As he raised a hand before it turned into a fist and fell. Then he closed his eyes for the seconds it took him to say in a strained tone,

"Don't say it, Amelia, don't you dare say it." I turned away from him and walked back to the table to grab my canvas book bag. Then I started stuffing the books I needed back inside it, as I told him,

"Consider this as me dared not to say anything else but, *bye Lucius.*" Then I folded the flap over the opening and hooked the strap across my chest before grabbing the lightweight jacket I'd brought because it was chillier in the mornings.

Then I started to walk away, not exactly getting far without him. This was because Lucius grabbed my hand in his and no matter how much I tried to get out of his grip, I couldn't. Then he looked down at me and informed me,

"Like I said, you can have your time, but it is going to be spent by my side…"

"Now and forever."

CHAPTER TWENTY-ONE

THE CLUE IS IN THE LUGGAGE

I walked out of the Bible Lands Museum where my friend Yosef worked and had been helping me with my research. Although, I certainly didn't expect when I walked in there this morning that I would be leaving hours later with Lucius' hand refusing to let go of mine. He had also taken my bag from me, making me suck in a breath at the contact when his arm brushed across my breasts. If he noticed, he didn't comment but then again, his eyes did brighten a moment, burning amber.

But now, with the way his hand gripped mine in what felt like an unyielding hold, it was as if he was worried that if he let go, then I would bolt, and he would only end up having to chase me. Which, in front of a load of tourists, wouldn't have been a good idea, not unless we wanted the police involved. But then what was I thinking, as this idea only crossed my mind for a second, because it was foolish to think that by screaming for help right now might have given me another head start. Because Lucius was the master at manipulating mortal minds, so it would have been pointless. He could have just created a wall of people to surround me before calmly walking up to me and throwing me over his shoulder and no one would have batted an eyelid.

Damn Vampire King!

So, instead, I stormed from the glass fronted building and started walking towards where my car was parked across the road. A plan that ended the moment Lucius pulled on my hand, stopping me. I looked back up at him, now seeing him with his sunglasses on and I swear my heart raced. But then with the smirk he granted me, it was obvious that he knew my heartbeat had kicked up a beat. Bloody hell, but could he look any sexier! Gods, if the sight hadn't been so hot to look at, then I would have hated him for it!

"My car is over there," he informed me, and I looked towards the chauffeur driven car parked where it shouldn't be and said,

"Good for you, it's a good sign you're aging well when you can remember things like that," I said sarcastically making him chuckle, before he started to lead me over to it.

"I can't leave my car," I told him, trying to pull back. Something that was useless clearly, as he looked towards the parking area and told me,

"We can get it later."

"Or we could just arrange where to meet and I will take my car and you take yours and I will see you there?" I asked in a hopeful tone making him pull his glasses down enough so he could look at me over them, his unimpressed look speaking for itself.

"I will take that as a no, then?" I commented awkwardly.

"It's nice to see that your powers of observation are still up to par, Love…as you can take that as a, *Hell no,*" he said before gripping my hand tighter and pulling me towards his car. So, with my bag over his shoulder and my hand wrapped tightly in his, I had little choice but to go where he wanted me to go. Especially seeing as most of my new life was in that bag he had hold of.

I had been staying in a small apartment only ten minutes' drive from here, picking it for that reason. Because coming here had always been in my plans as no one knew about Yosef. He was a friend that I sometimes reached out to if anything particularly interesting came into my sector at the museum, one that I knew he could help with. A job, I had to ask myself often if I would ever get to do again. Of course, the museum had given me time off, but I doubted they had been planning on it being three months!

The thought was a depressing one, as that job had been my whole life. A life that, from the looks of things, just got even more complicated.

But Yosef had merely thought I was on a sabbatical, due to a personal historical discovery I was funding with the help of investors. He worked in gallery three of the museum, one that was called symbolic communication, and housed seals used in trade and commerce, being one of the earliest examples of communication and featuring over 6,500 years of glyptic art. He also oversaw works in gallery four which was literate voices, the story of writing. A field of expertise which naturally leant itself as useful considering what I faced.

The history was all based on the development of writing and a gallery of chronicles showcasing the development of written communication from its earliest forms: cuneiform, hieroglyphic and alphabetic writing. So basically, the box in a nutshell. Of course, having the symbols pretty much memorized by now helped in this, seeing as I had thrown the box back in Lucius' face in my moment of trying to make a point.

So, Yosef had pulled a few strings and they ended up welcoming me to carry out my research with the promise that the museum would benefit from any discoveries I made. I now wondered if that included the angry Vamp King who was currently opening the door to the parked car and nodding down at it expectantly. Well, he was old, so it's not like he wouldn't fit in, I thought sarcastically as I folded myself inside. He soon followed and it quickly became apparent that Lucius didn't intend on giving me much space and he sat in a way that he was touching me. Which made this car feel as though it was getting smaller by the second.

"So, the deal is we go somewhere, we sit, and we talk and that's it…right?" I said which he ignored and told the driver,

"Back to the hotel." This made me mutter,

"Or I could just get ignored and you make all the decisions," I muttered mockingly, making him finally respond,

"Now that sounds like a good plan." I rolled my eyes at the window this time and ignored him.

"Relax, there is a restaurant at the hotel where we can sit and talk, besides, I need to retrieve my phone from my room." I looked down at the pockets on his shorts in a questioning way,

"It needed charging," he informed me, as if this mattered but it made me laugh,

"What's funny about that?"

"Only that it is probably the most human thing I have ever heard you say." He scoffed before removing his glasses and hooking the arm of them in the neck of his T-shirt, so they hung there.

"So, this hotel of yours, this isn't the part where you left out that it was in Germany or Portland, Maine…right?" I asked because I felt strangely as if I needed to speak. He granted me a grin before saying,

"It's the Notre Dame of Jerusalem Centre." Of course, I knew of it naturally as it was a beautiful building, with a lot of history.

"Waldorf Astoria all booked up?" I asked making him grant me a wry look before telling me,

"I have investments in the hotel." I scoffed a murmured,

"Of course, you do." But this wasn't what struck me,

"So, the Notre Dame huh…? Well, that's close then," I commented quietly, wondering if he was staying there because of how close it was.

"Seven minutes from the museum and ten minutes from your apartment," he told me, and I released a deep heavy sigh, making him chuckle.

"I didn't have a hope, did I?" I asked in a deflated tone making him pick up my hand, and raise it to his lips to kiss as he told me,

"No, you didn't, but if it helps, you gave it a good try, sweetheart." I yanked my hand from his and mumbled,

"Patronizing, condescending, arrogant…" he laughed before turning to me and saying,

"You can't say that I didn't warn you."

"Yes, because that makes a whole month of buses, cruise ships and car journeys so much better and seem so worth it!" I snapped making him shrug his shoulders just as we pulled up to his hotel that looked more like the entrance to some English castle.

"Yes, well it's lucky for you, that out of the both of us, my tenaciousness was fueled on the grounds of making you safe, whereas yours was just reckless and foolish," he said making my mouth drop open. Then without looking back at me or my astonished (had I just been slapped without realising it) face, he got out of the car, doing so the moment the door was opened outside the hotel. I then leaned forward to the driver and said,

"If I give you 4000 shekels, would you just speed away, like right now?" He granted me a wide eyed, questioning look at what was the offer of over a thousand dollars to drive me somewhere. But the sound of the growl outside told me what his answer would be.

"Don't fucking try it." Then Lucius' hand came into view and he said my name in warning, making me release a frustrated sigh before getting out of the car, after first slapping his hand away and ignoring his courteous gesture.

Oh, and let's not forget the part where I tripped over my own feet and fell into him anyway. The second his hands went to my hips to steady me, my breath hitched and he, in response to the sound, squeezed me tighter. Damn him and his ability to turn me into a mindless twit!

This meant that I had no option at salvaging this other than to take a deep breath and try and at least appear to be taking charge of my life. So, I tagged his sunglasses from the neck of his T shirt, flicked out the arm, put them on and tapped his cheek, before telling him,

"Thanks, handsome, now did you say something about a bar?" Then I started to walk towards the entrance, leaving him behind and left muttering to himself,

"Must be losing my damn touch." I grinned to myself and felt him catch me up just as I was looking up at the impressive entrance, his next correction was,

"And it was a restaurant, not a bar."

"Same jazz," I replied without looking, instead taking in the two turrets of pale stone blocks and the building in between, with glass doors set back through a stone archway. There were also two huge buildings that framed either side of the impressive entrance which I assumed were the accommodation wings.

Lucius opened the door for me, and I walked inside to find a lobby showcasing the same pale stone as on the outside. This was combined with pale marble floors to match. Two comfy looking seating areas framed both sides of the open centre space, one that led to the reception.

Lucius took my hand once more and walked us both through the lobby, going first to the receptionist and when her eyes widened, I could understand why. Damn sexy Vamp!

"Mr Septimus, welcome back, they have just finished adding the new luggage to your suite." He nodded and said,

"Very good, any messages?" She checked on the system and said,

"Just one, a call from a Mr Draven." I tensed at the sound of my father's name and Lucius' hand tightened on mine before he looked down at me, turning his head to the side slightly, before whispering,

"Easy, sweetheart." I took a breath and ignored the way he watched me as I swallowed down the hard lump.

"Can you make us reservations for dinner tonight at the Cheese and Wine, he asked, making me want to ask what he thought he was doing. Instead I told him firmly,

"I can't have dinner with you." Then I lifted my sunglasses to the top of my head so I could show him how serious I was when making that statement.

"Why not?" he asked, and the receptionist slipped up and also inquired,

"Yes, why not?" I shot her a look, at which she rolled her lips inwards before mouthing a silent 'sorry'. I gave her a nod before turning back to Lucius.

"The deal was that I let you drag me here for a drink or lunch at the most, but not dinner." The woman behind the desk looked at Lucius as if asking herself why this man would have needed to drag any woman anywhere. And maybe questioning why they weren't all lined up around the block or something, this at the very whisper of a mention that he was looking for a date.

"It is too late for lunch," Lucius told me, and the receptionist opened her mouth about to correct him, when he gave her a pointed look, which in turn made her look to me and quickly say,

"He's right...so I will just ring them...any particular time?"

"Never o clock," I answered.

"Eight o'clock," Lucius replied, ignoring my made-up time which sounded a much better option. She nodded and walked to the phone off to the side, no doubt wanting to put distance between us. Something that became obvious, seeing as she wasn't using the one that was right in front of her screen.

"Lucius, this was not..." I was stopped short the moment I felt his fingers under my chin, bringing my face up at the same time he lowered his before whispering,

"Trust me, sweet girl."

I swallowed hard again wanting to point out that I most definitely *did not* trust him or his pushy ways. But the way he had said it was enough to steal any response I may have had or would've been brave enough to voice. I swear, that even my poor neglected clit had just swooned. Because as much as I hated to admit it, my two-month dry spell hadn't only been linked to sex. For even my fingers seemed to have lost their appeal. This I put down to Lucius and just the thought of him being too painful to think about. Especially in that way. And well, seeing as he had featured in all of my sexual fantasies before he even became my boyfriend, then I was stuck with nothing else to work with.

Which meant that two months without even a single orgasm was enough to make a damn Disney princess cranky and ready to tell even the birds and talking mice to fuck off! But what I was currently discovering that made this even worse, was that I was now being forced to endure my very own walking, talking, smoking hot fantasy! And let's just say that expecting my body not to turn into a traitorous bitch and betray me was like asking for it to snow tomorrow, and it was summer in Jerusalem!

I swear, I wouldn't last the day without rubbing myself up against him like some damn cat in heat! Gods, but why the Hell had he turned up!?

It turned out that this internal musing ended up not just making me horny, but I also missed everything that was arranged. Only knowing this when Lucius started leading me to…well, I had no clue where. For all I knew he had arranged chloroform, chains, and a coffin to be in his room, ready to ship me back home…well, at the very least I expected it would have airholes otherwise that would have just been mean.

I let him walk me to the elevators before I finally came out of my own inner monologue, enough to say,

"I'm not going to dinner with you."

"Yes, you are," he stated glancing up at the numbers to see if it was on its way.

"You know, bullying a girl to go on a date with you is a little sad and giving off major desperate vibes…besides, why not ask the receptionist, she looked like she was checking you out…see what I did there?" I said nudging his arm and making him smirk down at me, ignoring my 'check out' joke and commenting in a cocky way,

"Why, you jealous?"

"Why, you delusional?" I threw back at him, making him chuckle.

"Besides, I am hardly dressed for dinner but hey, that's an idea, you just let me catch a cab home and then I will meet you back here later…yeah?"

"Nice try, sweetheart. Besides, the dress part won't be a problem," he told me as the doors opened and he pulled me inside the elevator.

"I hate to ask, 'cause I know I am going to regret it, but why isn't a dress going to be a problem, Lucius?" A bad boy grin was my only answer, making me then ask,

"Where are you taking me now?"

"To my room," he said making me instantly try to step out of the elevator, at the same time saying,

"Oh, hell no!" Only he tugged me back and slashed a hand in a way that made the doors close a lot quicker than they usually did, so I had no choice but be trapped in there with him. Then an arm banded across my front in a way that seemed as though it was becoming a habit of his. He held me to his chest and whispered down into my ear,

"What's wrong, sweetheart...scared?"

"Terrified," I admitted and then to save myself I added,

"They take murder very seriously here." It was after this that I felt myself shaking thanks to him throwing his head back and the sound of his laughter made my heart ache. Gods, but I loved it when I could make him laugh. It felt like I had just won a prize every damn time.

After this, he only let me go from this very intimate hold when the doors opened to what I gathered was his floor. I soon found my hand was in his once again and I was being led to what I discovered wasn't a room at all, it was naturally a suite.

And as far as suites went, it was a very nice suite, beautiful even. But its beauty wasn't what my eyes went to the moment I was pulled inside the room. No, it wasn't the stunning view of the city from the private terrace, or even the expensive looking luggage that was yet to be unpacked, telling me Lucius had just arrived.

No, it was none of those things. Instead, it was the items that shouldn't have been there, making me turn to the culprit in question and ask him in what I considered a dangerous tone…

"Why are all my bags here?"

22

Under My Wear

CHAPTER TWENTY-TWO

UNDER MY WEAR

I continued to take in the sight of all of my things as my mind struggled with the reasons why. It was obvious that they had all been packed up from the apartment I had been renting. My mind also did a quick sweep of the surprisingly modest living room that was the same pale stone walls, with oak wooden floors and soft furnishings in sunset colours. Artwork, which included painted nights of Jerusalem, next to fields of olive groves in the sunrise, adorned the walls and pottery and other ornaments were dotted around the room on chunky, dark wooden furniture with arched latticed doors.

But these accents of colour in the room were being overshadowed by the sight of my belongings.

"Why is all my stuff here, Lucius?" I asked making him shrug his shoulders and look as if he was trying hard not to smirk.

"I told you once before, looking smug is not an answer!" I snapped making that smirk now turn into a grin he was doing a shit job at trying to hide.

"I thought I would save you the cash," he said giving me his first bullshit lie.

"That's funny, 'cause see, I paid up for the next six months, so do you want to try another bullshit reason or just give me the gist of your dominant ass making decisions that weren't yours to make!" I told him, shouting at the end as I walked closer to him. And although he looked amused by the sight, he still started to back up as if I was a threat. Which I knew I wasn't, because he was looking as if all he wanted to do was burst out laughing.

"You had an infestation," he said making me shake my head, fold my arms, and tell him,

"Right well, unless I really pissed off the Gods since leaving my flat and unbeknown to me, they decided to release a plague of locusts I am unaware of, then there were no bugs in there this morning, Lucius." His lips twitched again before telling me,

"It was a rodent infestation." I raised a brow, silently calling him on his bullshit once more.

"I like mice," I said picking up one of my handbags and throwing it straight at him. He caught it head on, as it would have hit its mark had he not been fast. He moved it to one side and said around it,

"They were rats." I leaned down and picked up one of my shoes from the box and said,

"I like rats." Then I threw the shoe at him, making him drop the bag and catch the shoe.

"They were the size of cats," he said on a grin and this time I picked up a vase from a side table and shouted this time,

"I like mutant, cat sized rats!" Then I threw it at him, but instead of catching it as he had done the rest, he side-stepped, making it smash into the wall behind him. The second it burst into pieces my hands flew to my mouth as I shrieked, before dropping them to my sides and accusing,

"Why did you do that!" He laughed once and said,

"I think you will find you're the one who threw it."

"Yeah, but you were supposed to catch it, or it was supposed to knock you out, not smash on the wall! Shit…do you think it was expensive?" I asked as I started to walk past him getting ready to pick up the pieces, when suddenly he tugged me around the waist making me squeal in surprise.

Then, before I knew what was happening, I found myself pinned against the wall with one large vampire consuming my personal space and making it his own. Then he tore his sunglasses from the top of my head and threw them to one side. After this his hands were framing my face and he was tipping my head back and up to his, before he told me on a growl,

"Fuck me, but how I missed you!" Then he was kissing me, and my gasp of surprise only ended up being a welcome for his tongue to slip inside and taste every last bit of me. A needy moan of mine was absorbed by the kiss and only ended up spurring him on to take more of me. But my hands had remained by my sides, as I didn't know what to do with them, because I didn't think it was a good idea to give him the impression that I wanted him to be doing this to me, even if by the Gods, YES, I did and I fucking hated myself for it!

But it was if he knew because he pulled his head back and took my hands in his before raising my arms. When they were level with his shoulders, he placed them at the back of his neck. Then he put pressure on my fingers, prompting me to hold onto him after ducking his head lower. This was so he was free to pick me up by the waist, so we were at the same height. After which he started to walk me somewhere and before I could ask where we going, he started to speak.

"Now this is what is going to happen, you will go inside this bathroom, where you will find everything you need, then you will shower and get ready. After which I will take you to dinner, where we will sit, eat and talk about all the things that need to be said..." I opened my mouth to speak, getting out a barely heard,

"But..." before he shut me up by snapping his teeth at my lips making them close from fear of getting bitten. Then he went right back to speaking,

"...and I promise you, Amelia, you will listen to all I have to say or I swear, I will bring you back to this room, tie you to my fucking bed and keep you as my prisoner until you do... now do you understand?" he said, finishing by placing me on the vanity in the bathroom and catching my eyes as if to make sure that I had. To which I was only capable of nodding in return. Then he let me go and flicked me playfully under the nose and said,

"Good girl." After this he walked out of the bathroom closing the door behind him, making me turn around to face the mirror at my back so I could see my reflection and ask it,

"What the hell just happened?"

Naturally, the traitorous bitch had no answers for me.

I DIDN'T KNOW how long I took getting ready, or how long it was before I even started to. I just stared at the door before staring at myself in the mirror as if either one of these views would explain to me what was happening?

This was in hopes that the last few hours would somehow begin to make sense to me. The biggest question of all being what the hell was he doing. Fuck that, what the hell was I doing?! A question I had asked myself at least six times during this whole 'getting ready' order Lucius had given me. Now the question was, did I want to go on a date with him, Gods no! But did I want to walk back out the door and tell him this…? That was the 'Hell no' that won. As I wanted to do that even less. Because I couldn't face him right now.

So, instead, I focused all my energy on getting ready and yes, of course I went the extra mile in trying to achieve amazing results. This with the aim that with one look at me and it was powerful enough that I could bring him to his knees and crumple at my feet at the sight of my beauty! Then I could bolt for the door and do a runner. But then, in all honesty, I was a woman about to go on a date with her ex and wanted to look amazing, as after all…

I was only human!

Of course, achieving this would have been easier had my cyeliner stopped making mirror imprints on the arch of my eyelid every time I opened my damned eye. So this meant redoing one eye twice and using I don't know how many cotton buds to achieve this. Now, as for stabbing myself in the eye with one, well that was thanks to Lucius knocking on the door and scaring the shit out of me. But he did this to inform me that he had hung my black lace dress behind the door making me mutter in a mocking way,

"I guess I am wearing the black lace dress then." Then I stuck out my tongue at myself pretending it was Lucius, aka, Mr bossy 'date me' pants. Although, to be fair, it was the only fancy dress I had, so it made sense. But to know that he had obviously gone through my things, well let's just say, it hadn't exactly given me the warm and fuzzies!

The major thing that still hadn't made any sense, was why the bathroom was filled with my beauty products and the living room of his suite was filled with my luggage? Because as we had left the museum I had told him, one cup of coffee and that was it. Something he had agreed to. Well, so far it had started with a quick conversation over coffee, with the choice to leave after I have heard him out, now to somehow being in his hotel suite. Somewhere, I will add, where he obviously intended me to stay and go on a date with him. Like seriously, when had I allowed all of this to happen?

Of course, this was Lucius we were talking about. He might not be able to manipulate my mind with the power of his will, but he wasn't without his other skills in the art. Which was why I got to the point of not being able to put it off any longer. As I had already found my outfit hanging up, with my underwear hooked over the hanger making me want to growl at him.

I had to say that spending the entire evening with him knowing what my underwear looked like wasn't exactly going to add to the cool ice queen persona I had decided to go with. Especially when I opened the door and saw him standing there looking like sex on a stick. Gods, but why hadn't I just invested in a vibrator…or a sex shop?

He was wearing navy-blue suit trousers, a black leather belt and a crisp white shirt tucked in at the waist and naturally, rolled at the sleeves. Black dress shoes completed the sexy look. His trademark glove could be seen, this one made of black strapping that, damn him, only ended up adding to the sex appeal.

Of course, so did the dusting of blonde stubble kissing his jawline and the way his hair had been styled back. It parted a little at the side, as if he had got out of the shower and just run his fingers through it a few times working with where it fell naturally. And as much as I hated to admit it, it did make for the most perfect sight when I opened the door being faced with his magnificence. My heart fluttered and my lady bits…well hell, I didn't even want to think about what they were doing! Most likely drooling, spreading wide and wolf whistling to get his attention…had my pussy been a cartoon character that was.

I walked out to find him leaning casually against the arm of the sofa, his handsome features illuminated slightly by the screen of his phone that he was looking down at. But then, at the sound of me opening the door, his head snapped up. Then his eyes scanned the length of me, doing so slowly and with the keen eyes of a predator, one with the sole purpose of taking in every inch of me. And well, the moment that dark grin, the one that promised so much more than I was ready for, started to appear, I couldn't help but shiver. He didn't miss it either, as his eyes flashed amber before they shimmered back to bluish, grey steel.

Then he tossed his phone to one side, never taking his eyes off me before making his move towards me. It was like a killer on the hunt and I tried not to squirm under the intenslty of it all.

"You could make a Goddess shy away from your beauty, for it knows no bounds, my Khuba," he told me making me blush and drop my head, finally free from the sight of him approaching me. But then he wasn't happy with this and took hold of my chin so he could bring my gaze back to his.

"But these eyes…these fucking eyes. Gods, but the power they hold over me is fucking limitless!" he said before leaning down ready to kiss me again and I turned my head just in time to avoid it, telling myself that I couldn't let him do that again. Not until I have had my answers and discovered what was going on. Because his kisses were dangerous. They had the power to lure me in and make me forget. They had the power to give me hope, and I knew how painful hope could be.

They had the power to entrap me in the promise of him forever.

In the end, his kiss landed on my cheek instead and I ignored his growl of frustration at not getting what he wanted.

"Thank you," I said on a barely heard whisper as my emotions were making my voice too thick to push past my lips any louder. Then I took a much-needed breath and after stepping away, something he thankfully allowed, I granted him a look up and down before telling him,

"You look nice too."

"Nice?" he mocked making me fight a grin.

"Very nice?"

"Damn, but I must be losing my touch if the word nice comes up…in fact, I think I am hurt," he said teasing me by placing a hand to his heart as if I had damaged him. I laughed once and said,

"I think your ego will survive, big boy." To which he replied,

"Well, the big boy compliment certainly helps." Then he winked at me making me laugh,

"It wasn't a compliment."

"No, it was a compliment aimed at you," he said before slowly looking down at himself and making my eyes follow to see for myself what he meant.

"Lucius! Gods, can't you…" I said putting a hand in front of my eyes to hide the very obvious erection straining the material down his impressive length. He laughed unapologetically and said,

"What, hide it? And just where do you suggest I do that…? As I am not sure you will like my preferred suggestion so soon," he said with a grin at the horror on my face.

"Seriously, did you just say that?"

"What do you expect with you looking like that…? Besides, I know what lies beneath that pretty dress of yours," he said obviously flirting with me and making my mouth droop slightly.

"Yes, well you know I think I could have picked out my own underwear!" I snapped making him reach for my silk wrap off the back of the armchair we had been stood close to before he said,

"Damn, why didn't I think of that, then you would have been forced to walk out here naked." I scowled at him without any real heat behind it and said,

"I had a towel, jackass." He then placed the wrap around my shoulders and told me in return,

"Yes, and I have hands, beautiful…*very capable hands.*" He emphasized those words with a quick squeeze of the top of my arms, before letting me go.

I rolled my eyes making him lean down slightly so he could whisper in my face,

"And one of them is itching for punishment, so you want to roll your eyes for me again, sugar?"

I swallowed hard and told him,

"Not unless you want to see my ass running." His lips tipped up on one side before telling me,

"As delicious as that sight would be, especially with me chasing it down like the fucking beast you have the power to turn me into…I think I have had quite enough of the action these last two months." I sucked in a quick breath before coming back with,

"Right, well better tell Mr twitchy palm to cool off then… yeah?" At this he laughed and said,

"With your sass, then I'm not sure that is possible." This made me smile, before I walked towards the door and said over my shoulder,

"Make it possible," I threatened again, making him chuckle before following me. Then just as he turned to close the door, I heard him mutter,

"Even the Gods wouldn't have that power, sweetheart."

Wow, so this really was a date then.

"Well, this is nice," I said after we were shown to a private table that looked to have the best view. It was a rooftop restaurant called the Cheese and Wine and it had the most spectacular views across the Jerusalem skyline. And according to the menu it also boasted the best selection of imported cheese and wine in the city.

The large open space was inviting with its pale woods, wine barrels and pale stone walls. It was also open all along one side with a roller blind of bamboo above, unnecessary without the elements trying to ruin this perfect night. There were also warm yellow waves of fabric swathed over the wooden beams above the long tables, creating an inviting experience of the city. One that was offered with unobstructed views watching the setting sun cast its golden hue over the Old City and at the same time offering you the chance to enjoy fine food and wine. And like I said…

It was perfect.

Lucius gave me a warm smile in return for my comment and

took the place of the waiter by holding my chair out for me. The gesture had me unable to hold back a secret grin, knowing that this was Lucius' way. Along with taking both menus from the waiter, obviously choosing to hand me mine after first seating himself. Then the waiter asked what we would like to drink,

"Would you like a bottle of wine?" Lucius enquired making me say,

"Not unless you're having some?"

"I'm not really the wine drinking type of guy," he told me with a smirk making me nod in a way that silently said, '*yeah, I got that'.*

"Then surprise me," I challenged making him accept it and after scanning a finger down the list, he said,

"I'll have a Taybeh dark and a Long Island Iced Tea, for my girl." I had to bite my lip to stop myself from both smiling at being referred to as his and also what he ordered me. But the moment the waiter walked away, I decided to keep up with ice queen pretence, so I leaned in closer over the table and hissed,

"That was mean." He laughed and said,

"No, what was mean was calling me when I couldn't get to you and making me miss the opportunity to see you drunk again."

"So, what is this, your hope at take two?" I asked in a testing tone.

"I am not sure you could handle it again, sweetheart." I snorted a disbelieving laugh at this, which granted wasn't the most ladylike sound I had in my arsenal, but still.

"I know what you are doing." I told him making him shrug his shoulders and say,

"And what would that be?"

"You're goading me into trying to prove how much I can drink so you can get me drunk." Just then our drinks turned up and once alone again he challenged,

"Does this mean I should call him back and order you a water?" I narrowed my eyes at him, picked up my cocktail and said,

"Challenge accepted, Vampire." Then I pulled out the straw, dumped it on the table and took a long drink the old-fashioned way. This made him smirk, before he tipped the neck of his bottle towards me then took a long swig himself.

And with that one look alone in his eyes, making them flash amber for a mere second I knew…

I was in trouble.

CHAPTER TWENTY-THREE

WATER FIGHTS AND MEDALS

The moment I woke up, I found myself asking my brain if it remembered why I felt like I had made a lot of foolish mistakes last night? And if it could possibly have anything to do with the consumption of lots and lots of alcohol, seeing as it felt like my head had been used as someone's drum last night. Okay, so granted this was a lot of questions for my poor brain to handle, which was why I closed my eyes again, rolled over and pulled the covers over my head with a groan. But then I felt and heard something I knew I really shouldn't have and that's precisely when all my bad mistakes started to crash into me. Starting with the chuckled laughter and shaking of the body next to me.

"Please brain, tell me I am only dreaming again?" I muttered making him say,

"I must say it's nice to know that dreaming of me in your bed is a regular occurrence." I groaned before muttering,

"Who said it is?" This was said with the covers still over my head.

"You said the word *again*." I closed my eyes tighter and hissed a,

"Damn it." Naturally, this was Lucius I had woken up next to, so he laughed again. Then he whipped the covers from my head, making me complain with a moan, and not of the 'making me feel good' variety.

"Good morning," he said in a way that sounded far too awake for him to have woken when I had. Hence why I complained,

"Gods, but how can you sound so awake this early in the morning."

"Because it's actually the afternoon and you snore when drunk…that, my little Khuba, *is why."* I continued to keep my eyes closed, rolled away from him, and said,

"Okay, you can stop talking now." Again, this amused him. Then I felt him shift his body closer, as he draped an arm around me from behind, pulling me back against his chest…*his very naked, hard chest.*

"I find it cute," he hummed behind me, making me warn,

"Lucius, stop talking." Of course, he ignored me and leaned down to whisper in my ear this time,

"And endearing."

"Lucius, I said stop talking," I warned yet again.

"And also, even a little sexy," he teased making me turn quickly in his arms, so I could slap his big bicep and say,

"I thought I told you…omg you're completely naked!" I shouted the second I saw the tangled sheet reveal as much. The sight making me react totally irrationally considering our history as I started to scramble backwards. But seeing as this was me, I misjudged the fact we were completely on my side, which meant I fell out of bed with an umpf. Then, after the chuckling had stopped, his head popped over the side and he said in a cocky tone,

"I believe we have been here before." I threw an arm over my face and grumbled,

"Great, does that mean I am allowed to slap you again?"

"Mmm, well, seeing as I know where it ends...*most definitely,*" he purred making me groan, even though my cheeks were going red under the cover of my arm.

"Although, I do remember you wearing significantly less clothes at the time," he said and I felt him pull at the t-shirt I wore, making it tent over my breasts with a pinch of his fingers. It was huge on me and obviously one of his that I had no recollection of changing into.

"As it shall stay," I told him dryly making him mutter,

"Spoilsport...you know, you were far more accommodating last night."

"I will now go back to my earlier statement of...Lucius, stop talking." He laughed and carried on anyway...but of course he did, I thought rolling my eyes under my arm.

"In fact, it was harder to get you into clothes, seeing as you were determined to keep taking them off and throwing them at me." I lifted my arm and muttered up at it,

"Oh my Gods, you're evil." He ignored this and continued to add to my horror,

"I can honestly say, that in all my years, I have never felt so much like a rock star as I did last night."

"Correction, make that primeval," I muttered making him laugh.

"Are you intending to stay down there for the rest of the day?"

"Yes, at least until I am thirty," I told him, hearing for myself the grin... how, I didn't know but I would have put money on it being there.

"Then should I join you and we can make camp?" I couldn't help it, I laughed at that.

"I never took you for the boy scout type, Lucius."

"That depends, are they wine drinkers or beer?" This brought back some memories of how the night started, making me want to gasp in horror as they started to flow back to me. But instead of giving anything away I told him,

"The only grape you will find those kids drinking is of the Kool-Aid variety." Of course, he saw through my bullshit strained response and said,

"Your memories of last night are starting to come back to you, aren't' they?"

"No, they are not, and I swear if you mention the D word, then I will shoot you…I'm getting quite good with a gun now, you know."

"Yes, but like you said, they take murder quite seriously here…now come back on the bed," was his answer.

"No, I'm fine down here and given your last comment, I think it's safer for you if I…hey!" I complained the second I felt him get out of bed, lifting me into his arms before putting me back in bed.

"And just what D word is it you're referring to?" he asked, now I was back in his arms and I had to admit, there was most definitely worse places to be.

"Lucius," I said his name in warning, as he started to whisper,

"Dinner?"

"Lucius," I continued to warn him on a growl,

"Drinking?" he tried again, making me raise my hands to my ears and say,

"Lalalala, not listening." Then I felt him shackle my wrists and forcefully pull my hands down so he could whisper against my jaw this time,

"Dancing." I turned my face away and shouted,

"Gaaahh!"

"Be at ease, sweetheart, the night was an enjoyable one and that is all that matters," he told me, his voice sincere and comforting.

"Well, at least I wasn't sick this time," I pointed out making him chuckle.

"There is also that." I finally decided it was time to get serious, so I rolled back to face him, so we were both on our sides. Then I tucked a piece of hair behind my ear in a nervous gesture. He watched me do it silently, with a half-smile playing at his lips.

"Ask your question, Amelia."

"It's just…did we, I mean last night…did we, you know?" I said rolling my hand around in between us making him grab it in his and pull it close to his lips so he could start biting on the tips of my fingers. Then he repeated,

"Did we…? You're gonna have to be more specific here…I believe we did lots of things last night." I rolled my eyes, ignoring that spark of heated amber in his eyes and said,

"Did we have sex, Lucius?"

"See that wasn't too hard now, was it?"

"Kind of part of my question, Lucius." I responded dryly, referring to his obvious manhood that usually needed to be hard to achieve what I was getting at. Something Lucius clearly didn't have any difficulties with, seeing as the bloody thing always looked ready!

"As disappointing as it is for me to admit, the answer is no, we did not. As trust me, sweetheart, one you would have remembered and two, my preference in a partner during the act is for them to be a little more coherent than your drunken state allowed." God's, but I swear he was trying to get my cheeks to melt right off the bone! A fact he didn't fail to notice seeing as he was currently running the back of a finger down my heated skin.

"But I remember you carrying me to the bed and then us kissing and then...well granted, I don't remember much after that," I confessed.

"That's because before that part of the night could continue as I would have liked, your head touched the pillow and you passed out."

"And this?" I asked looking down at myself, referring to his t shirt.

"That was to hide the temptation from waking you up by continuing where we left off...it was for both our benefits, trust me, getting you out of your dress was torturous enough," he said and looked strained as if the memory flashed back to him. My chuckle prompted him to add,

"I'm talking medals need to be purchased and awarded here, Amelia." I blushed at this and tucked in my chin to smile. At this he got closer to me, lifted my face to his and whispered,

"Big, huge, fucking medals." So, I tried to talk past my smirk and said,

"I will see what they have on Amazon." He laughed at this and flicked my nose before shifting back and giving me at least a few more inches of space.

"Wow, I don't even remember what it was we ate for dinner," I said after my stomach chose that moment to growl.

"That would be down to the four cocktails before it and the three after it...don't worry, I made sure you ate, and you hydrated," he said nodding to the bottle of water next to the bed that was half empty.

"And the reason we are in bed together and you're...erm, well clearly naked?" At this he grinned, looking down at himself and the abundance of muscles on show...I mean jeez, a girl didn't have a chance! Especially when he lifted the sheet that was once again rested at his waist. Then he looked down at his body, one that was making a statement of saying hello to me in a very 'erected' and obvious way,

"Well, would you look at that, I am naked…oops." At this I laughed and shook my head at his obvious playful mood.

"As for sharing a bed, it's my bed, sweetheart." I looked around the room, and seemingly taking it in for the first time now I was sober. I looked up to see the beautiful mosaic masterpiece on the domed ceiling, making me wonder what I had said about this room last night.

It looked like some King's bedchamber, making you ask yourself what era of history you had woken up in. With its archways of mixed blocks of sandstone and rose coloured marble, framed with even more mosaic tiles in its carved alcoves. Even the floor of pale stone framing the centre square of rose/orange marble, made the room warm and tranquil. And like the rest of the suite, it was adorned with chunky wooden furniture, with the bed being no exception. The headboard was a ladder of thick twisted spindles that matched the two larger ones at the end of the bed. White sheets and a plush wine-red comforter that now lay crumpled at the foot of the bed and half draped over the bench seat at the bottom.

But his comment about it being his bed made me point out,

"Ah, so what you're saying is the extent of your gentlemanly ways is limited to opening doors and passing menus?" I asked after propping my head up on my hand with my elbow to the bed. He smirked and said,

"Do I look like the type of guy to sleep on a fucking couch…especially with such a temptation in my bed?" I tried not to blush again or bite my fingertips, instead giving him my sass,

"I don't know, Lucius, you're not the type of guy to drink wine and you're not the type of guy to sleep on the couch…"

"And your point is exactly?"

"Just peeling back the layers, handsome," I said with a shrug.

"Well, whilst you're peeling, then you should know that I am also the type of guy who puts his woman to bed when she drinks too much and passes out, instead of the way I had intended her to pass out. I am also the type of guy who hides that temptation and doesn't take advantage of the beauty at my fingertips." I released a shuddered breath I tried to hide, as his words hit their mark as intended.

"And just how did you intend for it to go?" I was almost too scared to ask,

"If you have to ask me that question, then I believe a history lesson will be in order." Another shudder later and I was backtracking.

"You know what, I think the answer just came to me, so I'm good." I practically squeaked out the answer making him smirk. Then I reached for the water, opened the cap, and said,

"Well, lucky for you, looking after drunken girls seemed to be your forte, and takes precedence over your less than gentlemanly ways...t-shirt or not." At this I started to drink the water, which ended in a high-pitched shout of horror the second after he said,

"Is that so...um, time for another lesson then." After this he grabbed me and just as he was quickly shifting me beneath him, the open bottle of water went everywhere. Splashing his face but mainly it went over me and ended up soaking the front of my white t shirt. One that quickly started to turn see-through.

"Lucius!" I called his name and then to prove how little he cared, he shook his head at me, making the water from his hair drip over me as he laughed. Then he grabbed the bottle and tossed it to the side, before running a hand through his now damp hair, pushing it back so that the longer parts weren't in his face. Gods, but the sight was one that would certainly feature in my fantasies…that was if I could ever get my fingers back up to the task of helping a girl out in sexual frustration!

But then my breath caught in my throat the second he started to scan down the front of my body. My pounding chest making my breasts rise and fall under the wet cotton, and well, his grin said it all even when his words followed,

"I must say, sugar, I am enjoying the view…*immensely.*" The way he said this last word was like a promise of what was to come and the way my nipples were now straining up against the wet material…well, I would say that the traitorous bitches were responding.

"Lucius." His name slipped out on a moan the second the back of his fingers skimmed across one taut nipple. But at the breathy sound of his name escaping my lips was when his restraint snapped. His lips were suddenly on me, his weight pressing me into the bed, and I found myself arching up to meet him. Then I felt the material on my top get tight as he quickly had it bunched in his hand at my back. It became so tight across my breasts that the wet material felt like it had become a second layer of skin, one he was very interested in exploring. I knew this the moment he left my lips and dipped his head down so he could take a wet nipple into his eager mouth. Doing so straight through the material and making me cry out at the intense pleasure that zapped through me like some sexual bolt of lightning!

"Gods," I muttered on a sigh and his lips spread into a knowing grin around my nipple before he started biting it and this time I cried out,

"Fuck!"

Now this made him chuckle before telling me above my flesh,

"That's better." Then he went back to it, driving me wild. And just as I felt myself getting lost in the feel of it all, something kept nagging at me. Something I wanted to ignore, knowing how desperate I had been for him. But as I felt his hand skimming down my belly, letting me know where his destination was, this was when it really started to scream at me. The fucking doubts! Which was why, in the end, it was my own words that woke me up from this dangerous fantasy,

"Gods, that feels so good…so good…Lucius wait!" I shouted at the same time shackling his wrist and stopping him from going any further. This was because a memory of last night finally made it through and now wouldn't leave me. It was one of the things I had asked him in my drunken mind,

"Why is it called a goodbye, when there was nothing good about it?" I repeated the question as it came to me and his head rose slowly from my breast. One look at my face was all it took for him to know the problem. As he too remembered the reasons I had even asked this of him last night.

We had our goodbyes and they had hurt…they had near fucking destroyed me!

"And there she goes again," he muttered raising himself up from me.

"I can't do this…I can't let myself…"

"Ssshh, stop, Amelia," he said sternly before taking me in his arms and holding the back of my head to his chest, before telling me,

"We are still due that chat you and I, which I will give you as I know you need it…." Then he eased his hold and tugged on my hair a little telling me to look back at him,

"Just as long as you realise that after we do, this…what we have right here…it doesn't change a thing." I swallowed hard and forced his name through my lips, intent on telling him I didn't even know what.

"Lucius, I…" he quickly interrupted me, obviously not taking any chances on what I was about to say.

"I am not going anywhere…End. Of. Discussion." His firm voice brooked no argument in the matter, so I didn't even try.

"Now this is what is going to happen, I am going to order us some room service whilst you have a shower."

"So, I need one then?" I asked on a laugh. He grinned and told me,

"You taste just fine to me, sweetheart, even if you do smell like a cocktail bar." Then he caught me under my chin and gave it a little playful shake before he left the bed, walking away now with his gorgeous ass on show making me say,

"Oh, come on! Seriously, give a girl a chance!" He chuckled to the sound of my rant and whilst completely naked stood there with the hotel phone in hand as he ordered a selection of food to be brought up. This was when I thought it best to get my ass up, one that thankfully wasn't on show due to his t-shirt looking more like a short dress on me…*a wet one.*

Then, whilst he was preoccupied, I ran into the bathroom and did what was needed, ending up in his shower once more. In fact, I was just enjoying the solitude and the feel of the powerful jets raining down on me when a very powerful and also, very naked figure walked around the shower wall and joined me. My hands flew to my girly bits making him raise an eyebrow and tell me,

"Even if I didn't already have every inch of you burned to my memory, then the image of you without your dress on from only last night will be…*everlasting,*" he said, whispering this last word down at me before taking my place and ducking his head under the spray, making it near hard to breathe at just the sight. Then I heard him clear his throat before asking with a knowing grin,

"You finished or do you want me to help?" I bit my lip, blushed, and told him in a shy voice,

"I've finished." Then as I turned from him, I felt a hand

span my belly as he pulled me back against his naked front as he rumbled in my ear a growled insight to his thoughts.

Thoughts that soaked me much more than the shower did, for his words felt more like a promise…

"Now that is a shame."

CHAPTER TWENTY-FOUR

TRUST TALKING TO TIE OUR SINS

After this sexual promise of his in the shower, I got out quickly leaving him to his knowing chuckle. Then I made quick work of getting dry, dressed, and looking somewhat human again. And I achieved this by tying my hair up into a high ponytail, putting in some new contacts, that I had been able to order online, and adding a light touch of makeup, concentrating on the dark circles under my eyes...*thank you, hangover.*

I decided this time to forgo the usual t-shirt and shorts that he had found me wearing yesterday, opting for something a little sexier...because like I said, *only human.* So, today's choice reflected on what I would have picked, had I known the love of my 'broken hearted' life would show up. Which was why I was naming this outfit, 'a little late to punish him with how nice I looked', deciding it was better late than never.

So, I snapped the pearl pop buttons together on my shirt dress that was a tight tunic style with a mandarin collar. The chest area had rows of embroidered flowers in the same pink, blush rose colour as the shirt and each was edged with white tipped petals.

The dress came to mid-thigh, so showed off a good amount of my legs and I added a belt to pull it tight at the waist, giving me what I hoped was an hourglass shape. The belt was three rows of plaited black leather that matched a pair of black leather ballet flats I slipped on my feet. But it was the pearl buttons that only started in line with my nipples that made it what I hoped was sexy, as it certainly offered an eyeful of cleavage…thank you balcony bra!

Then, once I was ready, I found Lucius sat in the living room waiting for me and he was also on the phone. He saw me the second I entered, and I found myself quietly congratulating myself on the choice of outfit. This was because the heated look in his eyes made them look as if they were burning for me. The way he took his time scanning my body and making a show of letting me know that he liked what he saw. Then, without looking away from me, told whoever was on the phone,

"I want it here by morning… make it happen." After this he hung up, making me wonder what it was he wanted to 'make happen' this time. Huh, maybe it was the shopping list of chloroform, chains, and the coffin I had first been expecting.

"Come here, pretty girl," he ordered gently, and I soon found the tip of my thumb in my mouth before I realised I was giving in to the habit. Then I ignored the twitch of humour playing at his lips and walked closer to where he sat on what was a warm yellow coloured sofa, one that matched the rest of the room's sunset tones.

Then he rose from the seat, seeing that my response to his order wasn't what he wanted as I left space between us. Then, before he could face me, I veered off towards the private terrace, one that was overlooking the wonderful view of the Old

City of Jerusalem and what was known as the Mount of Olives. It was a mountain ridge east of and adjacent to Jerusalem's Old City and it was named from the olive groves that once covered its slopes.

The mountain ridge had also been used as a Jewish cemetery for over 3,000 years and held approximately 150,000 graves, making it central as was the tradition of Jewish cemeteries. It was one of the places Yosef had taken me to and explained its history to me. This included several key events in the life of Jesus, as related in the Gospels, events that took place on the Mount of Olives and is described as the place from which Jesus ascended to Heaven. So naturally the mount has been a site of Christian worship since ancient times and seeing it now on the terrace with Lucius at my back was…well, a startling contrast of events, given his own history and the part he played. Which was why I wanted to ask him, how he felt about being back here?

It was why I wanted to hear his own story being told by his own words. I wanted to know everything about him and being here together only ended up fueling that burning desire to know and adding to what I knew was dangerous curiosity.

"Time for us to talk, little Šemšā," he said and unfortunately, I knew what this talk would include, and it was nothing about what my mind was currently focused on. Which was why, that after Lucius had said this, I suddenly wasn't feeling hungry. In fact, one look at the doorway that led into the bedroom and I was tempted to fake a headache, blaming it on a hangover and hoping that I could just go and hide in the bed for the rest of the day.

Of course, the second I felt a hand span the small of my back, then I knew the chances of this were slim at best. Besides, he wasn't the only one who needed answers. But this was where my problem lay, as I wasn't sure I was ready to relive that day, no matter what he had to say about it. But I did, however, need to know what his intentions were now. Because if he didn't intend to take me back to my parents, then what was his plan...*why had he come at all?*

Well, I think one thing was obvious and that was Lucius still felt strongly for me. As clearly no-one would go as far as he had done. Not only by still trying to find me after all this time, but also in the way he kissed me. The way he had missed me. I was hurt, but I wasn't stupid or blind enough not to see sincerity in his actions. So, to say that confused seemed to be a constant state of my mind this last twenty-four hours was naturally a huge understatement.

"Let's just take this one step at a time, should we?" Lucius suggested, obviously feeling my anxiety and resistance. Especially seeing as I hadn't yet taken one step towards the table.

"That sounds good," I answered before letting him lead me onto the private terrace that had been set up for us with a large selection of food spread out on the round dining table...*including cheese.*

"Didn't we have enough of this last night?" I asked on a laugh, nodding at the large platter and making him smirk.

"Ah, so you have started to remember?" he asked as once again he held out a seat for me to take.

"I haven't forgotten it all, no," I replied trying to will myself not to blush because of it.

"Well, you're the one who demanded I order the English cheese board, getting very excited about cheddar if I am remembering correctly," he informed me as he took his own seat next to mine.

"Mmm, the cranberry cheddar was yummy, oh and village oak."

"But not the Stilton if I recall?" he laughed at the memory of my face as I scrunched up my nose, because eww.

"Oh yeah, now that was some potent stuff…Hell, we should have taken some with us in case we need to knock out the witch, she's like a bad penny that one and bound to show up again," I said making him scoff,

"Yes, well, unfortunately I think it's going to take a lot more than cheese to defeat the bitch."

"Smelly cheese, don't forget that part." He smirked at me before motioning to the platters and saying,

"Hence why I told them to leave that particular choice off the board." My eyes went to where he pointed and I grinned big,

"Aww, you ordered me my cheeses again, you big romantic you!" He laughed at this and muttered,

"Easily pleased I see." At this I picked up one of the fresh rolls and threw it at him, making him spill half his coffee on the table.

"Oh shit, I'm sorry… but seriously, can you go back to being super reflex Vamp and start catching shit again?" I complained making him grant me a look before telling me,

"Or another idea…crazy I know, but you could refrain from throwing things at me and solve both our problems." I rolled my lips inwards trying to hold back the grin and said,

"Yeah, but Lucius, this is you we are talking about, chances are high that I *will want to throw stuff at you again."* He paused, mopping up his coffee with a napkin and grinned at me.

"Then how about I create an incentive not to."

"Not sure you have anything to bargain with, but I am open to hearing my options," I replied before taking a bite of the apple I had plucked from the fruit bowl. He watched this with hungry eyes flashing like the burning sun before he leaned in close. Then he took hold of the arm of my chair and suddenly tugged it closer towards him. I yelped a little before he gave me his incentive,

"How about you get to keep your delicious ass without finding it over my knee, wearing a pretty shade of red in the shape of my hand...*incentive enough for you?*" he asked before taking hold of my wrist and taking a huge bite out of my apple, doing so with it still in my hand.

"Erm, yeah, that sounds like a good trade," I said making him nod once before letting me go. But when I tried to shift my chair back, his hand shot out to the armrest and stopped me.

"I like you close," was his only response to this and it was one that had my heart pounding. After which I poured myself a cup of tea, needing to do something with my hands. But I still had to clear my throat before asking him,

"How's your coffee? Better now it's in a cup, eh?" At which the intense moment left us, and he burst out laughing.

"It's fine, but my palm is itching again."

"You know you should get that looked at...I bet they have a cream that could help," I said before taking a sip of my tea and then winking at him over the rim of my cup. He lowered the paper he had started reading, in Hebrew of course, and replied with,

"Duct tape could also help, now eat your lunch before I make enquiries on where to get some." At this my lips twitched as I fought a smile at our banter, knowing just how much I had missed it. After this I took his advice and piled a plate up, making sure to get a good amount of that cheese I liked.

It also helped me relax more because we hadn't just sat down and started discussing the giant anvil sized question mark hanging over our heads. This was until my belly was full and I couldn't stand it any longer.

"So, I take it you didn't just decide to pick Jerusalem as

your next holiday destination and just happened to find me when sightseeing at the museum did you?"

"Unlike a nerdy little beauty I know, I don't usually step off a plane and travel directly to the first museum I can find," he told me making me tempted to ask why he did then, only I wasn't brave enough.

"That's a shame, there are plenty of treasures to be found at them," I teased to which he lowered the paper, stole my gaze, and said,

"I believe I found the only treasure I was looking for, now let's talk about the part where I am keeping her." After this, and I swear it was a good job I hadn't been trying to swallow food as I think I would have choked!

"Lucius I…" I stumbled on my words as I didn't know what to say to that. But in the end, it didn't matter as it turned out that Lucius had plenty to say about it.

"Alright, so before we get to the root of why you ran from me, I want you to first ask yourself an important question, setting aside those doubts of yours that are obviously flooding your mind." I cleared my throat first, and forced out,

"Which is?"

"Why would I be here now if I was in love with another and why am I not trying to get you back to Afterlife if I was doing it solely for that mistaken love?" I swallowed hard and felt that weight in my chest that you do when facing difficult questions.

"If I am honest, I have been asking myself the very same thing since you showed up and told me that you're not taking me back to Afterlife." At this he looked pleased, making me state,

"I am not unreasonable enough not to ask myself obvious questions, despite what I saw that day."

"What you *think* you saw," he quickly corrected.

"There are very few ways to interpret what I saw and heard

Lucius, you must know that?" I told him making him release a frustrated sigh.

"I get that, but you must also know that you're not the only one who feels betrayed here." At this I jerked back in my seat, one I shifted further away from his and said,

"You're joking right?!"

"Do me a favour, Amelia, and just for one fucking second put yourself in my position."

"I'd rather not," I snapped folding my arms and looking away from him. Yet he continued on as if I hadn't.

"Say I was the one who saw an innocent moment of comfort you accepted from a friend, only the way it looked was much more than what it was. Say I was the one to listen to a conversation between you and this friend that sounded like some forbidden love being confessed, when in fact, every single word that was said with me in your mind?"

"I think you can stop talking now," I said hating where this was going…destination guilt trip that's where!

"No! You are going to fucking listen to me, like you should have done the second you stepped out from behind that staircase!" he snapped getting angry, rising from his chair, and then making me do the same. So, I backed away as he started to stalk towards me.

"Every word that was said between me and Keira was about you! About the love that both you and your fucking mother spent all your time convincing me to keep quiet about, when it went against everything inside me to do so!"

"Lucius, please let's just…" I started to say before he interrupted me as he came even closer, causing me to edge my way around the table trying to keep it between us.

"And look what fucking happened!"

"Calm down, Lucius," I told him as his eyes started to change, only this time it was two pools of crimson sun that were staring back at me. That's when all that calm cool shell of his totally evaporated, and I knew it was from weeks and weeks of this building up.

"Calm down?! You think that I have had one fucking chance to calm down this whole time! Fuck sake, Amelia, the one and only time I felt anything close to fucking calm was when I saw you yesterday before having your hand in mine!" I sucked in a quick breath and said,

"What did you expect me to do, Lucius, I saw you kissing my fucking mother for Gods' sake!" At this he roared and flipped the table between us making me scream as it smashed against the wall. I raised my hands up to prevent anything from touching me, but this wasn't a problem as Lucius was right there in front of me.

"No! Put me down!" I demanded the second I found myself over his shoulder, hitting his back as if this would help. Then long strides later I felt myself falling the moment he bent forward, making me cry out in surprise before landing on the bed, bouncing twice as I did. After this I quickly felt my wrists being shackled by his hands before I had chance to use them to aid my escape from the bed. Then my arms were being pinned above my head and suddenly my leather belt was being tugged from my waist.

"Lucius, what are you…?"

"Silence!" he snapped as he yanked the length from under me, jerking my body. A second later and his intentions became obvious, as he wrapped it around my wrists with speed. He bound my hands and then tied me to the wooden spindles on the bed frame.

And it was only once I was unable to go anywhere, that he took a breath and sat back on his knees. I swallowed down a lump put there by both fear and lust and took in the sight of him, wisely doing as I was told by keeping quiet. He continued to take large purposeful breaths, obviously needing to ease his demon. And after making a point to look at my bound wrists, he finally spoke,

"There…"

"Now I am fucking calm."

CHAPTER TWENTY-FIVE

BOUND TO BLOOD

I tugged on my arms, discovering there was no give and now that he had calmed down, I let my own anger show through.

"Great, so glad I could help with that one!" I snapped, jerking once more at my bound wrists to make my point. One he didn't look to take seriously.

"Now, I ask of you Amelia, how would you have felt being in my position had I been the one to run from you, run from the love you had tried to so hard to convince me of feeling…how would you have felt had I been the one to run before giving you the chance to explain?" At this I turned my head away, hating that he could be right…because if it was true, which from his actions now, it seemed to be, then how would I have felt? I hated being forced to feel that doubt, one that was just as painful as my own beliefs.

"I see my words are starting to sink in, something that would have sank in a lot sooner had you not run from me and given me the opportunity to explain."

"You could have just lied to me again, Lucius," I told him with a grit of my teeth making him release a sigh before shifting so he was now stretched out next to me. Then he started brushing back the loose strands of my hair that had escaped during our tussle before leaning forward so he could smell my hair.

"Yes, and you could have chosen to trust me," he said, speaking against my hairline before pulling back.

"Trust is earned, Lucius… not demanded," I informed him, referring to more than our time together but our history as a whole.

"You're right and will no doubt take me a long time to do so again." I scowled at him and snapped

"I haven't lied to you!"

"No, but you ran from me and it will therefore take me a while to trust that you won't do that again," he informed me calmly, which only managed to make me angrier than if he had been back to shouting at me.

"Oh, so what, you gonna put me on a leash?!" I snapped making him grin,

"Don't give me ideas, *Pet*…" he said putting emphasis on the word before adding,

"…I think you would look fucking sexy wearing a collar with a chain attached from it, to my fist." I sneered at him and snapped,

"Yeah well, this bitch bites, Lucius, and not in a way you will fucking like!" Then I looked down at his cock, making my point by nodding to his hard erection that was pressing against his jeans. However, having him throw his head back and laugh, had me asking,

"Seriously, you're Bipolar aren't you?"

"Around you, starting to feel like it sweetheart," he commented wryly.

"Let me go," I demanded, seeing as he seemed to be in a better mood again.

"No… now tell me your fears, and let's get this done." So much for good moods, I thought irritably.

"I don't want to talk about it like this!" I snapped, yanking on my hands, and making the bed shake a little. The corner of his mouth tipped up into a dark grin as he told me,

"I like you like this."

"Well, I don't!" I shouted, making him snap back in sight of my anger,

"Yes, well I have just spent eight weeks hunting your ass down and that, Amelia…that, *I didn't like so much!*"

"Fine! Then I will just live like this then…can't wait until I need a pee!" I snapped making him chuckle and making me hiss under my breath,

"Bipolar, asshole."

"Yeah, well this asshole has you at his mercy, so maybe think about that the next time you want me to feel the sting of venom from your tongue," he threatened making me scoff,

"What I want is for you to release me so you can feel the sting of my hand as I slap you!"

"Yes, and we always know where that gets you, and sweetheart, if you wanted me to kiss you, then all you need to do is ask…or beg, depending on my mood."

"I wouldn't beg you for anything!" I shouted up at him, at the same time raising my head as much as my restraints would allow, so as to put action behind the statement.

"Oh, I bet you would, especially as I have a feeling that my girl has been suffering from the loss of my hands…*and my lips…*" he said lowering himself to my collar bone and kissing across it after first popping a few of my buttons open, freeing one shoulder. I purposely held back a moan and muttered instead,

"You wish." Then I felt his knowing grin against my skin before he kissed his way up my neck and along my jaw before coming to my lips.

"No, I don't wish, I know... *for I have felt that same loss, my girl."* He whispered this last part before kissing me. But I refused to participate, which is when he started to coax me to.

"Open up for me, sweetheart." I shook my head keeping my mouth closed. Because I was angry, and I was hurt and most of all I was confused. But throughout all of these things, I refused him because I knew that nothing would be solved with a kiss, one that would only end up playing on my emotions. So, I held strong, turned my face away and said,

"Release me." He started kissing my jaw once more, nipping at it until his fingers took hold of my chin so he could force me back to his lips.

"Open for me, and I will think about it." I shook my head once more, gritting out a hissed,

"No" and his reply was a bad ass grin that should have told me that he was a long way from being done with me.

"But you look so beautiful when you open that pretty mouth for me," he said, his tone smooth and dangerous. So, I made a point of rolling my lips inwards and shaking my head.

"I always get what I want, Amelia, *remember that,"* he warned and just as I was about to shake my head once more his hand was suddenly cupping my sex and before I could shift away from it, he slipped a hand inside the waistband of my panties. Then the second he touched my clit I gasped, and of course...

He was there ready.

His tongue invaded my mouth and his kiss turned hot and heavy in seconds. The sounds of him growling combined with my desperate moans meant that with only a few minutes of having his fingers drumming that fuckable beat against my sex,

I was on the cusp of screaming his name. When suddenly, his hand cruelly disappeared.

"No! Please!" I shouted as my sex fluttered in little pre come spasms. He chuckled and I swear I hated him for it but not as much as when he said,

"See, sweetheart, I knew you would beg for it!" I growled up at him as he rose back to sitting on his knees. Then just as he yanked open his jeans, I snarled because I was furious,

"Go to Hell!" He grinned down at me, after first yanking his grey t-shirt over his head, before suddenly my panties were torn down my legs, making me gasp. Then he positioned himself in between my thighs and I couldn't help but squirm at the sight. He slowly lowered himself down over me and said,

"Without you…My Khuba, *I was already there!*" Then he thrust up inside me and swallowed my cries of pleasure with his fervent kiss. The sheer size of him made me glad that he had got me all hot and bothered first as I was soaked, and needed to be, as Gods, had he always been this big?!

But then his kiss stopped and instead he lifted himself up so he could look down at me, slowing down his thrusts. Then he placed his forehead to mine and whispered the most beautiful words I could have heard in that moment, erasing all others before it,

"Finally, I'm home." I closed my eyes, as I felt the tears start to rise, the emotions almost too much to bear but ones I treasured all the same. I tugged on my arms, forgetting that they were tied as I wanted to touch him. So, knowing this, he yanked hard on the leather tied to the bed making it snap. After which I was then free to lower them, hooking my still bound wrists over his neck, before lifting myself up and whispering over his lips,

"Home."

His response was to groan a throaty sound, before crushing his lips to mine and consuming me with all that was Lucius.

After this he didn't hold back in making me his once more, claiming a lot more than just my body, but my heart right along with it. He couldn't seem to get enough of me, his hands were everywhere, on my ass, lifting me to his thrusts and making me cry out every time he hit those delicious nerves. Doing so now in a way unlike he had ever done before, and I felt something coming that I never had before.

"Lucius I...I don't know..." He chuckled no doubt at my innocence and pulled my hands from behind his neck so he could pin my wrists to the bed. After this he whispered down at me,

"It's alright, just let it go, let it gush for me...*trust me.*" After which he continued, moving in a certain way that made his cock entice something from deep inside me. I didn't quite understand what it was but the urge to release something more than just my orgasm was overwhelming me, as if I feared it. Then I was crying out in both horror and an almost blinding pleasure unlike I had ever experienced before as it erupted from me. He pulled his cock free and looked down to watch as my release sprayed up all over us, making him smirk down at me as if he wasn't just pleased, *he was fucking ecstatic!*

"Oh...Gods I...I..." I didn't know what to say but before I could utter my mortification, he decided for me what would come next.

"Now again," he declared making my eyes widen before he was filling me again and doing the same over and over making me scream and beg and plead with him, Yes! No! Gods, anything just for him to never stop. I don't know how many more times I came this way and each time he would pull out to watch, as if he had opened the floodgates and broken something within me. The way he continued to force them out of me, telling me after each one,

"Again!" But I was soon shaking my head and telling him,

"I can't…no more, I can't…oh Gods! Gods, Lucius I am… Fuck! AH…AH…AAHHH!" I screamed as the biggest and longest orgasm ripped through me and I swear it had the power to tear me in two! I ended up dragging in big lungful's of air, panting with my sex quivering around him as he looked down at me and said,

"I told you, you would remember it, and now… it's my turn!" he said, after releasing my wrists so I finally had the use of my hands…hands he had plans for. I knew this after he suddenly ripped open my dress shirt, the sound of the buttons snapping open all at once echoing in the room. My heaving breasts seemed to strain up towards him, rising with every thrust he made with his hands at my hips yanking me down onto his length.

"Free them for me and offer yourself for my teeth," he ordered nodding down to my breasts and with fumbling hands I did as he asked, pulling them both free from the black silk cups.

"Lift one to my lips, offer it to me, my fuckable, sweet girl," he said making me bite my lip as I shamefully did as he asked, as though he was my master and I was there to please him. A thought that only made my sex quiver around his cock when he stilled a moment. Then he took what I offered him, making me cry out at the first pinch of pain and then when it morphed into utter bliss! I found my hands in his hair, gripping onto him, with the strands fisted through my fingers as I anchored him to me.

"Yes, yes, Gods yes!" I cried out as his hips continued to a steady rhythm that he chose, obviously wanting to make our first time back together last as long as possible. But then I wasn't sure how much more pleasure my body could take. So, I lifted up to his ear and whispered,

"Come honey, come inside me…I want you to claim me again, the only way you know how." My words did something to him. I knew this from the sound of his growl around my

abused nipple. I also saw this after he lifted his head to look down at me, his eyes blazing into mine. Then his hand was in my hair, yanking it to the side before telling me,

"Mine...always...*Fucking. Mine!*" then he swooped down and finally...*finally*...he made every last piece of me his, like his dark words of passion promised he would. A promise sealed by the bite of my Vampire King. His fangs pierced my neck and I cried out,

"YES!" Then he started drinking down my blood making me come undone around him, for it felt as though I hadn't just come home, it felt as if I had discovered the heart of it! Every pull of blood he sucked down seemed to tug at my last orgasm, making it last until I was a shaking mess like a fucking crimson leaf in the storm that was Lucius.

But wait...

Where had that thought just come from?

I didn't have long to think on it before Lucius tore his bloody lips from my neck and just as he held me so tight to him, I knew the last thrusts of his cock were all it would take before he came inside me. But before he did, he held my head to his neck and said,

"I'm yours, every fucking piece of me belongs to you! I love you, Gods, how I fucking love you! Now claim me! Bite and claim me now!" He roared just as he made me bite down on him and the second his blood burst across my tongue, he fisted my hair and roared!

"RAWWWHHH!" It was a sound that this time had the power to crack the walls above the bed. He bellowed his release as he continued to power into me, draining himself of every last drop until he was seated deep within my core.

After this I felt him lower my head gently back onto the bed, easing my lips from his neck. I couldn't help but smile to myself at the sight I left, looking up at the crescent shaped cuts on his neck that I had made.

My mark.

My claim.

And one look at his bloodstained lips and I knew mine were the same. Something that turned into a crimson kiss, as he placed his lips to mine, this time in a sweet tender way that spoke only of the love he had declared to still have for me. One that this time couldn't be denied, despite all my doubts.

What had just happened between us couldn't have been faked…

It just wasn't possible.

"Are you alright?" he asked softly after pushing all my hair back from my damp forehead. I couldn't help but nod before saying in a breathy tone,

"So, you missed me then?" to which he threw his head back and burst into laughter… gut clenching, belly shaking, laughter. The kind that I felt everywhere, including my sex seeing as he was still seated deep within me. Then, when his amusement had eased, he licked his lips until the blood was mostly gone. Then he kissed my forehead and what he said next had the power to heal my heart for good.

Healed from the hurt the second he whispered tenderly…

"Every damn day, baby."

CHAPTER TWENTY-SIX

BOY SCOUT AMBUSH

The rest of the day was spent together and would have no doubt been in his bed, had it well...not been for the mess he had forced me to make. Geez, but just thinking about it made me start squirming and from the knowing spark of power in his eyes, then he knew it too. But since then we'd had sex three more times and I had to say by the time night started to fall, I was feeling it, both between my legs and with how tired I was.

But then, I most certainly wasn't regretting it, as it had been like being reunited with an addiction. One, that granted was dangerous for my health considering the amount of my blood he had consumed. Although, he had also made sure I fed from him every time as well and I had an idea this was his way of trying to get back that bond. The exchange of our essence and what strengthened that link between Chosen Ones.

It was clear he wanted that connection back and I was only too eager to give it to him. But sex, after the first time, had been a mixture of frenzied sex in the shower, then playful sex on the sofa and last of all, making love. It had been slow, sensual, and adoring. And it had also been on fresh clean sheets back on the bed. This was after the chambermaid had come in and I had told her we were sorry, that I was clumsy and spilled water on the bed…all in a rush of words. Something Lucius ruined the second he said in perfect Hebrew,

"What she is trying to say is that I fucked her like a beast, and she loved it, but now she is shy because we made a mess." Something I learned once the horrified woman left the room making a sign of God and I'd asked what he had said to her. I knew some Hebrew but nothing like Lucius' skills. Of course, I had been mortified hearing this and hence how we ended up having playful sex on the sofa, which I made sure we didn't make a mess on, this time.

But now, we had just finished making love. And honestly, it had been so utterly perfect that I felt myself getting emotional and having to hold back the signs of it. However, with the moonlight pouring in through the open windows and the hum of the city outside, it was a moment that I would never forget.

Especially with my body curled to his side and with him looking down at me the way he was. The way his gloved hand tipped back my face so I could look up at him, then he ran a covered thumb over the apple of my cheek and said,

"Gods, but how I have missed these stunning eyes of yours…no wonder I would dream of them every night, looking up at me the way you do now." I blushed and turned my face quickly so I could kiss the palm of his bound hand, making him tense a little at the contact. Contact, I had never braved to attempt before, but then as soon as the gesture was done, he relaxed, lowered his hand, and pulled me tighter against him. Then he kissed my forehead, calling me,

"My Sweet girl." I grinned before teasing him,

"Yeah, but I bet you weren't calling me that only two days ago." I felt him smile and admit in a knowing tone,

"No, I was not calling you that, Amelia."

"I never asked, but how did you find me?"

"Apparently dumb luck can happen to us all," he replied making me hit his belly, although little good it did me with all those tight abs bunched like a brick wall of muscle.

"Hey!" I shouted, making him question,

"And did it happen any other way?"

"Well no, but still, give me a little credit here," I grumbled, knowing that dripping blood into that box had been more luck and less intelligence.

"Oh, my girl, I have given you enough credit over these last eight weeks to last you a lifetime…Of course I have also cursed your name equally so."

"Gee, way to go in making a girl feel…" he quickly cut me off, reminding me that we may be in each other's arms, but we still had a long way to go before trusting each other again.

"Hunted? Because that is precisely what you were. I told you that I would never give up, I warned you that I would find you and now here we are. You're locked in my embrace and soon to find yourself this way every night that follows it, for I promise you, my Khuba, letting you out of my sight will not happen…not for quite some time."

"You think I would run from you now, after what just happened between us?" I asked making him point out on a growl of words,

"I believe that is the second time for such a thing to happen between us and yet it still ended in you running." I hated that he was right, because we had been like this together once before and I had run from it the first moment I had seen…well, what I thought I had seen. Something in itself that still needed to be explained. Yet, when I was just about to open my mouth to ask, he shook his head and told me,

"Not tonight, let us face everything else tomorrow, for today was perfection and tonight I get to sleep with you in my arms. Let us just enjoy the now." I couldn't argue with that and well, I also couldn't argue with him playing with my hair the way he was, finding myself sinking into all that was Lucius,

And loving every breath I took doing so...

Sleeping in his arms.

THE NEXT DAY started pretty much the same as the one before, in the sense that we woke up late and Lucius and I were in bed together. Although the differences were that our first meal of the day wasn't then followed by destruction, arguing, and being tied up before sex. No, it just started with sex, then came the meal and we skipped destruction and arguing altogether.

But by late afternoon, I found myself being led down to the lobby where I was faced with what Lucius had planned and it included a huge heavy duty 4x4. I watched as it was driven and parked directly in front of us making me comment,

"Well, this is unexpected." His knowing grin was my only reply to this, and I couldn't help but take a moment to look down the length of him. It was slightly cooler today, so he was now wearing stonewash jeans and a plain charcoal T shirt, that was tight on the arms. But he wasn't the only one who'd dressed for the cooler weather as I was wearing tight indigo jeans that were rolled at the calf, and a plaid shirt in burgundy red, navy blue with hints of white in the lines that separated the two colours. I wore the shirt open and knotted under my bust with a white vest top underneath. White and red sneakers matched, although from the looks of things, I was missing hiking boots and a beige safari hat!

"Are we going hunting or something, 'cause despite popular belief among rogues and Mercs, I don't actually consider killing a sport?" I commented at the sight of the huge Mercedes 4x4. Lucius burst out laughing before grabbing the knot in my shirt and tugging me to his front before telling me,

"You wanted to know what was next, this is next." I frowned in question then asked,

"Is this why you had me pack a small bag, because you know, I was only kidding with that boy scout stuff and didn't really peg you for the camping type," I said as he started to lead me around to my side. Then he opened my door after the man who had driven here handed Lucius the keys.

"Just wait and see," he told me before grabbing me by the waist and lifting me into the car, adding yet another bossy order,

"Sit your sweet ass down, beautiful."

"Wow, bossy much…you know, you are lucky you are hot, Mister." I grumbled with a smirk I couldn't hide after he got in the car and started her up. This was before we headed out to I had no idea where. I lasted all of about five minutes when I said,

"Oh, come on, this is killing me here! Lucius, where are we going?" He chuckled at my outburst and told me,

"Where do you think, Mount Hebron of course?" My eyes widened at the sound of the name that was written on the map, as it had been the one I had spent weeks researching.

"We are?!" I said, the excitement in my voice easy to hear.

"Once the blood started to run through to the map, you recognized the mountain track from the picture in my office, didn't you?" he asked making me look sheepish.

"I might have done," I answered in a cryptic tone that didn't match my obvious reply.

"It was my home, you know," he said after a few silent minutes, making me tense and hold myself rigid, as for the first time he was giving me something of himself...*a piece of his past*.

"But I take it you know where I was born...being the clever little scholar you are," he added playfully.

"Queriot, a town located south of Jerusalem in Judea," I told him making him grant a sideways grin.

"Also known as Kerioth, but it is nothing more than ruins now," he said without any melancholy in his voice, just more matter of fact.

"What was it like?" I asked, making him look thoughtful as we drove through the city in a heavy duty truck that looked right now nothing more than overkill.

"The same sun baked, dry earth in seemingly endless summers, to snowcapped mountains in winter, so basically the weather is what I remember the most, that and olives." I laughed at his dry humour.

"In truth, I don't often find my mind going back there," he admitted surprising me.

"Too painful?" I asked softly, surprised and thrilled that he was finally opening up to me.

"Too old, more like," he said scoffing first, then going on to say,

"When time seems everlasting, it changes you. Your memories seem more like distant tales whispered from ear to ear until they become barely even the truth in which they were born from."

"So, what you're saying is that you don't miss..."

"Stale flat bread and herding livestock...no, Amelia, I don't miss that," he said amused. I honestly tried to picture it, knowing he didn't even look close to being the same man he once was...*Judas Iscariot*.

I confess that since being here I had become obsessed in discovering all I could about who was only classed to most as being a traitorous historical figure during the days of Jesus Christ. So, needless to say, that more often than not, it just ended up making me angry. Besides, I didn't want to learn about it from books or what the bible claimed it to be. I wanted the truth of it from the man himself.

"So, I take it we are going to the mountains and following the map, because you know I have tried to follow the same route and it's still too vague…for starters the tracks don't even look to exist anymore," I told him making him reply cryptically,

"That's because they don't." Naturally, this made me frown in question.

"So where are we going then?"

"Harei Yehuda," he told me, marking the end of our discussion. I knew this when he said,

"After today, will you do me a favour, Amelia?"

"What?" I asked in a tone that said I was almost afraid to.

"I want you to call home, talk to your father and…"

"My mother?" I finished off on a whisper.

"She is worried and upset, she is also desperate for you to discover the truth and believes she has something important to tell you that will help you understand." I looked out of the window and watched as we continued through the built-up parts of the city. Then I felt him reach across and take my hand, raising it to his lips to kiss. After this, he held it there and asked in a sincere tone,

"Please?"

I released a deep sigh and nodded, telling him,

"I will… I promise when we get back that I will call her." He granted me a warm, tender smile that created small creases at the corners of his eyes before he thanked me. One kiss more and my hand was given back to me so he could drop his sunglasses down from his head before changing gear. Twenty minutes later and I soon understood why it was we needed a four-wheel drive, as we started heading up the mountain.

THE DRIVE UP the mountain had been beautiful and offered amazing views, if not a little bumpy. Hence the heavy duty ride, one I discovered had been what Lucius' 'Make it happen' order had been all about yesterday. I also discovered that Lucius most certainly knew his way around this part of the world. He drove to places that seemed like the road would go nowhere and it was only when we pulled into a clearing that I finally asked,

"Are we here yet?" He laughed once and inquired,

"Be honest, just how long have you wanted to say that?"

"Erm…about five minutes into the drive." He smirked and told me,

"We have a few hours until night falls."

"Wait…so we are camping?" He put the car into park, took off his glasses and said with a wink,

"Boy scout, remember?" Then he got out of the car taking a moment to scan the area. I watched as he made his way around to my side before he opened my door and helped me down.

"Well, this is cute," I said following him to the back of the car and scanning the clearing that was framed by trees which sloped down over the ridge the clearing was situated on top of.

"I used to travel through here with my father as a boy," he told me, shocking me enough that my steps faltered.

"You did?" I asked after first needing to clear my throat. Gods, but I could barely even think of Lucius as being human, let alone just a boy!

"Of course, over two thousand years have passed, so it's of little surprise that the place looks different now, far more trees and such," he told me after opening up the back doors revealing what looked more like a rugged camper. Then he continued to get things out of the back that looked like…fold out chairs?

"Holy shit, we are camping!" I shouted making him laugh.

"Don't get too excited, sweetheart, we are just spending some time here before night falls." Then he pulled out a basket and I shouted,

"And you brought a picnic!" making him mutter under his breath,

"Easily pleased once again."

I ignored this and skipped up to him, placed my hands at his back and reach up on my tip toes by his ear so I could whisper,

"You know, if there is cheese in there, then chances are you are gonna get lucky in the wilderness, Mr Septimus." At this he turned his face to look at me over his shoulder and with an arrogant grin he asked,

"Is that so, Miss Draven?" I gave him a wink and kissed his cheek, before grabbing the chair and taking it over to where we were setting up, 'picnic camp'.

After this Lucius made short work of using what was inside the camper style 4x4, that I learned was a Mercedes-Benz G professional that meant it had been stripped of its back seats, so it could be converted by Grey Wolf camping interiors, with a custom pop top roof that had a bed in it. It also had two 20L jerry cans filled to the brim, a Forcetec ladder to the roof and rails to match. Oh, and just in case we happened to get stuck in a downpour, it had Mud Tec reinforced ramps attached to the sides. They were ready to be taken off and used to get us out of any sticky, muddy situations, by putting them under the wheels. But in my opinion, it just added to making the gun grey vehicle look meaner.

Now, I knew my cars and also my bikes, as growing up with so many diesel heads in the household, well something was bound to stick, seeing as I was a walking, talking, living breathing, information sponge. But even with this being said, I wouldn't have known anything about this car, if Lucius hadn't decided to share with me after I had asked him about it.

This also signified the first of many conversations once we sat down together. As soon we were sat looking out into an incredible view of the mountains, we both had a beer in hand and consumed half of the food Lucius had arranged for us. It was hours later, and the sun was just beginning to set, bathing the view in warm colours of pinks, oranges, and hints of red as the shadows of the mountain ridges turned to shades of blues and purples. It was beautiful, but for once this wasn't what I commented on.

"So, what did you do up here with your father and what was he like?" I asked seeing as he was in a chatty mood. I noticed him glance at me from the corner of his eye before taking a swig of his beer and looking back over the vista of colours.

"He did most things fathers did at that age with their sons, he taught me to hunt, to be cunning and to be fast." I raised a brow in question, prompting him to tell me,

"I was something of a troublemaker." I burst out laughing at this and couldn't help but continue to chuckle after it.

"I am shocked, of course," I said making him scoff,

"Yeah, I just bet you are."

"So, what you're saying is that you have always been one of the bad boys, eh?" I said teasing him. His amused look said it all. Then after a minute of thought he continued,

"I questioned everything, including authority."

"Noooo…that doesn't sound like you at all." He gave me wry grin and said,

"I wasn't one to conform, unless there was a cause I believed in." I took a breath and decided to see how far this conversation would go.

"Is that why you followed Jesus?" I braved to ask. He gave a smile and told me gently,

"Not ready to go there just yet, sweet." I granted him a little nod of understanding and decided to switch to when he first became who he was today, thinking this was a good way to keep him talking.

"So, you didn't deal with authority well…Must have been the natural born leader in you then," I commented taking another swig of my beer. But then he shocked me by saying,

"I never wanted to be a leader, least of all a King." I frowned before pointing out the obvious,

"Lucius, you were a Roman Emperor."

"Yes, but only under the order of your father did I become so, my little scholar," he told me making me nearly choke on a swallow of beer. He chuckled at my reaction.

"I didn't know that," I said, pointing out the obvious.

"Two thousand years of history, sweetheart, there is a lot you don't know," he said making me release a sigh because I knew it was true. I mean just how many layers could a guy that old have?

"Hardly seems fair seeing as you know everything about me," I complained on a sigh, making him remind me,

"I'm talking now I believe." I grinned at him and agreed, tipping the neck of my beer at him,

"That you are." I took a sip and then said,

"And not that I want to seem ungrateful or at the risk of making you stop or regret that…"

"You want to know, why now?" he cut me off from my rambling,

"Yeah, I want to know why now," I repeated wanting to know why he was all of a sudden Mister chatty past pants and was letting me into the world of Lucius.

"Let's just call it the first steps to gaining back that trust that has been lost," he replied making me realise that he was doing this for me...or so I thought, until he added,

"Besides, I realise that expecting you to be content at only knowing the past thirty years of my life is unrealistic."

"Oh really?"

"Well, given your curious nature, your love of history and tenaciousness at getting what you want, then yeah, it was unrealistic." He teased making me shout,

"Oi!" This before throwing the first thing my hand grabbed from the table, which was a half-eaten pastry.

"Gods, woman, will you stop throwing shit at me!" he complained as it missed him by an inch as it went sailing past his face.

"I will, when you stop pissing me off, handsome!" I threw back at him without an ounce of malice, making him grumble,

"Fuck, wish she would go back to slapping me...ends better."

"Who are you even talking to?" I snapped making him grant me a dangerous grin. Then he placed his bottle down next to his chair, doing so without taking his eyes off me.

"Oh no...no you don't..." I started to say moving from my chair and starting to walk backwards, keeping him in sight as he rose from his seat, ready to start stalking me.

"No...you...don't...Lucius, ah!" I shouted as I turned to run back to the car finding myself grabbed from behind and thrown over his shoulder.

"Well, look at that, caught you again!" he shouted. Then, just as he started walking me to the back of the car, his entire body went rigid. This was something that made mine do the same and only realising why, when we heard a voice say,

"I can say the same thing." I looked down at Lucius and told him,

"See, I told you that you should have packed the smelly

cheese." He growled low after pulling me down the front of him, so I was plastered to his chest. Then we both started to take in the full extent of our problem as the small army of shadows started to surround us.

I released a sigh and said,

"The bitch, witch is back."

CHAPTER TWENTY-SEVEN

DEATH FALLS UPON US ALL

"Well, I have to say, it's about time you two got back together, I was getting impatient," the witch said stepping from the tree line curled in what looked like the shadows she commanded. It was as though she had just appeared out of nowhere. This made me think back to the way she had escaped the river of blood in the vault, telling me then that she most likely had created some kind of portal.

She wore her usual red cloak. The same one I had seen her wearing in both my dreams and the nightmare reality. I didn't know what she meant about us being back together or why she would need for us to be, but I knew one thing, I wasn't the only one who didn't like her comment. I knew this when I felt Lucius get tense.

"Aww, well, would you look at that, honey, she was rooting for us," I said sarcastically making Lucius scoff.

"We meet at last for I have been curious about when the bitch I intend to kill would turn up," Lucius said in a calm tone that the hard muscles beneath my palms told me he was anything but.

"I wouldn't be so cocky, Vampire, after all, it's not like I came alone," she said, now raising up her hands and out from the shadows stepped the army of rogues she had brought with her, one we both already knew were there. I didn't know how it was possible for me to know this as it wasn't as if I had any supernatural gifts to help in this department. But for some reason, I just had. As if I had felt them humming against my skin, one that gave new meaning to the saying making your skin crawl.

"Good, for you will need a fucking army," Lucius told her.

"Now. if I had known that was all it would take," she said in cocky tone.

"You mistake me…for you will need the fucking army just to give you a head start before I rip your fucking heart out, witch!" Lucius snarled the threat making one of the figures that suddenly emerged next to her start laughing, one unfortunately we both knew well.

"See, I told you he is arrogant," she said turning her head towards the witch. However, one look at her and I just groaned in annoyance before commenting dryly,

"Ah, well, it's clearly not a party without Bitch face…well, this should be fun, I was looking for another shot at killing that bitch!" This had the desired effect as it made Lucius chuckle and Layla furious,

"We will see about that, you little cunt!" Layla snarled stepping towards me, only to find herself stopped when the witch's hand rose, ceasing her movements.

"Not yet, we need her," the witch warned, making Lucius growl low in his throat, pulling me tight to his frame.

"Yeah, to fucking bleed!" Layla said maliciously.

"Silence!" the witch snapped after turning her head to the

side and slicing a hand down in front of her making Layla cower slightly,

"Wow, so crass...seriously Lucius, you had terrible taste in women before you met me." Lucius didn't look away from our enemies, keeping his eagle eyes on them, whilst agreeing with me,

"That I did, love."

"Enough of this! You know what we want, Vampire, now show us the way," the witch snapped, and the jerked motion made her hood slip back a little. But what was then odd was the way in which she hurried to cover herself back up, yanking it forward with a fumbled motion. I frowned in question as it was almost as if she didn't want to show her face. Was it because of the scars...? Did she consider it a weakness...or perhaps it was more than that?

"Explain to me why I should, do you think your little army scares me?" Lucius challenged.

"No, but what does scare you, Vampire, is losing your Chosen One and can you really risk fighting them all without risking her life...besides, here's a little example to back up my claim." The witch then made a motion with her hand and suddenly there was a whizzing sound before pain burst in my shoulder at my back, making me push into Lucius from the impact.

"AAAHH!"

"Amelia!" he shouted as I fell into him, and when I lifted my face off his chest the first thing I asked was,

"Where did all the blood come from?" Lucius looked down at me and the second he saw that I was hurt, he did so with blood thirsty murder in his eyes, as his demon started to come through.

"I wouldn't do that if I were you, for I have ten more aimed at her that you can't see and won't have the power to stop. Now, show me the way and I will let you heal her," the witch told him, making him close his eyes and snarl as he twisted his neck to the side in a painful way. It was then that I knew he was actually fighting with his demon side in order to try and stay in control.

But the pain was starting to rip through me, making me fall limp against him and as a result, his arm tightened around me. Then, pushing past the pain, I used my strength to reach up so I could put a palm to his cheek,

"Hey, it's okay, come back to me...yeah?" I said trying to help him focus as he struggled to hold himself back from allowing that part of him to take over. I knew this when the black veins started to branch out around his crimson eyes and snake down his neck where his skin seemed to ripple with the increasing power building. But at the sound of my voice he started to pull through and was soon looking down at me, half as a demon, half as the man I loved, before whispering my name,

"Amelia...I'm so sorry."

"It's okay...I'm okay, it's just...ahh...my..." I finished this as I tried to reach around my back to pull whatever I could feel was stuck there.

"Ssshh, it's okay, I will heal you," he told me softly.

"Tut, tut, not yet, Vampire... now show us the way, as I am sure it was not a walk you could have ever forgotten," the witch said with a smirk in her voice making him growl.

"She's got a fucking arrow in her shoulder!" he snapped making me frown. Holy shit... was that what it was, no wonder it fucking hurt!

"Yes, and she will continue to bleed the longer it takes you...quicker if you remove the arrow." The witch said making Layla laugh,

"I can't fucking wait for that show!" I hissed her way, and said to Lucius,

"New rule, no ex bitch faces on date night." He gave me a small strained smile before cupping my cheek and rubbing a thumb over my cheek,

"Sweetheart." His tender endearment was interrupted the second the witch snapped,

"Time to get moving!"

I felt the rumble of Lucius' growl against me before he swept my legs up and even though he did so gently, I still cried out in pain as he took me in his arms, being mindful of where the arrow was sticking out of my flesh.

"Ssshh now, it will be alright…I will take care of you, my Khuba," he told me softly at the sight of my pain. I nodded twice and laid my head against his chest as he carried me. Then I tried to ignore the strange feeling, like a wave of heat, as if someone had shot a firecracker in my shoulder not an arrow.

Lucius started walking and I glanced over his shoulder to see that the witch was following along with the shadows of rogues behind her. Layla at her side, of course, dressed all in black like some fucking ninja! Gods, I hated her! Unfortunately, it looked like we were outnumbered here as there were seriously too many shadows to count and with my injury, then in all honesty, I couldn't be bothered anyway.

Lucius continued walking, and we left the clearing as the last of the sun said goodbye to the day and a full moon replaced it. This at least gave us enough light to see and the car behind us soon became a shadow in the distance. Lucius continued to take long strides along what looked like an old footpath that was most definitely overgrown. He was trying to stay along the tree line instead of going into the thick of the forest, and I soon realised why.

He kept looking up at the night sky as we walked, which

was when I realised...*he was being led by the stars.* That had been why he was waiting for night fall.

"Well, look at you...total...boy...scout." I said feeling lightheaded, from what I gathered was losing blood. Lucius gave me a little shake and said,

"Come on, sweetheart, keep talking to me now, yeah?" I took in a deep breath and let it out again.

"Any pain when you do that?" he asked, me making me frown in question,

"No," I told him with a little shake of my head. He then went on to ask,

"Any shortness of breath?"

"Well, yeah but that's most likely down to the arrow sticking out of my body," I replied making him smirk,

"Not lost your sass...also a good sign."

"A good sign of what, that I am still living and able to verbally abuse you?" He chuckled again and I looked behind him, making him say,

"Don't look at them, look at me." I knew why he said this as he didn't want me to panic. A little late for that, seeing as I had already been shot and didn't exactly see how we were going to get out of this.

"It's kind of hard not to, I mean they are kind of noticeable," I told him, making him repeat the order,

"Ignore them and tell me how you feel?" I chuckled but it ended on a groan thanks to the burning pain that tightened when I moved.

"Without laughing," he advised.

"Well, don't say that, as now all I will want to do is laugh!" He shook his head as if he was questioning my sanity when I explained,

"It's the same as telling someone who's scared of heights not to look down, they always do!"

"Alright, sweetheart, I think I am getting your point here… now tell me, any sharp pain when inhaling or chest pain, which is more severe on one side?" I frowned again and said,

"No, just a burning pain…why?"

"Because your heart rate has increased." I laughed once, winced again, and ignoring his raised 'I told you to keep still' brow, I said,

"Again, if I were to venture a guess that would be from the arrow sticking out of my shoulder."

"I asked because there might have been the possibility of a pneumothorax."

"A collapsed lung?" I translated in form of a question.

"Yes, but seeing as you seem to be breathing without difficulty then I would say that, thankfully, this isn't the case."

"Any other fatal worries I should know about, Doctor Phil?" I asked and his replied shocked me, because clearly, he had heard of Doctor Phil…unless I had mentioned him in some cocky reply before?

"I'm not worried about your state of mind here, sweet."

"Yeah, but he is the only famous doctor I know about, other than the one from Doctor Who."

"Who?" he asked making me repeat,

"Yeah, Who." He frowned and said,

"Actually, now I am worried about your brain." I was about to laugh when he shook his head silently reminding me that laughing wouldn't be fun for me right now.

"Doctor Who is a TV show, I wasn't confused or forgot. Now go back to your other worries," I told him without telling him how sexy the whole doctor act was.

"Other than a fucking witch that can pull arrows from a veil of another realm?"

"Ah, yeah, well that does sound bad, as I gotta say, this being shot business isn't fun for me." He gave me a tender look before looking up at the stars again, changing his direction a little. Then we started to make our way towards a large open space as a field spread out in front of us. I half expected us to find Maria from Sound of Music being followed by a bunch of singing kids and a broody guy she fell in love with. Forget Nazis, an army of Vampires being led by a pissed off witch with a grudge, was where the real horror was at, I thought sarcastically.

"Now, tell me what your other worry was, other than yes, the army, the witch and raining arrows from another realm... wow, must say, didn't see myself saying that sentence today." Again, I received another grin before he said,

"My concern was if it had hit the brachial artery, then there would have been dramatic blood loss, requiring the application of a tourniquet to prevent exsanguination but the arrow is continuing to slow down the bleed rate, so this is good."

"Wow and here I was thinking I was the smart one...see, total boy scout," I said making him laugh after which he told me quietly,

"Amelia, listen to me, they can't see you from here, so they won't know what you are doing."

"Why, what am I doing?" I asked whispering back.

"I want you to pull the neck of my shirt down and bite my chest as hard as you can." Suddenly my fun day was getting better.

"Hardly time for a hickey, handsome."

"Amelia, you know what I want, now it won't heal you completely, not until I can remove the arrow, but it will help with the blood loss."

"And the orgasm that usually follows it?" I asked making him reply,

"It won't be enough all at once."

"I guess that's why they didn't use a gun to shoot me with, huh, clever really."

"Right, well, before we praise the enemy too much, can you get on with it, as we have a way left to go and you will need strength for both the journey and when we get there," he advised in a tense tone.

"Why?"

"Because I have a plan," he said making it wise not to ask but instead to praise the right person who was on my team.

"Of course, you do…my man always has a plan," I said making him grin, flashing his fangs that I knew were the parts of his demon he hadn't yet released. After all, the threat was still at our backs.

After this he nodded down at me, telling me to start so I did what he asked. I yanked hard on the neck of his t shirt, gripping the material as if this would help. Then I first kissed the small section of bare chest making him wink down at me in thanks before I bit down on his flesh as hard as I could. He didn't even flinch as his blood dripped and pooled in my mouth. I continued to suck at him and started to feel better the more blood I took. But then when I started to pull back, he snarled down at me,

"More."

"Lucius, no, you need your strength too and I am feeling better." His snarled response told me I wouldn't win.

"More, Amelia, now do as you're told." I rolled my eyes at him before going back to sucking more, grinning around his flesh when he said,

"My itchy palm will owe you for that one, my sassy girl."

After this I didn't know how much farther we ended up going but I must have fallen asleep at some point with my face nestled against Lucius' chest, one that had healed long ago.

"I think this is close enough!" The witch's voice startled me awake and I quickly opened my eyes to see where we were.

I gasped in horror as we had now been plummeted right into my nightmares.

A single dead tree.

A missing bloodied noose.

A body no longer swaying at the end of it.

The place where Lucius first died.

CHAPTER TWENTY-EIGHT

BORN A KEY

Lucius felt me tense so hard it felt like my bones would snap and the pain in my shoulder intensified.

"Easy, sweetheart," he told me, making me grab onto his t-shirt, bunching it in my fist as I whispered,

"But this place...it's...it's,"

"I know where it is, love," he told me stopping me from saying it and I looked to see if there was any pain in his eyes, where there seemed to be only deep rooted anger that was desperate to break free.

"Now put her down!" the witch demanded, and I looked over his shoulder to find a large arc of rogues all stood like silent sentinels, making me feel as if something wasn't right with them.

"Lucius, all the Vampires, they seem..."

"I know," he said with a tense lock of his jaw. Because it was as if he already knew where my thoughts were headed, and he shook his head telling me not to speak of it now.

"Put her down, Vampire!" the witch ordered again.

"No!" he snapped back on a growl, but then she started to raise her hand and said,

"Very well, another arrow should do it." Layla clapped her hands as if this was the most fun she'd had in years…Gods, the bitch clearly needed to get laid if that was the case!

"NO! DON'T!" Lucius roared making the witch fold her arms and say expectantly,

"Well…"

"Fuck! Alright, alright just don't fucking hurt her!" Lucius said, his panic clear to see as he started to lower my feet to the ground. Then he held me steady until I was able to stand on my own, something that made me feel lightheaded again.

"Now move away from her."

"If I do that, she will fucking fall!" he snapped.

"Then she will fucking crawl to it! Now move it!" the witch demanded making him do as she ordered for fear I would get hurt again. He mouthed down at me,

'It will be alright.'

"Now, walk towards the tree!" The witch ordered me this time and I had to say, I really didn't fucking want to. The image of my nightmares coming back to me was enough to make me terrified to go anywhere near it. Lucius took one look at me and knew it. Which was why he started to argue,

"I fail to see the fucking point of all of this!"

"The Tree of Souls will show itself…you will see," the witch replied in a certain tone.

"The Tree of Souls is a fucking Vampires' fairy tale, it doesn't fucking exist!" he snapped but I could see the witch's grin from here, a flash of white beneath the hood.

"Don't be so sure."

"I have had my people searching for it for centuries, and nothing…trust me, I am fucking sure!" he snarled back folding his arms across his chest and looking as if he was close to splitting his t-shirt! He looked fit for murder and rage and total demonic execution. Meanwhile, I was left with no other option but to continue trying to make my way towards the tree I knew had taken Lucius' human life. It was a haunting sight, that single dead tree all twisted and bare, looking more like the sun bleached bones of what used to be some Hellish beast reaching up out of the earth trying to escape damnation.

"Perhaps you weren't looking in the right place," Layla said getting in on the action.

"You think the first fucking place I looked wasn't the place I fucking died and was resurrected…It's. Not. Fucking. Here!" He growled forcing out each word and trying to make his point when releasing his wings as more of his demon erupted to the surface.

"Then, if you are right, no harm will come to her…now walk the rest of the way, Princess," the witch told me, and I snarled myself at the name and cursed myself for stumbling as I did as I was told.

"Don't you fucking move, Luc!" Layla snarled in warning as Lucius struggled to watch me trying to stay on my feet.

"Fucking foolish beliefs!" he snapped making her tell him,

"Or just the lack in them, for you will see, lover." Now hearing her calling him this made me close to saying to hell with the rain of arrows, I wanted to rip her head off!

"The tree is nothing but a fucking relic!" Lucius' demon was the one to respond this time.

"Then why is it still here, dead as it may be, but it is still here… even after all your attempts at destroying it…still here it stands," the witch reminded him, letting me know just how Lucius had felt about it remaining after all this time. And he didn't respond other than to growl at her because of it.

"No, it is your lack of faith that forced you to turn your back on your own past, and now you will see, all you needed was the right key…the blood of…"

"Shut the fuck up!" Lucius shouted, making the witch chuckle.

"What is she talking about?" I asked still making my way towards it and only a few feet away now.

"Nothing, she knows fucking nothing but lies!" he snarled, referring to the witch, but his tone suggested more panic than anger.

"My lies, oh Vampire…she has no idea the fucking lies you have told her…the same ones you have since the day she was born!" The witch snapped back making me frown in question just as I had no choice but to reach out for the tree trunk, as I fell into it.

"Lucius?" I whispered his name before asking,

"What is she…" suddenly I was cut off when he roared back at the cause of all our problems,

"SILENCE!"

But through his roar I stumbled back, falling further back against the tree, and looking up in horror as its large branches loomed above me, like twisted limbs of some monster trying to grab me, ready to tear out my soul and drag me back down to Hell. They were moving, swaying…or was that just me,

"Amelia?" I heard my name being called through the darkness of my nightmare, but I couldn't see it. I continued to move, trying to free myself from whatever gripped me now, but it seemed useless!

"Amelia!" Lucius shouted my name this time, done so in panic and the second a blinding light erupted from beneath me, I screamed as suddenly I started to fall…no, not fall, but just like my fears, I was being dragged. Like the earth beneath my feet had started to crumble away, giving way to the roots of this tree that was pulling me under. They were like the hands of death wanting to claim its next victim and I was powerless to stop them.

Then I was screaming as I started to fall through the earth and beyond.

"NO!" I heard the scream of the witch in the distance above as I disappeared from sight and I closed my eyes as my heart dropped to my stomach! I continued to fall, screaming only one name,

"LUCIUS!" Then suddenly I felt a hand gripping my wrist as I was slowly being lowered to the ground. I wanted to ask myself who it was that gripped me so tight, but I was too afraid to open my eyes. But then my brain started to work past the fear of death and what I felt wasn't bare flesh around my wrist…

But one of leather.

Lucius.

Lucius had caught me.

My eyes flew open to see him above me, my wrist in his hold with the great shadow of his wings above him. Then I felt my feet touching the ground and I looked down to see that he had lowered us into what looked like a giant underground cavern. Lucius followed me down until his feet were also on the ground and before I could ask what happened he pulled me in to his chest to hold me close.

"Gods, Amelia, my Khuba, my love… I could have lost you!" He sounded so torn and worried that I simply let him hold me, knowing that we both needed the comfort right then.

"I'm so sorry, Amelia…so, so, sorry."

"What for, you didn't…"

"For this," he said and before I had time to react, pain exploded in my shoulder as he tore the arrow out, doing so in what I knew was most likely the kindest way possible. However, that didn't stop me from screaming as the pain cut through me like a knife forged in the pits of Hell! I watched as he threw it to the side angrily, before taking hold of me once more. Then he started to shift my body around so he could reach my lips.

"Ssshh…calm, calm now, it is done, now here, I want you to drink."

"But… I already …took…" I slurred my words, feeling myself falling under and so close to giving way to the unconsciousness my body was craving. He had been right about the arrow, it had been slowing the blood loss.

"Ssshh, drink Amelia, it will make you feel better," he said, and I soon found myself cradled in his hold where we must have slipped to the dirt floor. I heard the tear of flesh as he bit into his own wrist before I felt it being placed to my lips,

"Drink, Amelia," he urged again giving me a little shake as my eyes had closed and my body started to slump in his hold.

"Drink!" This time when he shouted, he did so with panic in his tone which jarred me enough to do as I was told. So, I latched onto the opening in his wrist letting the blood gush into my mouth, doing so with so much flow I didn't need to suck but only swallow. I opened my eyes briefly to see why this was as he was fisting his hand over and over again to get the blood pumping quicker, so I had no trouble feeding.

But then the moment I felt myself starting to heal came the next part that flooded my system. And with it a lot more than just fixing my body. It also became about the rush of my mind as it released a surge of dopamine, making me scream out as I came without even being touched. My brain continued to work overtime in producing a potent and effective recipe of different hormones and neurochemicals all creating a mind blowing experience.

I don't know how many times I cried out his name or how long after I remained shuddering in his arms as my body came down from the high. But I felt him whispering tender words down at me as he stroked back my hair with his palm.

"And some say sex isn't the key to a prolonged healthy life," I said after I was feeling slightly less breathless. I felt him chuckle before scoffing an agreed,

"Fools." I smiled before turning my head and shifting now so I could look at him. Thankfully, the colossal cave had a strange glow to it, as if something was reflecting off the rock walls I could see. We were both on the floor with me sitting in the spread of his legs as his back looked to be against a huge collection of boulders that reached up to the top of the underground cavern. It was like some naturally formed ladder or huge stepping stones up in a spiral.

"Ah, I see that was the safer route down then…as opposed to just falling." He followed my gaze back up to the top and said dryly,

"Yes, so it would seem."

"Lucius, all jokes aside here…what is this place?" Lucius looked around and took in the same space I did. It was a huge cavernous place and even though not exactly as big as The Son Doong, which was a cave in Vietnam and known as the biggest cave in the world…this would have been a contender for sure. Although, it was yet to be discovered how long it was, as Son Doong was over 5.5 miles long, had a jungle and river, and could fit a 40-story skyscraper within its walls!

This however was merely the first cave and up above was nothing but the roots of a tree that seemed too big and too plenty for what it had been above. They snaked and coiled over and over until it was a twisted mess of ancient roots all branching out in every direction. They then flowed down the walls of the far side, until you could only just barely see them beneath the tree.

"It was true, all this time," Lucius muttered in awe.

"Lucius?"

"This is the Temple of the Tree of Souls," he told me in a tone of astonishment, something rarely heard coming from Lucius.

"The place you said for centuries you have had people looking for?" He gave me a look that said it all,

"I might have lied slightly."

"Only slightly?" I laughed,

"I have known about this place since my rebirth," he admitted.

"Then why?" I asked with a shake of my head, relishing in the absence of pain in my shoulder.

"Because there was no way to access it, trust me, now that has been the centuries of trying part. I only knew of its existence."

"So that's why you never believed that this could be the place the map was leading us to?"

"Not until the blood proved it to be otherwise, for I knew it would be pointless. It was little more than a myth, and barely a memory for me. I am still unsure as to what it is exactly that is down here," he admitted, and I would have pointed out that assumption was most likely leading to the possibility of a big tree of some kind. Which was why I asked,

"Then what is the Tree of Souls?" He released a deep sigh, rubbed a hand down his face and told me,

"The Tree of Souls refers to the tree you saw, the one that took my human life and changed history for all of Heaven and Hell and the beings born from such. Just as with Jesus' death it changed humanity."

"So, it's symbolic, like the cross."

"Of sorts, but there are those, like the witch, who believe the Tree of Souls to be a fable, a tale that speaks of unspeakable power for anyone who rules over it."

"And that's why she wanted access to this place, she believes it is down here?" I asked making him nod but then something said earlier came back to me, and I asked,

"Wait, you said barely a memory…you've been here before?" At this he looked awkward, as if he didn't want to admit what he was being forced to. But considering our current circumstance, well he couldn't really shy away from facts right now. He released a sigh and told me,

"It was where my body was brought after it happened."

"What?!" I couldn't help but screech, as he helped me off the ground.

"I don't exactly remember much, Amelia, and that isn't solely down to age, for try to remember that I was dying at the time." I wanted to ask so many questions, but I didn't know where to start, so he continued on for me.

"The witch, she didn't know what would happen, for if she did then she wouldn't have been ready as I was, as I merely remember rising through the ground, something I believed for years to be nothing more than dreams of warped history, twisted into something it was not. Now I know I was not only wrong, but I believe that those dreams were preparing me for this moment…so I would be ready and know what to do." I thought on what he was saying and asked myself the same thing, if the dreams of him and the tree were somehow to prepare me?

"What did happen when I fell?"

"My blood combined with yours must have been the key and she knew it, which is why…"

"I didn't really have to do anything but bleed under the tree…yeah okay, gotcha…so what now?" I asked looking back up at the rock formation that potentially we could climb, but there didn't exactly look like there was a handy trap door up there and even if there was, the welcome party wasn't of our choosing.

"I suggest we see where it takes us, look over to the far side, there seems to be a doorway." Lucius nodded to a place too far away for me to see and my look said it all as he granted me a coy grin and said,

"Trust me, human, it's there." I elbowed him in the ribs for the comment, making him smirk. Then he took my hand and we started to cross the huge cave.

"Did you notice the rogues, how they all looked different?" I asked making him nod, now looking bleak when he said,

"She is more powerful than I thought possible in a witch."

"What did she do to them?" I asked, hating that so far, she seemed impossible to beat.

"I don't know how, but she has taken control over them completely, it is worse than we first imagined."

"Oh great, more good news," I grumbled in annoyance.

"Take some comfort in this, for if her plan has been to get down here all along, then she must be pissed now seeing as that didn't happen. So, at the very least we had prevented what I assume to be the…"

"Grand Finale?" I finished off for him.

"Yes, or the part where she tries to fuck up the whole world by ruling over Vampires." I shivered at the thought and forced myself to ask,

"You really think that's her master plan…not to just kill them all?"

"After seeing how she has reduced the rogues to nothing more than mindless drones, then I am starting to lean heavily towards that conclusion, yes," he said as he helped guide me over some of the bigger rocks. And as we got closer to the other side, I could see now what his vampire eyesight could see before mine.

There was an opening that looked to be man-made, but the details had long ago been lost due to the sides being consumed by the ocean of roots from above. It was almost like they were flowing down in waves, with the thicker roots entwined and coiled with the thinner vines. They all cascaded into the entrance now as if a vortex had sucked them through.

"Well, this looks welcoming," I commented dryly, making Lucius grip my hand tighter in his as we passed through the doorway which looked at least ten feet tall. Then, just as the darkness started to consume our senses, flames erupted all around us as torches lit in carved holes. These were situated in the rock walls and each was framed by the root system, like little windows. The hallway was also the same height as the door, with the flickering light being closer to the root covered arched ceiling.

We continued down, both tense and ready for anything… however, like most things, when that 'anything' happened, neither of us was prepared for it. As the moment we walked through the opening at the end, something seemed to slam in between us both, forcing us apart and causing us to separate. I fell backwards landing on my ass with a grunt of pain that jarred my bones and I rose to my elbow, first having to shake my head to get my mind back into gear.

"Wh…what happened?" I asked, coughing first as the loose dirt had been kicked up around me from the compacted earth on the ground. I looked up to find Lucius on the ground which in itself set me into panic. So, I got to my feet and ran towards him, only to be met with the same invisible barrier that separated us both, slamming me back once more on my ass.

"No!" I shouted as I pounded a fist to the ground in my anger. And when I lifted my head, it was to find Lucius still on the ground, unmoving and,

For the first time…

Unconscious.

CHAPTER TWENTY-NINE

TREE OF SOULS

I ran towards the image of Lucius on the floor asking myself why he hadn't got up yet and panic set in that something was majorly wrong! I wanted to bang my fist on what I now could see was a shimmering layer of air between us. As if it was nothing but dust particles innocently getting caught in the sunrays. It looked as light and airy as if I should have just been able to wave my hand through it all, but I knew this not to be true…No, I had learned my lesson finally after being put on my ass five times and well, that shit gets old quickly!

"Come on, Lucius, honey, wake up for me!" I pleaded again but nothing. I could at the very least see that he was still breathing which was currently the only positive I was seeing here.

"WAKE UP!" I shouted stopping my fist just in time from banging on what seemed like nothing more than glittery air.

"He cannot hear you…"

"Not like we can."

"Mmmawahamm"

I spun around quickly at the sounds of three different voices, the last being nothing more than an indistinguishable mumble of sounds. My hand flew to my pounding heart as fear started to creep its way in, because really, I had no clue what I faced down here. I may not have had anything to fear in my father's world but down here…well, I wasn't in fucking Kansas anymore!

"Wwwho's there?!" I said trying to get the first word of that question not to sound so shaky. I turned around in the dark space, one that was barely illuminated enough from the opening we had just passed through, one Lucius was currently lying unconscious in.

"We are the Keeper of three…"

"We see, hear and speak of all that the blood of Kings commands."

"Mmnsebm" Again the mumbled voice followed, making me wonder of the point of it. I also found myself frowning at the creepy words that sounded hissed and scratchy.

"Yeah, well lucky for you then, as I can't see shit!" I snapped and suddenly at my complaint, the huge room sparked into life.

"Gods," I muttered in sight of all the huge torches that were being lit by unnatural means. Large disks of gold, the size of cars, sat in curved iron twists of metal and started to fill with a flaming liquid that poured from above. I followed the flow up and saw that the flaming waterfalls each came from holes in the rock face and there were seven in total. Then, once the disks had been filled with enough fuel, the waterfalls stopped, leaving flames to lick and snap at the air. But it offered enough light for me to see now where I was, and it could only be one place…

"I am in the Temple of the Tree of Souls." The place was

real! It wasn't a fabled tale after all or a memory that had deceived Lucius.

"She knows…"

"She is clever."

"Sss mmise."

The three voices said again, making me awkwardly say,

"Uh…thanks…I guess." Well, at least they seemed to like me, so big plus on that one, especially if that meant I wasn't going to get eaten anytime soon. My voice echoed around what I could now see was a carved temple that looked to be as old as time itself!

The markings along its walls belonged to every known civilization since the time of man and there were many even I didn't recognise. But giant pillars the size of redwood trees were all carved in every type of symbol, hieroglyphics and script known and unknown. They framed the open space and there were far too many of them to count, which spoke for how big the Temple was.

As for the floor, it was a series of broken slabs that had been uprooted and split from the dark black roots that looked charred as if they had been set alight. I followed them all the way to the centre of the room which was the whole reason the Temple had been built. For it hadn't been for the tree above, where Lucius had died as Judas, it had been from this tree grown from his ascension.

It was an enormous stone grey tree that reminded me of the one in Afterlife, the Temple of Souls. Clearly souls needed a lot of temples I thought sarcastically. But this tree was most definitely different as, like the roots that had led us here, the whole tree looked to be made of them. So instead of having a trunk and branches, it was simply a giant series of roots in the shape of a tree, only at the top there were so many silver leaves, there must have been millions. Each one seemed to flutter and shimmer as if caught on some imaginary wind, and at the very top of the tree was what looked like a single blood red rose. One that could only be seen as it was the only colour on there. That and a strange strip of shadows that seemed to swirl around the centre part of the tree, making me question if this had something to do with the shadows I had seen surrounding the army of rogues?

But then as I stepped closer, I started to notice more.

"The tree…what…what is wrong with it?" I asked at the sight of the black charred roots that weren't just contained to those under my feet and slabs, but also to the base of the tree. It was like a darkness rising up from the ground below and reaching all the way to the first set of branches of the tree. Reaching to where thousands of leaves had turned to black and even now, I could see as one started to fall to the ground and then crumble away to ash. Then seconds later there was another.

"Hurt…"

"Infected."

"Mmawam."

The three said making me step further into the space and as I started to walk round the tree, I could now see the huge split at its core that looked like an opening. The closer I got the more I could see for myself that it was in fact a doorway, one as big as the one we had just both tried to step through. An ominous red glow came from the darkness within, as if daring you to take a look and find out where it led. Well, that was one rabbit hole I was most definitely staying away from, I thought with a shiver.

I looked back to Lucius and asked,

"Will he be alright?"

"He sleeps through his death no longer…"

"The Blood of the King still beats."

"Mhom hamme." The mumbled part was a little pointless and I couldn't help but wonder why. So, I asked,

"Where are you all?"

"She seeks the seekers…"

"Keepers of three must we be,"

"Memme mh."

Then I saw only one huge figure as tall as Ragnar appear from behind one of the massive pillars. He was wearing a long worn cloak that covered all of its misshapen figure. I could feel my mind working overtime just trying to distinguish which part was which, and why there was only one that had appeared, when three voices could always be heard. When suddenly I didn't need to ask again, as the cloak fell away and revealed the true horror of who it was I was speaking to.

"Holy shit," I muttered, taking quick steps back as the figure of three bodies combined emerged. It was like the tree in a way, where three torsos conjoined as the shape of a triangle and were twisted up in six arms and four legs, as it was clear, only two were needed for walking.

But this wasn't the only thing about the creature that was horrifying, it was the three heads all grouped together and, like the body, were off centre and not quite in a line. It also became clear to see why one was always mumbling.

"Gods in Heaven," I uttered in shock as I took all of him or should I say all of them in. One of the twisted limbs was reaching up for the face closest. Its hand was tucked inside his mouth, dragging his jaw down making it impossible for him to speak. Pained, angry eyes wrinkled the features on his face making the skin on the bridge of his nose rippled.

As for the other two heads, another hand had reached up the head of the next, one that was turned towards the side and in between the other two. The hand was positioned over the top of his head with its fingertips embedded in the eye sockets, in a painful grip blinding him. The last and top head had two hands reaching up and not only covering its ears, but had the fingers tugging down at the flesh so they hung limp and unused. But strangely out of the three, he looked the less pained and was obviously the one that relied on sight.

So, it seemed for them to exist at all, they had no choice but to work together as a whole. For two could speak, two could hear and two could see but only one of each was useful to the three. Which told me that perhaps they communicated as one mind, as all communicated.

"See no evil, speak no evil and hear no evil," I whispered as it dawned on me, making them hiss and at first, I thought I had insulted them. When it became apparent it was actually a strange chuckled sound.

"She is funny our queen of blood…"

"She will save us."

"Meesss."

"What do you mean, I am…" They interrupted my question by telling me,

"You are our Master's Chosen One."

"His blood born and first of your kind."

"Mhossone." I frowned at this and looked back to Lucius who was still passed out on the floor.

"I don't understand," I admitted shaking my head as if there was some temple sized puzzle piece I was missing here.

"We are keepers of the…"

"Yeah, yeah I got that bit, so skip ahead…no pun intended," I said making them snigger a hiss again. So just as they were about to yet again repeat themselves, I held up a hand and said for them,

"Yeah I know, I'm funny, now get to the part where you explain what it is you think I have to do with any of this," I told them as my irritation was mounting.

"The Tree of Souls dies from the Venom of God."

"Yes, the Venom is what kills us."

"Mmmauanu."

"What did he say?" I asked, referring to the mumbling one, checking I wasn't actually missing out on the helpful one of the group.

"He said that it must be stopped before the infection reaches the branches of our queen." I frowned and looked to the blood red rose that seemed to be at the top of the tree.

"The blood of your queen?" I muttered wondering if they had this wrong, was it something to do with my mother…was she the rose, the only human that Lucius had turned?

"So, what you're saying is that this Venom of God is poisoning the tree…wait, so the rogues, we were right, they are turning." They all started nodding enthusiastically and in truth, it looked painful. Then they told me,

"Each leaf is a soul collected."

"And a soul collected turns black when the infection takes hold."

"Mnmmham"

"And what about that one there…" I pointed to yet another leaf that fell and crumbled away to ashes before it hit the floor.

"Ah, they destroyed another one."

"Yes, another soul lost."

"Mnonnem." They sounded sad as they shook their heads all at the same time, making the big body sway. But this was when I started to get it.

"So, each leaf is a vampire Lucius turned and when they turn black that means they are rogue but when they fall…"

"Then they die."

"They are no more."

"Mubbfubm"

I raised a brow questioning the mumbler, when the first one to speak every time told me,

"He agrees."

"Right...okay, so there must be a way to stop it?" I questioned thinking that if this was an infection we just had to find a way to cut it off before it had more chance to spread. That was the only way we would save the Vampires and with it my mother.

"A solution there is..."

"But travel to where it all begun you must go."

"Mellmen." The Keepers told me nodding as if they were happy they had finally got through to me.

"And where is that...is it...through there?" I asked as I nodded towards the doorway at the core of the tree.

"It is and hurry you must."

"Time is the key, and we have been waiting for you."

"Mhaanm." I held my hands up and started shaking my head,

"Now just wait a second, I think you have the wrong girl, or sex for that matter as it's Lucius that you need, it's his blood that...?" I was suddenly cut off, and in a way where their words started to make my heart pound.

"That he stole from you."

"For his sacrifice can only be undone by the sacrifice of the blood of the pure born."

"Mmhamum." I frowned at this in a questioning way before pointing out the obvious,

"But I am just human." The two that were able gave me a smile and it definitely was more creepy that the comforting one I think they were aiming for. Because they then told me,

"No, you are the rose that blooms."

"The blood stolen will set us free,"

"Muah."

"I don't understand…what are you trying to tell me!" I said now looking up towards that single flower and asking myself,

"Is that not my mother's soul?" They tilted their heads at my question the way a dog would when hearing a new sound. Then they dropped a bombshell on me and said,

"No, it is yours."

"The pieces of soul he stole from you."

"Mnmnhm" I gasped as my hands flew to my mouth at the same time I was shaking my head. Because no, it was impossible…he would never…he wouldn't. So, I told them,

"Lucius!? No…No that…that can't be…I am just a human! I was born this way," I said stumbling back as I said this, unable to keep my eyes from that fucking flower.

"The Venom of God left you human."

"It took from you our Queen born."

"Mhh."

I shook my head again, trying to make sense of what they were telling me. All that time wondering, asking myself how could I possibly be human? How not a single piece of my father had made it through into my life? That surely it was wrong. Surely a mistake had been made. Feeling all my years as if something was missing and now…now as I stared up at the blood red rose, I was starting to feel it. The river of blood in my veins. The one I had somehow managed to call forth that day in the vault.

How had I done that?

How had I fucking done that if I was nothing but human?!

Which meant that I had only one last question left to ask,

"What am I? What part of my soul did Lucius steal?" The question left my lips and my gaze went to the thief in question, knowing in the depth of my heart that he had known. All this time, since when I was born, the first time he ever saw me, not as a teenager but as a baby. He had somehow stolen that part of me, making me human!

And he knew.

He fucking knew!

It was why he had walked away. Putting the life he had put at risk at arms-length.

So now, as I repeated the question, I did so with my own Venom,

"What am I!?" I screamed it this time, having the power to rock the Temple floor, forcing Lucius to begin to waken from the force of my furious question. I could feel this place start to seep into my veins as anger started to shake my body as I trembled, awaiting what I knew was my stolen destiny and all from the man I loved.

And he knew.

All this time, *he had lied.*

"Amelia?" he said my name, shaking off the effect of our separation as I had done before him.

"What part of me did he steal?" I asked more calmly now, seeing as he was rising from the floor. He quickly took in the sight of me, but he froze as he heard that question.

"Amelia...what are you...?" His question was cut off quickly when he took in the sight of the Tree of Souls and the Keepers. He scanned the whole space in seconds and that was when it hit him.

"NO!" he roared making me close my eyes against his cry of anger,

"No, Amelia look at me! Look at me, don't listen to them and I will explain."

"I don't need you to explain, Lucius, I just need you to tell me what part of my soul it is you stole from me," I said, looking down at my feet as the tears started to cloud my gaze, making the patterns on the floor merge as one. I swallowed hard and finally looked back up at him, seeing for myself the face of the guilty staring back at me. But despite this, the first part of my answer came from the Keepers, making me suck in a startled breath when they told me, all at the same time, speaking as one…

"The Angel in you, is what he stole."

At this my legs gave way and my knees hit the floor as if with that truth everything in me came crashing down all at once.

But the truth was far from done as Lucius was then the one to add to his list of crimes against me,

"I stole the soul of an Angel and that of…

"A first born Vampire."

To be continued

ABOUT THE AUTHOR

Stephanie Hudson has dreamed of being a writer ever since her obsession with reading books at an early age. What first became a quest to overcome the boundaries set against her in the form of dyslexia has turned into a life's dream. She first started writing in the form of poetry and soon found a taste for horror and romance. Afterlife is her first book in the series of twelve, with the story of Keira and Draven becoming ever more complicated in a world that sets them miles apart.

When not writing, Stephanie enjoys spending time with her loving family and friends, chatting for hours with her biggest fan, her sister Cathy who is utterly obsessed with one gorgeous Dominic Draven. And of course, spending as much time with her supportive partner and personal muse, Blake who is there for her no matter what.

Author's words.

My love and devotion is to all my wonderful fans that keep me going into the wee hours of the night but foremost to my wonderful daughter Ava...who yes, is named after a cool, kick-ass, Demonic bird and my sons, Jack, who is a little hero and Baby Halen, who yes, keeps me up at night but it's okay because he is named after a Guitar legend!

Keep updated with all new release news & more on my website
www.afterlifesaga.com
Never miss out, sign up to the
mailing list at the website.

Also, please feel free to join myself and other Dravenites on my Facebook group
Afterlife Saga Official Fan
Interact with me and other fans. Can't wait to see you there!

facebook.com/AfterlifeSaga
twitter.com/afterlifesaga
instagram.com/theafterlifesaga

Acknowledgements

Well first and foremost my love goes out to all the people who deserve the most thanks and are the wonderful people that keep me going day to day. But most importantly they are the ones that allow me to continue living out my dreams and keep writing my stories for the world to hopefully enjoy… These people are of course YOU! Words will never be able to express the full amount of love I have for you guys. Your support is never ending. Your trust in me and the story is never failing. But more than that, your love for me and all who you consider your 'Afterlife family' is to be commended, treasured and admired. Thank you just doesn't seem enough, so one day I hope to meet you all and buy you all a drink! ;)

To my family… To my amazing mother, who has believed in me from the very beginning and doesn't believe that something great should be hidden from the world. I would like to thank you for all the hard work you put into my books and the endless hours spent caring about my words and making sure it is the best it can be for everyone to enjoy. You make Afterlife shine. To my wonderful crazy father who is and always has been my hero in life. Your strength astonishes me, even to this day and the love and care you hold for your family is a gift you give to the Hudson name. And last but not least, to the man that I consider my soul mate. The man who taught me about real love and makes me not only want to be a better person but makes me feel I am too. The amount of support you have given me since we met has been incredible and the greatest feeling was finding out you wanted to spend the rest of your life with me when you asked me to marry you.

All my love to my dear husband and my own personal Draven... Mr Blake Hudson.

Another personal thank you goes to my dear friend Caroline Fairbairn and her wonderful family that have embraced my brand of crazy into their lives and given it a hug when most needed.

For their friendship I will forever be eternally grateful.

I would also like to mention Claire Boyle my wonderful PA, who without a doubt, keeps me sane and constantly smiling through all the chaos which is my life ;) And a loving mention goes to Lisa Jane for always giving me a giggle and scaring me to death with all her count down pictures lol ;)

Thank you for all your hard work and devotion to the saga and myself. And always going that extra mile, pushing Afterlife into the spotlight you think it deserves. Basically helping me achieve my secret goal of world domination one day...evil laugh time... Mwahaha! Joking of course ;)

As before, a big shout has to go to all my wonderful fans who make it their mission to spread the Afterlife word and always go the extra mile. I love you all x

Also by Stephanie Hudson

Afterlife Saga

A Brooding King, A Girl running from her past. What happens when the two collide?

Book 1 - Afterlife

Book 2 - The Two Kings

Book 3 - The Triple Goddess

Book 4 - The Quarter Moon

Book 5 - The Pentagram Child /Part 1

Book 6 - The Pentagram Child /Part 2

Book 7 - The Cult of the Hexad

Book 8 - Sacrifice of the Septimus /Part 1

Book 9 - Sacrifice of the Septimus /Part 2

Book 10 - Blood of the Infinity War

Book 11 - Happy Ever Afterlife /Part 1

Book 12 - Happy Ever Afterlife / Part 2

Transfusion Saga

What happens when an ordinary human girl comes face to face with the cruel Vampire King who dismissed her seven years ago?

Transfusion - Book 1

Venom of God - Book 2

Blood of Kings - Book 3

Rise of Ashes - Book 4

Map of Sorrows - Book 5

Tree of Souls - Book 6

Kingdoms of Hell – Book 7

Eyes of Crimson - Book 8

Afterlife Chronicles: (Young Adult Series)

The Glass Dagger – Book 1

The Hells Ring – Book 2

Stephanie Hudson and Blake Hudson

The Devil in Me

OTHER WORKS BY HUDSON INDIE INK

Paranormal Romance/Urban Fantasy

Sloane Murphy

Xen Randell

C. L. Monaghan

Sci-fi/Fantasy

Brandon Ellis

Devin Hanson

Crime/Action

Blake Hudson

Mike Gomes

Contemporary Romance

Gemma Weir

Elodie Colt

Ann B. Harrison

Ingram Content Group UK Ltd.
Milton Keynes UK
UKHW011258160523
421838UK00001B/172